Phantom Algebra

by

Dan Rice

*The Haunting of Pinedale High
Series*

Cover Art by *Teddi Black*

The Wild Rose Press, Inc.
PO Box 708
Adams Basin, NY 14410-0708
Visit us at www.thewildrosepress.com

Publishing History
First Edition, 2025
Trade Paperback ISBN 978-1-5092-6302-8
Digital ISBN 978-1-5092-6303-5

The Haunting of Pinedale High Series
Published in the United States of America

Dedication

To Alex for providing insight into the elite youth
athlete mentality.

Chapter 1

Bad Love

Zuri never imagined she'd find love in the podunk, milk-white municipality known as Badger Hollow. Not only was Toby Alkorn gorgeous, he was the best kisser on the Great Plains.

That's what all the girls said, those who had kissed him, and there were many—and those who only dreamed about it, which was about everyone else. Zuri and Toby had kissed plenty since they started dating. She couldn't honestly proclaim Toby as the best kisser on the Great Plains, but she had kissed a few boys, and he was the best by far.

On that hot and humid August afternoon behind the stadium bleachers and across a country lane from a veritable sea of corn, Toby was irresistible. With his blond hair damp with sweat, Fighting Badgers football uniform stained by grass and dirt, and face still red from exertion, he exuded masculinity.

Even his body odor was a turn-on, which was something new for Zuri. She had been around plenty of sweaty boys and men, smelling their repulsive musk at the boxing gyms where she had watched her father train and been trained by him back in the good days before everything fell apart. Before Zuri and her mother became the hunted, pursued by a father who wanted his child back and haunted by an estranged husband out for death.

Toby's fragrance only increased his magnetism. He caressed her buttocks, neither gentle nor rough. Just right, really, setting her body all tingling. But then he shoved his hand down her track pants and started aggressively groping. That was a step too far, and she firmly removed his hand.

"Oh, come on," he moaned.

Raucous laughter and boisterous banter came from his teammates who at that moment were emerging from a gap between the high bleachers.

"I'm not doing any of that in front of them," Zuri whispered.

"Come on." He pouted, his lush lips making the expression cute, almost sexy. "All right."

Toby dropped his hands and backed away. A few catcalls came from his teammates anyway. Zuri could have melted with embarrassment. It was hard enough being an outsider and practically the only brown face at school. The last thing she needed was a reputation as a slut. Toby flashed her a proprietary smile that made her feel icky. She didn't belong to anyone, and she certainly wasn't an object to be possessed.

Toby turned to his teammates. "None of that, my boys."

The catcalls died down.

"That was an amazing throw, Tobe," a compact wide receiver glazed.

"That arm is going to win us the state championship!" shouted a hulking defensive lineman with chest and shoulders made broad from years of farm work and high-protein meals.

Toby mimed throwing a football to the team.

"Second in two years!"

As the players scrambled to catch the imaginary football, chanting, "Repeat, repeat," heady pride surged through Zuri. Being athletic herself, she admired Toby for his athleticism and natural leadership on the field. He was only entering his junior year and already had division one colleges scouting him.

The team moved on, heading to the parking lot where parents waited to take them home or their personal vehicles were parked. A tight end with tussled hair and acne-sprouting cheeks hung back. "Bruh, some of the boys are headed to Badger's Dairy Freeze. You coming?"

"I'll be there in a bit."

Toby made a gesture with his hands that Zuri couldn't see. She didn't like the smile on the tight end's face as he turned away, heading for the parking lot. Toby turned back to Zuri, smiling mischievously.

"What?" she asked.

He took her hands in his and pulled her to him, pressing his chest against hers. "It's just the two of us now."

"What about the coaches?"

"Don't worry about them. It's no secret they keep a cooler of ice-cold beer in the equipment shed to drink after a good practice. We had a good practice today, real good. Did you see that throw? For the touchdown? Fifty-five yards at least."

"You know I was watching."

Toby leaned closer, pinning Zuri against a metal support post. The cool metal pressed unpleasantly against her spine. His lips crushed against hers, dispelling her discomfort. He was an excellent kisser, even when he was a little rough. Zuri could keep kissing him all afternoon and well into the night, but Toby wanted more, cupping her left breast. It was the hand shoved down her pants and underwear, pawing at her groin that set off alarm bells. Zuri had been to second base loads of times, but Toby charged toward third. That was not a place she planned to go, not yet.

When she placed her hands against his chest and pushed, it was like trying to move a brick wall. Toby outweighed her by at least sixty pounds, and he wasn't moving.

Thrusting her head back, Zuri banged the posterior of her skull against the metal support, managing to break her lips from his long enough to gasp. "Stop."

"Stop what?" Toby groaned and pressed his lips against hers again.

Moving like a greased eel, Zuri slipped free of his grasp and stepped around him with the practiced ease of a pugilist. Toby spun around to face her, his back to the bleachers. His upper lip curled into a sneer. "What? I thought we were having fun," Toby whined.

"I had enough fun for today," Zuri said. "Why don't you go cool off at Badger's Dairy Freeze with your boys."

"Nah." Toby shook his head. "I've been plenty patient with you. Now it's time for you to put out."

Zuri backed away, recognizing the predatory tone in his voice. She'd heard rumors about this side of him, but hadn't really believed them. Up until now, he'd always been so nice. A gentleman far less coarse than many other boys she'd made out with.

Powerful hands clenched into brick-sized fists, Toby lurched for Zuri. He drew back his right hand for a punch. Like when Zuri sparred, fought in the ring, or partook in back-alley brawls to keep up her skills when no gym was available, the whole world slowed, like everyone moved through water except for her. She moved like a video playing at three times speed, calmly backstepping a pace and placing her right leg behind her. When he came into range, she fired a near-perfect high kick.

Just as the fray set into motion, the head coach emerged from the bleachers and took in the scene of his star quarterback throwing an honest to God punch at the new black girl in school. "Alkorn, what in the hell are you doing?"

The coach's voice boomed, a bullwhip of command used to cow arrogant teen athletes, a trumpet to be heard across fields and over the rowdiest crowds. But it was too late. Before Toby's fist connected, Zuri's kick landed cleanly against his left jawline. She felt a surge of satisfaction as the impact jolted her leg from foot to hip. Even her hero, Malee Chaiyathorn, couldn't have landed a better strike.

Toby never saw the blow that knocked him out cold. He fell to the concrete, head hitting the ground with a sickening thud. Zuri stared in shock at her now-former boyfriend. *What have I done? What have I done? What have I done?*

The head coach lumbered past Zuri, huffing and puffing from exertion. He didn't smell of alcohol, only ripe sweat.

Chapter 2

Justice For…

Zuri shifted nervously, blood pressure sky high and palms clammy, as she waited in the sheriff's office in an uncomfortable chair next to her mother, Amari. A rattling window-mounted air conditioner kept the small, spartan space cool, cold really, especially after the heat and intense humidity of the afternoon and early evening. Before them sat an old rectangular metal desk with a faux wood desktop covered with paperwork, a small flatscreen monitor, a wired keyboard, and a wired mouse. The laptop the devices connected to was practically hidden by the dozens of sticky notes affixed to it. Behind the desk was a heavily padded executive chair that appeared far comfier than those designated for guests. On the wall were plaques proclaiming the accomplishments of the sheriff and the department as a whole.

"Fighting, Zuri? Knocking a boy out?" Amari whispered. "You told me you were done with fighting."

"It wasn't like that, Mom," Zuri said. Up to now, she'd neglected to tell her mother about Toby Alkorn—and wasn't keen on mentioning that it was her boyfriend, whom she'd been seeing for almost two whole months, she'd knocked cold. Well, former boyfriend. "He's not even hurt. He was sitting up when the medics arrived."

Amari turned to stare into Zuri's eyes. "You beat him up. I know what it is like to be beaten, or have you forgotten?"

Zuri dropped her gaze to the linoleum floor. For a moment, she felt out of breath like she had run a record-setting time in the one-hundred-yard dash. How could she have forgotten? That terrifying incident that rent her family apart was burned into her memory and made her feel helpless.

The door to the office opened with the loud creak of hinges needing oil. Both women started to stand, but Sheriff Tobias Johnston told them in his chocolatey baritone to remain seated. Zuri dropped back into her chair, but Amari stood straight for a second, then sat again. The sheriff was a big man, easily over six feet, and built like a keg. He wore blue jeans and a button-down blue cotton shirt with a badge affixed to the right breast. He wore a Stetson, which he took off and placed on the desk atop some paperwork. His hair was salt and pepper, as was his trim beard.

Sheriff Johnston sat in the executive chair that creaked softly under his weight. "So you're the girl who dropped Toby Alkorn."

Zuri met his stern gaze for only a moment before deciding studying her hands in her lap was a better option. She shifted in the chair, hyperaware of the hard seat pan making her butt sore.

"Feeling a little ashamed of what you've done? That's good," the sheriff said. "Good citizens don't go around beating people up. Have you been doing that a lot, Zuri? There have been reports…nothing definitive. Do you know anything about that?"

The chair her mother sat in squeaked. Zuri could feel

Amari's eyes on her and squirmed. Of course, she'd been in a few fights—back alley sparring matches, really—since arriving in town six months ago. She had to keep up her skills.

"You don't need to answer that," Johnston said. "I'm just thinking out loud."

"What is going to happen to my daughter, Sheriff?" Amari asked.

"The whole event was recorded. Now, I have yet to see the video. But…well, Mrs. Williams, to put it plainly, Toby Alkorn has a bit of a reputation when it comes to interactions with young ladies."

Zuri looked up. "Video recording?"

"That's right. My deputies say the recording corroborates your story, young lady, as does what Coach Malloy told us. Toby Alkorn attacked you, perhaps intending to sexually assault you. You defended yourself. Hell, his fist was flying for your face. Guess he didn't account that you're as fast as a fly escaping a swatter."

Zuri had never seen a camera behind the bleachers. "But what camera?"

A ghost of a smile graced the sheriff's lips. "The kind of camera we law-enforcement types deploy when we want to surreptitiously detect illegal activity."

"You're trying to catch the snowflake dealers," Zuri said.

Amari glanced between her daughter and the sheriff. "Snowflake?"

Johnston frowned. "Snowflake is a slang term for fentanyl, Mrs. Williams." The sheriff leaned back in his chair. "Let's get back on track. As I said, Toby Alkorn has a reputation. Accusations have been made against him before. But nothing that's ever stuck. His daddy, well, his daddy is a leading citizen and very influential, if you take my meaning."

Zuri melted into the chair. She didn't want to hear what the sheriff had to say next.

"This boy attacked my daughter," Amari said, voice rising. "There's video evidence. Witness testimony. She defended herself."

"That's true. That's true. However, your daughter knocked out Toby, and they are in a romantic relationship."

"What?" Amari faced Zuri. "Why am I just learning about this?"

"I'm not in a relationship with him anymore," Zuri muttered, wishing she could fade into the ether like a specter.

"That complicates things a bit," Johnston said. "It allows people to say…sure things happened, but it was all a misunderstanding. Young people being high on life."

"What are you saying, Sherriff Johnston?" Amari asked.

Johnston shifted in his chair and picked up his Stetson by the brim in both hands and moved the hat in a circular motion almost like turning the steering wheel of a car. "The likelihood of Zuri's involvement in this unfortunate event being forwarded to the prosecutor is about zero. That's good. That's great. But it doesn't mean a case will be brought against Toby Alkorn unless your daughter decides to press charges. Put plainly, there isn't a jury that could be convened in the whole state that would convict Toby Alkorn of anything. If there was a smoking gun with his prints all over it, a dead body, and half a dozen witnesses stating he pulled the trigger, I'd say there's only a fifty-fifty chance he'd get convicted. That boy, scum that he is, is nearly untouchable due to his abilities as a quarterback and his daddy's influence in these parts."

Johnston set the Stetson on the desk, walked around the table, and squatted before Zuri. "I want you to know I believe your story. All you were doing was defending yourself. You've heard of Juliet Stone?"

Zuri nodded. Everyone knew about Juliet Stone, and like everyone, Zuri didn't believe the tale until this afternoon.

"She's living in Nebraska now." Johnston shook his head. "She's my third cousin if you can believe that. She accused Toby Alkorn of doing to her what he tried to do to you. It was investigated, but nothing could be proved. I believe it happened similar to what was recorded happening to you. Now, she and her family have moved away because good old leading citizen, Mr. Alkorn, wouldn't leave them alone. What he did was subtle but effective—a bank loan her father needed for his business suddenly became unattainable, moneyed folk taking their kids out of her mother's daycare and a few episodes of bullying at Juliet's school. She and her family are in Nebraska now. The Alkorns are still here in Badger Hollow." Johnston glanced between Zuri and Amari. "I apologize for what I'm going to say now from the bottom of my heart. But I'm expressing what I see as reality in these parts. Juliet was a white girl who was related to the sheriff. She made an accusation I believe but couldn't make stick. You're not white, and as much as it pains me to admit it, there are people in this town, in this county, and in this state who won't believe you or won't care, no matter the evidence, for that reason."

Chapter 3

A Pen Name for Mother

Less than a week after the meeting with Sheriff
Johnston, Zuri listened to the old hybrid's engine whine
as Amari coaxed the minimum interstate speed out of the
rundown vehicle. Other automobiles zipped by, almost
as if the hybrid stood still. Some drivers honked, a few
made obscene hand gestures; occasionally, one swerved
their vehicle dangerously close in front of the junker.
From her station riding shotgun, Zuri was sorely tempted
to swear at the drivers and reply to each crass hand
motion with one of her own. Amari, however, was
sanguine, never losing her cool, even when a semi
pulling a double trailer whipped in front of them and
immediately slammed on the brakes. Zuri swore, which
earned her a chiding from Amari in an infuriatingly calm
tone.

The weather would've been pleasant enough if the
vehicle's AC worked. As it was, the sun beating down
from a blue sky with only a few wispy white clouds
heated up the car's interior with startling efficiency.
Even before noon, mother and daughter sweated, despite
having the windows rolled down. Having the windows
down meant the constant, heavy thrum of road noise.
Every time a vehicle sped by spewing stinking exhaust
fumes, the Williams women were assaulted by the

stench.

The landscape they traversed appeared entirely flat from their vantage on the highway. Farmland, fields lush green or fallow brown, for as far as the eyes could see. Irrigation equipment on giant wheels spewed water onto the crops. Sometimes, a barn stood near the road. Most were ramshackle affairs, surrounded by rusted farm equipment that appeared not to have been used for decades, with bowed roofs and missing siding, but not all. A few were splashed with vibrant red paint and white trim. The well-maintained barns impressed Zuri, and she wondered idly why some farmers allowed their barns to fall into disrepair while others kept their barns postcard perfect.

Ruminating on the landscape didn't distract Zuri for long from the pinprick of dread, an icy singularity in her abdomen that chilled her despite the heat, the humidity, and her dripping sweat. She did what any self-respecting teen would do with a smartphone in hand. She doom scrolled social media.

Well, she didn't doom scroll for long, quickly being hooked by her mainstay, clips of the Thai kickboxer Malee "The Jade Tiger" Chaiyathorn beating the bejesus out of other young women in the octagon, using a combination of punches, classic Muaythai kicks, and grappling submissions. Zuri idolized Chaiyathorn, dreaming, both while awake and asleep, of being as gorgeous, humble, and deadly in the ring as The Jade Tiger.

While watching the clips, Zuri held the phone in her left hand and shadowboxed with her right, throwing jabs, hooks, and elbows. If there had been room, she would have launched kicks and even a flying knee, but the hybrid was too small, even if it hadn't been crammed with their meager possessions. Amari noticed her daughter's rambunctiousness and couldn't suppress a smile. The anxiety in the pit of Zuri's stomach faded as she watched Malee win fight after fight, primarily by knockout, after wearing down her opponents with devastating kicks. Zuri considered the kick she had delivered to Toby Alkorn's chin and decided her idol would have approved of her technique.

But too soon, they passed into a cell coverage dead zone, the video froze, and Zuri's trepidation returned with a vengeance. Dread formed a knot in the pit of her stomach that her mother's new job would summon Big Jake, estranged father and husband, like an enraged demon torn from the bowels of hell by a séance. They had been on the run from him for three years. Uprooting themselves every few months in the name of staying one step ahead of Jake. Before the incident with Toby, they have been getting ready to settle down in Badger Hollow for the long term, or, at least, that's what Zuri had thought.

"Why didn't you tell me you were looking for a job?" Zuri asked her mother.

Amari glanced briefly at Zuri before returning her gaze to the roadway. "I didn't want to get your hopes up. Or worry you." She shrugged. "It was always a long shot."

"I thought we weren't supposed to keep secrets from each other," Zuri said while giving the stink eye to a driver flipping them off while passing in a sleek blue sports car.

"Secrets?" Amari scoffed. "What about your secret boyfriend? Why didn't you tell me about him?"

Zuri crossed her arms before her chest. "He wasn't much of a boyfriend."

"The best kisser on the Great Plains is what I heard."

Zuri looked at her mother, eyes wide. "You heard about that?"

"Girl, I worked at the Smiling Badger Café. Schoolgirls came by all the time on Friday and Saturday nights. Gossiping. Giggling. I can't tell you how often I heard that boy's name. It's a wonder I didn't hear yours."

"They can have him," Zuri said with finality.

Amari shook her head. "I hope he gets the help he needs before he hurts someone. I really do."

"Hurts someone again," Zuri said and added disparagingly. "Is that why you stayed with Dad for so long? Because you thought you could help him?"

"Is that what's bothering you?" Amari's voice rose as she spoke. "You're afraid he might find us because of my new job? He would've found us long ago if he was looking, Zuri. Besides, my advice column will be written under a pen name. Dolores Clattenburg." Amari laughed. "Can you imagine a more outrageous name?"

"I hope you don't give relationship advice," Zuri said snidely, checking her cell phone for service and finding two bars.

"Oh, you think I don't have advice to give about that? I've been around the block a few times, Zuri. We both have with your father, but we're still here. We're still together. We're still breathing."

Zuri didn't listen to the last of her mother's words. She was back on social media, searching for clips of Malee to watch for the hundredth time or more. But she couldn't escape the scene playing out behind her eyes. Her father, Big Jake, straddled Mom on the kitchen floor and threw bone-crunching punch after bone-crunching punch, like The Jade Tiger pouring it on for a knockout.

****

After over eight hours on the road, they stopped at the cheapest motel they could find on the outskirts of Indianapolis. Zuri carried a bag of toiletries to the room for her mother, pleasantly surprised to find the space clean and not smelling too bad. It was far from the worst place they had stayed since fleeing Big Jake.

Full of pent-up energy, Zuri told Mom she was going for a run. Amari knew saying no would only lead to an argument, so she told her daughter to be careful. Zuri ran, occasionally throwing punches, for over an hour past parked cars, grocery stores, and warehouses, all the time barely taking in her surroundings. She daydreamed of training in the gym again when they reached Pinedale, North Carolina. A real gym with heavy bags, speed bags, and a ring to spar in, maybe even a coach to train her. She only turned back to the motel when the cool night air caressed her cheeks, and she realized it was dark. After using her phone to map a route, she ran back to the motel by streetlights and the glaring headlights of passing cars.

Amari was half asleep when Zuri entered the room, which was cooled by an AC unit droning under the window next to the door. After groggily telling Zuri about the ham sandwich and a bottle of water on the rickety table next to the window, she promptly fell asleep. Zuri wolfed down the stale sandwich without tasting it. She chased the food by gulping the water until the bottle was empty.

After a quick shower, Zuri crawled into the unoccupied twin-sized bed. Still full of anticipation of training in the gym, she fell asleep, but her rest wasn't undisturbed for long.

Zuri knew she dreamed. She had suffered many nightmares since Big Jake had nearly beaten Amari to death. But this phantasmagorical scene was something new, and she could not force herself awake. A man she recognized yet did not know stood over her in a white suit and a boater hat on his crown. His neatly trimmed hair and beard were salt and pepper. His eyes were blue and cold as shards of glacial ice. Clenched in his right hand was a bowie knife, keen edge glinting in the eerie light of the Buck Moon. The man snarled, lips moving as if he spoke, but no sound broke the vision's dead silence. The knife rose and fell, stabbing, slashing.

Zuri threw spindly arms of ghostly white before her to ward off the blows. When Zuri woke the following morning, she vividly recalled the nightmare and wondered why her arms were white in the dreamscape.

Chapter 4

Bigger and Better

Zuri rose early to fix her mother breakfast before Amari's first day at The Pinedale Gazette. The duplex they rented from an elderly lady in the adjoining unit was the largest space Zuri had lived in since they fled L.A. and Big Jake's fists three years ago. It had taken all of their meager savings to pay the security deposit on the rental. They were living on Amari's one rarely used credit card until she cashed her first paycheck from the new job. Fortunately, the unit was furnished, if sparsely, and included in their possessions were a pot and pan to cook with, three chipped bowls often used to eat instant ramen from and a handful of mismatched utensils.

The previous day, Zuri had snuck out late in the evening while her mother obsessed over what to wear on her first day in the office. Amari had a smattering of clothes from when she worked as a cub reporter freshly out of college, but although she could still squeeze into the clothing, none fit right, and all were outdated. Zuri headed to the corner convenience store about five minutes away on foot, feeling guilty about having eleven dollars and some change that she hadn't told her mother about. She stopped at the entrance to the store to admire the sky, turning cotton candy pink as the sun fell behind clouds and then the horizon.

She scoured the small refrigerated section for bargain eggs, finally settling on a six-pack that cost over half her cash. After calculating that she had enough to afford a small package of cheddar cheese, she went to the register. The clerk, a woman as wide as she was tall, made small talk about the sunset that she observed through the establishment's windows and relieved Zuri of all her money, save a dollar and a few pennies.

She still felt a little guilty about the money as she beat two eggs in a chipped white bowl with a fork. The sound of movement came from her mother's bedroom. That's what Zuri liked most about this place, her own bedroom. She only had one of those once since fleeing L.A., and that one had possessed a permanent dog piss odor, so her current digs were a definite upgrade.

"Zuri," Amari called from the short hallway leading to the unit's two bedrooms and one bathroom.

"I'm in the kitchen," she replied.

The kitchen and dining area were an open layout, basically one room. A small entryway adjoined the dining room. Zuri poured the beaten eggs into a heated frying pan. Soon, the aroma of cooking eggs wafted up from the stove. Zuri smiled. It was nice to live in a place where she had her own room, and the most pungent smell was the scent of her cooking.

The splash of water and the drone of the fan came from the bathroom. "Zuri, are you cooking?"

"I'm making an omelet." Zuri used the bottom of her T-shirt as an oven mitt as she maneuvered the pan so the eggs coated the surface. "Hurry up and shower."

"Eggs? When did we buy eggs?"

"Last night when you were trying on fits. I found some cash in my school backpack." That was only half a lie. Zuri had always known about the money.

She finished making the omelet a few minutes before Amari completed showering and dressing. The teen was sorely tempted to eat the food but resisted, instead filling a pot with water to boil for instant ramen. Amari emerged into the dining area, finding the still steaming omelet at her place at the table.

"This smells and looks delicious, Zuri," Amari said. "What are you doing?"

"Boiling water for ramen."

"Nonsense. Bring a plate over, and we'll share."

Zuri sat while Amari stood over the table, carefully cutting the omelet in two with a fork. Amari remarked on her work attire, deciding the pants were a little too tight in the hips. Zuri thought her mother had never looked more professional.

They ate together in silence, savoring the food. Even without seasoning, they both agreed that it was the best meal they had in ages. Too soon, their time together ended when Amari checked her phone.

"I need to leave." Amari stood. "I can't be late on my first day. Thank you for breakfast, Zuri."

Zuri looked up from the last bite of gooey cheese and fluffy egg on her plate. "Mom, he's not going find us here, is he?"

Amari pushed in her chair, knelt beside her daughter, and embraced her. "We're safe here. He would've found us long ago if he were looking."

"But what if he starts looking." Zuri nestled her head against her mother's shoulder.

"Then we'll face him together," Amari said.

****

Zuri left the duplex several hours later after cleaning

up the kitchen and watching inspirational videos on her phone, namely, clips of The Jade Tiger training or beating people up in the octagon.

The big news of the day was Malee Chaiyathorn had earned a shot at the flyweight title, and only the contractual details needed to be worked out for a bout against the current champ in November. This gave Zuri chills. A title shot for her hero. Rhythmically clenching and unclenching her right hand, she dreamed of one day following in Malee's footsteps.

Zuri's feet took her to Pinedale Fight School, located about twenty minutes away in the center of a rundown strip mall with most of the stores completely empty. Unlike many other strip malls past their prime Zuri had encountered across the country, this one lacked graffiti, broken windows, and piles of trash. A few cars dotted the cracked parking lot with barely visible striping. All were parked in front of the Fight School and a nail salon, two empty storefronts down from the gym.

Biting her lower lip, Zuri stared at the gym and baked in her rather baggy and ratty blue tracksuit under the midmorning sun. Through the windows with the words Pinedale Fight School, boxing, kickboxing, BJJ, and MMA stenciled in large white block letters were heavy bags, speedbags, and a muscular man jumping rope. Zuri desperately wanted to enter the gym and work out, but she had no money to pay the fees.

She'd told her mother she planned to find a part-time job, but Amari had been adamant when she said no. Zuri was expected to concentrate on school. As long as she earned good grades, Amari would pay for the gym membership once the paychecks started coming in.

That made Zuri nervous. While learning the lay of

the land, she had overheard snatches of conversations from other teens, claiming Pinedale High was academically challenging and haunted. She'd even seen a boutique selling souvenirs commemorating the haunted school. Haunted? What a bunch of BS for tourists with more money than sense. Zuri only believed in things she could strike with her fists, feet, knees, and elbows. Pinedale High being academically challenging, on the other hand, that she was ready to believe, and thinking about it made her clench her jaw.

"Hey, you want to work out?"

Startled, Zuri spun to face a man in gray sweatpants and hoodie with the hood up, shadowing his face. The hoodie was stained with sweat. Instinctually, she backed away, heart reverberating in her chest, eyes scanning for the best escape route.

"Sorry, sorry." The man raised his hands and threw back the hood, revealing a lean face with sharp angles and bright, intelligent eyes. "I didn't mean to scare you. Just…I've seen you here before. Do you want to come inside? Get a feel for the gym."

His smile was disarming and kind. He also reminded her of one of her favorite things about Pinedale: she wasn't the only brown face anymore. As small as it was, Pinedale was cosmopolitan compared to Badger Hollow.

Zuri wanted to say yes with almost every fiber of her being. "I don't know. I'm broke. You know, the fees."

"Tough being broke." He nodded toward the gym. "I tell you what. I know the owner pretty well. I'll ask him if you can train this once to get a feel for the place. Maybe he can cut you a deal until you have money to pay."

"I don't know."

He raised his eyebrows. "Come on. We've seen you shadowboxing. You got skill."

Zuri cracked a smile. "Sure. I'll go inside."

Chapter 5

Sucker Punch

A week later, Zuri was already a fixture at Pinedale Fight School. She arrived between nine and ten a.m. after fixing breakfast for her mother, often instant ramen since that first paycheck hadn't come yet, and cleaning the duplex. She slugged the heavy bag, worked the speed bag, jumped rope, and did hundreds of sit-ups each day. When she left in the late afternoon, she jogged home, tired, sore, and hungry. But the next day, she was back for more and loving every second of it.

When she first entered the gym, she had been invited inside by none other than one of Pinedale's favorite sons, a welterweight boxer, Demarcus Kelly. Not only did he know the gym owner, an elderly man known only as Mr. Tito, but he was also trained by him.

Mr. Tito, wearing thick-lensed glasses, threadbare khakis, a short-sleeve polo, and flip-flops, had come out of the back office with Demarcus by his side. "Show me your moves."

"Ummm…like shadowboxing?" Zuri asked after looking around and seeing the gym's two heavy bags and three speedbags were already in use.

The muscular man she had seen through the window earlier jumping rope growled as he landed monster punches against a heavy bag that Zuri suspected might split under the impacts. She noticed the ring was empty and added, hopefully. "I can spar someone."

"Nah, shadowboxing will do. Demarcus and some of the other fellas say you have some sweet moves. I don't see too good, so I'd like a demonstration."

Zuri went through her standard shadowboxing routine, starting with left jabs and straight right hands before adding more variety to her punches, and throwing elbows and Muaythai kicks. She quickly worked up a sweat because the gym was hot and stuffy. The entire time, Mr. Tito appraised her, like a rancher inspecting a prize steer. That was a good thing. It meant he evaluated her as a fighter, not a piece of ass or, worse, a little girl pretending to be tough.

Mr. Tito nodded. "Enough. You're good, but you already know that. Despite what it says on the windows, this is primarily a boxing gym, although classes are offered in all the martial arts listed."

Zuri nodded enthusiastically, thinking that if her mother approved, she could land a gig teaching Muaythai or BJJ with a little luck.

Mr. Tito motioned for her to come closer and whispered. "Demarcus says you're short on money."

She nodded.

"You've got skills. I can help you refine your boxing," Tito said. "I'll let you train here for a couple of months, gratis. After that, we'll discuss how much it will cost you. Sound good?"

A ten-thousand-megawatt grin split Zuri's face. "Yes! That's great, Mr. Tito. Thanks."

"Come to learn and be respectful. Those are the number one and number two rules here," He pointed to words painted in big black lettering on the back wall behind the boxing ring. "Number one, come to learn. Number two, be respectful. Number three, no weapons. Number four, keep the gym clean. Number five, Mr. Tito's interpretation of the rules is final. Can you abide by those?"

Zuri bounced on her feet. "Yeah. Yeah, no problem."

"Good. Given your skill, I expect to see you here often," Tito said and puttered back to the office in the rear of the gym.

Zuri faced Demarcus. "Thanks."

"No, thank you for coming in," he replied. "It's not right to allow a talent like yours to go to waste."

In the present, Zuri jumped rope, hoping to reach one thousand repetitions without a misstep before quitting. Her body was slick with sweat and her black sports bra soaking wet due to her hours of exertion, in the sweltering gym. If it was hot outside, the gym was always warmer and the humidity stifling, almost like a sauna.

Soon, she lost herself in the rhythm of the exercise, concentrating on the slap of the rope striking the floor. At two hundred reps, her calves started to burn. Not in a bad way, but in a good way. The getting stronger way. The burning subsided as she closed in on four hundred reps, but her legs were tired. All she needed to do now was push through to her second wind. She focused her mind on the rhythm, on the count, on jumping at precisely the right time. Unlike many of the other gym patrons, she never listened to music while working out. That was one of the lessons her father imparted to her when her family was still a family. *You train how you fight. You fight how you train. You don't have music to listen to in the ring or the octagon.*

"Oh, lookee here. Ain't she snatched?"

Zuri ignored the unwanted attention. Some harassment was part of the price of training at a fight gym, like the repellant body odor wafting off her harassers. Back when she had trained with her father, no one ever dared say a word to her. Most of the young men, even the ones she would have liked to have attention from, hardly even looked at her. Everyone had known that you didn't mess with Big Jake's daughter unless you wanted a monumental ass whipping. The kind of beating that could send you to the hospital, and you might never recover from. In the three years since she and Amari fled Big Jake, Zuri had faced harassment at every gym she trained at.

"At least she's dripping in that sports bra and short shorts."

Zuri focused on her exercise and her body movement. She wished the boys weren't fixated on her physique. Pinedale Fight School wasn't so bad, really. The older men, who always made her feel really icky at other gyms when they checked her out, minded their own business. Some of the boys, though, the teens around her age, were full of themselves and enjoyed commenting about her body when Mr. Tito, the other oldsters who trained fighters, and Demarcus weren't around.

"That girl thinks she can fight."

Zuri lost her rhythm, tripping on the rope. She shook her head, angry with herself. That's what the boys wanted, to knock her off her game by getting under her skin. Dropping the rope, she faced her antagonists, three boys all close to her age, led by a surly youth about Zuri's size named Mason Rider.

"I can fight."

"Ooooooh," the boys said in unison and started laughing.

"Hey!"

The boys startled and backed away. It was the big, muscular man, a bull of a man really, with a thick neck, barrel chest, and arms the diameter of small trees. From the lack of sweat dripping from his face and staining his workout gear, he had recently arrived.

"The young lady doesn't want to listen to whatever you boys are saying." He crossed his thick arms over his broad chest.

"Mind your own business. This ain't school," Mason said with a whine.

"True, Mr. Rider, but don't forget that I know who you are and where you go to school. As for the two of you, I know you both by reputation. You are all lucky to have Mr. Tito as a benefactor. I would hate to have to tell him that you were violating rule number two. Be respectful."

The boys hung their heads and slunk away, Mason muttering. "Yes, Mr. Copeland."

Zuri was tempted to snap that she didn't need anyone's help to handle bullies, but she knew better. That was her anger speaking. A young woman in a fight gym needed allies, even if she didn't want them.

"Thanks," she said.

"If they keep bothering you, tell Mr. Tito. His rules are the law here," Copeland said, grabbing a free jump rope from where the ropes were stowed on the wall by hooks.

They jumped rope side-by-side, Zuri noting that the big man was good at the exercise but not nearly as skillful as her. Zuri finished about twenty minutes later, heading to the door after putting away her equipment. At the exit, she ran into Demarcus and an older gentleman who helped Mr. Tito train the gym's top boxers.

"Hey, Zuri," Demarcus said with a winning smile.

"Hi," Zuri mumbled, trying not to stare at the handsome man too hard.

Demarcus turned back to the trainer. "My mom loves that new advice column too. The writer has a really weird name."

"Dolores Clattenburg," the trainer said. "The wife might contact the paper. Ask if this lady can come to her book club."

The words hit Zuri like a fist to the sternum. She wanted her mother to be successful, but she couldn't shake the feeling that Amari's success would draw the ire and fists of Big Jake.

****

Two weeks later, Amari cashed her first paycheck just in time to buy Zuri school supplies at the local discount retailer. As expected, money was tight, and Zuri worried they wouldn't have enough to pay for the gym. She still didn't know how much Mr. Tito would charge.

Upon hearing the teen's concerns, Amari replied. "Don't worry. We'll figure something out. Money is scarce, but that's nothing new. I'm making more money than I have in years. We'll make the paychecks stretch. You worry about holding up your end. Good grades."

"I could try to land work teaching Muaythai or BJJ at the gym," Zuri said hopefully.

"You worry about your grades," Amari said. "That's all you need to do."

The Friday before the start of the fall semester, Zuri

worked the heavy bag at the gym, alternating between kicks and punches. Pinedale Fight School was abuzz with activity. It had been for the last week as the gym's top amateur boxers prepared for a tournament at the end of September under the watchful eye of Mr. Tito and a handful of other grizzled old men. Zuri found the atmosphere intoxicating: the energy, the slap of gloves striking flesh, and the hard-won wisdom imparted by the trainers. But she found it impossible to avoid Mason, which was something of a buzzkill. The lad was a top prospect trained by Mr. Tito himself. Mason avoided approaching her, but she often felt his gaze upon her voyeuristic and judgmental.

"Zuri! Zuri!" Mr. Tito calling her name from the ring broke her concentration. "Zuri, do you wanna spar?"

She smiled. "You bet, Mr. Tito!"

She nearly ran across the gym to the ring, ignoring the quizzical gazes of the men loitering nearby, who had been watching the sparring matches with intense interest. She ducked under the ropes into the ring and spied her adversary. It was none other than Mason Rider complaining to Tito about having to fight a girl. The old trainer dismissed Mason's complaints. "You're sparring, not fighting."

An oldster entered the ring burdened with a bag full of gear. He looked at Zuri with a gaze that told her he had seen it all a hundred times or more. "Sit in the corner."

His tone broached no argument, so she retreated to the corner, where she found someone had placed a stool. She sat while the oldster carefully wrapped her hands without saying a word. When he was done, he asked her if she was good. Zuri nodded, eyeballing Mason across the ring. The bully was full of energy, bouncing on the balls of his feet and swinging his arms. Mason saw that she watched him and smiled, revealing a blue mouthguard. They would be boxing, giving him the advantage.

"I'm going to get my ass kicked."

The oldster shoved the right glove over her hand and started lacing it. "He keeps his left hand low. Uses his speed to avoid punches. He's fast, but you're faster. Lead with a straight right hand."

As the oldster fitted her headgear, Mr. Tito strode over. "Thanks for filling in, Zuri. The regular sparring partner has the flu." He looked at her meaningfully. "Remember. You're boxing. Sparring. No elbows. No kicks. No grappling."

"Got it, Mr. Tito."

No sooner than she said the words, the oldster jammed a bright red mouthguard into her mouth and whispered. "Straight right."

In the center of the ring, Mr. Tito told Zuri and Mason to touch gloves. Zuri reached out her hands. With a maniacal glint in his eyes, Mason threw a punch, catching Zuri cleanly on the cheek below her left eye. Zuri stumbled backward but stayed on her feet, knowing immediately the blow would cause swelling. With surprising agility, Mr. Tito scrambled between her and Mason and berated the boy.

"I thought you said begin, Mr. Tito," Mason whined.

Tito waved aside teen's excuse with disgust and turned to Zuri, examining her face. "Do you want to continue? No shame in backing out."

Zuri blinked until her vision refocused. There was

no backing out, not when facing a bully, especially when you're a girl. "I'm good."

Tito nodded and glanced between his charges. "Remember, this is a sparring match."

Straight right. Straight right.

Chapter 6

A Blast from the Past

On the Monday following her sparring match with Mason Rider, Zuri walked down a long, relatively steep hill on the route to Pinedale High. Birdsong came from the trees lining the street that would provide shade during the heat of the day a few hours later. The sun rose above distant tree covered mountains. The highlands seemed to fold over each other creating a picturesque effect. Zuri searched up the beautiful landscape on her phone, discovering she gazed upon the fabled Blue Ridge Mountains.

Along the road the houses were large and well-maintained with uniformly tidy yards. The type of dwellings Zuri had rarely entered. Even back in L.A., when the money was good from her father winning fights, they always lived in small, often rundown apartments near whatever fight gym he currently trained at. Many were the nights Zuri had struggled to fall asleep while listening to the rumble of nearby trains.

A dog yapping behind a white picket fence startled her. Heart thumping in her chest, she doubled her pace to put some distance between her and the mighty defender, which, on a quick glance, turned out to be a tiny dog with long hair, perhaps a terrier. Zuri decided it was better to cross the street to where a few empty lots were situated side-by-side rather than risk exciting more guard dogs.

Zuri looked both ways while stepping off the shoulder into the road and was forced to leap backward as two boys flew past on scooters. Stepping awkwardly on a rock, she rolled her ankle and stumbled, but avoided falling onto her butt.

"Watch out, dumb ass," a pimply-faced rider called over his shoulder.

Shaking her head, Zuri murmured. "Welcome to Pinedale High."

The boys raced onward, slowing only enough to barely make the right turn at the hill's base. Zuri continued on her way, quickly becoming lost in her thoughts again.

After being sucker punched by Mason, Zuri had executed the advice to lead with straight right hands. As the oldster had said, Mason was fast, but she was faster, and for whatever reason, be it arrogance or laziness, the boy never raised his guard high enough to block her shots. Instead, he tried to dodge them, which he did sometimes, but not nearly enough. Her right hand crunched into his face time and time again, sending satisfying jolts up her arm into her shoulder. With gratification, she watched the maniacal glee fade from his eyes, and panic set in as he realized he was getting his ass whooped by a girl. Mr. Tito ended the sparring match after one round, not wanting Mason to get beat up with the tournament only weeks away.

But the revelation after the match had doused Zuri's joy at showing up the bully. After berating Mason for his shoddy defense, Mr. Tito ambled over to help Zuri remove her gloves. Smelling of aftershave and sweat, he spoke as he worked. "You did good in there, Zuri. Maybe too good for Mason, but you taught him a hard lesson. Something I've been working on with him for months. Keep your hands up!"

"He does keep his left low," Zuri agreed.

Tito wrenched the right glove off her hand and dropped it to the canvas. "The angles you throw the right hand are unorthodox. I've only seen it once before." He looked her questioningly in the eyes. "Zuri Williams. You're not Jake Williams's daughter, are you?"

Zuri's mouth dropped open. "Ummm..." What to say? She collapsed in on herself, shriveling like a raisin. Did she dare lie and risk being caught? Did Mr. Tito know her father? Would he phone Big Jake as soon as she left?

The oldster looked at her questioningly and said. "It must've been...God, almost twenty years ago one of my fighters, an up and comer, fought Jake Williams. Jake was a journeyman boxer, a dangerous puncher but my guy had the skills and speed to handle him. At least, that's we thought. It was a right hand thrown from a strange angle that knocked my guy out cold. Bang!" Tito smashed his right fist into his palm. "The fight was over in one shot."

Zuri shook her head. "Ummm...no." Her skin was dark enough few people would suspect her father was a white guy. "I've never heard of Jake Williams."

"Huh." Tito's eyes narrowed and he shrugged. "Make sure you ice your cheek below the eye. It's going to swell."

And swell her cheek did despite her applying ice and her mother fretting over how her daughter would look like a junkyard dog on the first day of school. Zuri had considered telling Amari about Tito's tenuous connection to Big Jake but decided not to. Her mother was already upset about her battered face and might use the linkage to her estranged husband as an excuse to ban Zuri from the gym.

In all honesty, the blackeye wasn't too bad. It looked worse than it felt. When Zuri reached the bottom of the hill, her bruised cheek wasn't paining her at all, and the swelling below her eye didn't impede her vision. When she hooked a right at the hill's terminus, Zuri clearly glimpsed the two shiny scooters and discarded backpacks on the side of the road next to a stormwater retention pond full of cattails. The scooters' owners participated in a fray at the pond's edge, pushing a shorter boy back and forth between them while attempting to relieve him of the backpack strapped to his narrow shoulders. Zuri clenched her jaw, knowing she shouldn't be involved in a tussle on the first day of school, but she could never abide bullies.

Breaking into a jog, Zuri called. "Hey, leave him alone!"

The larger of the bullies shoved the smaller boy onto the ground. The kid barely missed falling into the pond. Both the boys faced Zuri. The smaller of the two, with the pimply face, gave her a toothy grin, showing off braces that glinted in the morning light. The bigger teen simply made meaty fists and scowled. They looked like they might be related, but Zuri wasn't sure.

"Oh, look, it's the dumb ass from up the hill. We were having some fun with our friend Luis. Weren't we, Luis?"

The smaller boy, sporting thick, wavy black hair styled in a mullet of all things had regained his footing and scrambled out of the bullies' reach. The lad was a little pudgy around the midsection and his eyes were bright, intelligent, and afraid.

"Were you having fun, Luis?" Zuri asked.

"Not really," Luis said with a fearful glance at his tormentors.

Zuri crossed her arms before her chest. "Luis wasn't having fun. Why don't you boys get on your scooters and scoot over to school."

The toughs exchanged a look and laughed. The pimply faced boy took the lead. "Sure. We'll scoot over to school, but not until Luis goes for a swim. You know, to get his backpack."

"Let's go, Luis," Zuri said, crossing to the other side of the street and heading toward Pinedale High. Luis scampered up beside Zuri, putting her between him and the bigger teens.

"We aren't through here!" the pimply youth bellowed.

Footsteps crunched over pebbles. Glancing to the roadway, Zuri saw pimple face charging, his hands balled into fists. Dodging his wild swing, Zuri brought up her knee, allowing him to ram his groin straight into her bony joint. The tough went red in the face and doubled over, clutching his gonads.

"My balls," he wailed, dropping to his knees.

"Oh, wow," Luis said, delight in his voice.

Zuri stared down the tough still on his feet, who glanced between pimple face writhing on the concrete and her. Shaking his head, he backed away and unclenched his fists. Unfortunately for him, his retreat took him straight into the pond. Yelping in surprise, he tried to leap out of the water but only managed to fall backward with a splash.

"Oh, my god," Luis said, giggling. "This is the best walk to school ever!"

"Let's roll," Zuri said, heading out at a quick pace. "We don't want to be late to school on account of these two losers."

Luis jogged to catch up to her, breathing heavily. "Thanks for saving me from the Anderson brothers. I'm Luis Torres." He extended his right hand toward her. "What's your name?"

Zuri considered Luis's proffered hand, suspecting this boy wasn't high in Pinedale High's social strata. Befriending him wouldn't earn her status with the popular crowd. But his intelligent eyes were kind and guileless, and he seemed close to bursting with unbridled enthusiasm and energy. Despite herself, Zuri didn't only feel sorry for Luis being bullied, she liked him.

Zuri took his hand in a firm grip. "Zuri. Zuri Williams."

"Ouch!" Luis said after they had finished shaking hands. "You have a strong grip. Wow. No wonder you handled yourself so well back there. You're strong. Hey, do you think we can walk home together? The Anderson brothers won't mess with you, but if they catch me alone…"

"Sure, Luis. At least part way. I'm going to the gym after school."

Luis skipped out ahead of her and started walking backward. "Let me guess. You work out at Pinedale Fight School."

Zuri laughed. "Did my face give it away?"

Luis scrunched up his eyes. "Your face? No, you're pretty. But you can fight."

"Are you trying to flirt with me, Luis?"

Luis's eyes and mouth went wide. "No, I…"

Luis tripped over his feet, and Zuri darted forward, grabbing a flailing arm to save him from falling.

"That's twice in one day you saved me from physical harm," Luis said.

"More like twice in five minutes," Zuri scoffed.

Chapter 7

The Office.

Buses pulled into the front parking lot of Pinedale High. Like other high schools across the United States, teenagers drove vehicles given to them by doting family members or purchased with funds from part-time jobs into the student lot. A smattering of adults with name badges attached to lanyards around their necks proclaiming them school officials intermixed with the student body, their presence helping ensure a minimum level of decorum. Near the school's main entrance, a wiry resource officer in a dark blue uniform observed everyone entering the building. Zuri spotted him from the sidewalk that took her and Luis past the buses toward the building's entrance. A white dude with a badge on his chest and a gun on his hip didn't make her feel safe, even if he did have a friendly smile and chatted good-naturedly with some of the teens.

During the fifteen minutes it took her and Luis to walk from their dust-up with the Anderson brothers to school, she had learned quite a bit about her new friend. First off, he could talk. He was a true motormouth, which suited her fine because it saved her from having to say much at all. Second, he was a math whiz, taking online math courses at a university in Raleigh all summer and would continue his college-level study during the school year. High school math was too easy for him. Oh, and he was captain of the chess team. All this convinced Zuri that her initial suspicion was correct. Befriending Luis wouldn't earn her any points in the high school status structure, but she didn't care. She liked him even though he was obviously a nerd's nerd. His enthusiasm for math and learning in general matched her interest in the pugilistic arts.

And that was freaking cool.

Near the school grounds was a cornfield packed with stalks that pierced the sky like a phalanx of spears. The corn only served to remind Zuri of Badger Hollow, which was not something she cared to reminisce about. Not on her first day at a new school. New school, new beginning.

Beyond the cornfield stood a dense forest. Despite the woodland's location near the heart of Pinedale, it possessed a wild quality Zuri had rarely seen firsthand. The morning sunlight didn't penetrate the forest. The trees were far too tightly packed for that. Her initial vibe upon glimpsing the woods was foreboding, a throwback to a primordial time when predators other than humans stalked the wildlands. Yet, it wasn't all scary dread. The deciduous trees added splashes of colors from fiery reds to golden yellows that blazed like beacons in the light, whispering in silent voices, "Come hither and play beneath our branches."

"Are there any trails through the forest?" she asked.

"Yes, but don't go in there," Luis said, bumping into her side since the entrance was a chokepoint, mushing the approaching students into a packed crowd.

"Why?" She had to raise her voice over the multitude of conversations in order to be heard.

Luis looked at her skeptically. "I know you're new here, but you must have heard."

"Heard what?" Zuri scoffed. "That the school is haunted?"

"Ummm…yeah, and the woods are too. The students who go in there don't come back."

"Whatever," she replied dismissively. But Luis's earnestness never faltered. Either he was one hell of a liar, or he absolutely believed the school and the forest were haunted.

As they mounted the stairs to the main doors, he asked who she had for homeroom. Zuri pulled out her cell phone from her pants pocket to check her schedule, which she had received via email a week earlier.

"Oh, Ms. Donaldson! She's nice," Luis said. "You'll like her."

"Hey, no cell phones out on school grounds. Put it in your backpack, young lady, and don't take it out again."

Zuri looked up to find the school resource officer eyeballing her. When his expression hardened, she immediately knew he'd seen her black eye.

"Sorry." She unslung her backpack and stuffed the electronic device inside the main compartment.

"Come here, young lady," the officer commanded.

Luis came to her defense. "Officer—"

"Get to class, Torres," the officer said, leading Zuri inside the building.

She looked over her shoulder at Luis and shook her head, mouthing the word, "Go." She didn't want him getting into trouble because of her. Flashing a curdled smile, Luis followed the flow of students down the hallway.

Feeling her peers watching—and knowing she was already branded with a bad rep—Zuri followed the unsmiling man into the front office. The staff were either too busy or too polite to stare, but she knew she they judged her all the same. Only troublemakers were escorted around the building by the resource officer. He led her toward a door labeled SRO near the back of the office. But then she saw her salvation, maybe. A different door, this one open a crack and labeled Mr. Copeland, Guidance Counselor.

Could the guidance counselor be the behemoth who worked out at Pinedale Fight School and came to her aid when she was being harassed by Mason and his posse? She remembered the bully calling the big man Mr. Copeland and how Copeland implied he knew the youth from a school setting.

"Listen, officer, I know you think I've been in a fight or beaten up by somebody," Zuri said. "But I haven't. I was in a sparring match, and my opponent sucker-punched me. That's why I have this bruise."

"You were in a fight?" the officer said. "We need to have a talk about—"

"Not a fight fight. A sparring match at Pinedale Fight School."

The officer rounded on her, clearly unhappy to be interrupted.

"Mr. Copeland, can back me up." *Please, be in your office. Please, be who I hope you are.*

The officer's expression softened and turned inquiring. "Mr. Copeland did mention joining that gym. Okay, let's see if he's in."

Zuri nearly collapsed with relief when she recognized Mr. Copeland's voice responding to the officer knocking on the door. With his impressive bulk, Mr. Copeland made his small office look all the smaller. He rose from his chair to greet them. Zuri's situation was resolved in less than three minutes, maybe under two, but only after the bell rang for first period.

Great.

Late for my first class on my first day at a new school.

The officer left, stating he might have a word or two with Mr. Rider, but he didn't bother apologizing for making Zuri late to class.

"Do you know your way to Ms. Donaldson's classroom, Zuri?" Mr. Copeland asked.

She shook her head. "No."

Copeland leaned over his desk, quickly writing a note, which he handed to her. "This excuses you for being late. I'll walk you to class. It's the least I can do."

"Thanks, Mr. Copeland." As they maneuvered through the office, she added. "Were you in the military?"

Zuri had noticed a picture hanging on the wall behind his desk of several men dressed in military gear and carrying weapons in a desert landscape. One of the men might have been a younger version of the man standing at her side.

The counselor opened the front office door for Zuri. "Retired. I served for twenty years. Hank," Copeland called over a middle-aged fellow in a jumpsuit with the label janitor on the right breast. "Can you show this student to her classroom? Room 104."

"Sure thing, Mr. Copeland," this Hank said with an easy smile.

Copeland retreated back inside the office, leaving

Zuri with the janitor.

Hank pointed at her. "Let me guess. You're Zuri. Zuri Williams."

How did Hank know her name? Had Mr. Copeland told him? She didn't think so. Maybe Luis had mentioned her to him, as odd as that seemed.

Hank laughed at her confusion and started down the hall. "This way, Zuri, this way."

Chapter 8

Black-eyed Pea

Zuri left the algebra class hanging her head. No doubt about it, that subject was going to kick her butt. Depressing to think that it was only the first day of school, and she already knew that her chances of earning grades good enough for her mother to pay for the gym were about zilch. Feeling defeated before the first round had even started, Zuri followed the river of students flowing toward the lunchroom. A whiff of cheap cologne lodged in her nose, compounding her misery. Altering her course to escape the smell, Zuri bumped into the upper arm of a tall blonde girl.

"Watch out!" the girl snapped.

"Zuri!" Luis calling her name saved her from having to slow and apologize to the other girl.

Luis trundled up beside Zuri, his cheerfulness and infectious smile beating back her darkest thoughts. "What happened with the SRO?"

Zuri explained Mr. Copeland backed up her story that the blackeye was from the incident at the gym, not from her fighting, or being beat up by her parents, or anything like that.

"He's a good guy," Luis said. "He helped me sign up for the college math courses and the paperwork that said I don't have to take high school math."

The way Luis said high school math made it clear that he considered lower levels of math beneath him. Zuri was tempted to ask for his help with algebra—after all, Luis had made it very clear on the walk to school that he loved to study—but she didn't want him thinking she was an idiot.

They passed through open double doors into the lunchroom. Circular tables were arrayed around the room, each with three or more chairs. A few students already sat at tables, talking and eating cold lunches. Luis waved to a petite, mousy girl and an absurdly thin boy sitting shoulder to shoulder at a table beneath a banner on the wall that displayed the school's mascot: a giant green python on a purple and teal checkered field. The girl smiled and returned the wave; the boy nodded.

"That's John and Edith," Luis said. "We can sit with them."

The back corner of the room identified this as the outcast table. Great. They queued in the line for hot lunch, and Zuri kept her opinion to herself. The line moved efficiently but too slowly for her. Instant ramen for breakfast couldn't keep hunger at bay for long, and the scent of greasy food made her mouth water and her stomach rumble loud enough that she was afraid Luis might hear it over the din of hundreds of students eating, talking, being kids.

"Hey, what's with that janitor? Ummm..." Zuri tried to think of his name, but hunger pangs distracted her.

Luis raised one eyebrow. "You met Hank already?"

"Yeah, that's his name. Hank. Mr. Copeland asked him to walk me to class. It was the weirdest thing. He knew my name. First and last." Zuri shook her head. "I don't remember Mr. Copeland telling him my name."

"That's like his shtick. Hank just knows things out of the blue. Like your name." Luis glanced around as the line meandered forward and leaned close, adding in a hushed undertone. "Some people think Hank is a ghost. I don't know about that. I've never seen him look...look ethereal. He must have overheard your name while you were in the office."

"You're probably right." Zuri glanced at Luis, bemused. "Why do you keep talking about ghosts? Are you trying to scare me? Like hazing the new girl?"

"You haven't seen a ghost yet?" Luis asked. "Heard any strange noises? Bumped into something unseen?"

Zuri rolled her eyes. "The weirdest thing that happened to me is Hank knowing my name. You told me he's not a ghost. I got to tell you, Luis, I only believe in things I can see with my eyes and hit with my fists."

"Give it time," Luis said. "You'll see."

Zuri was tempted to sock him in the shoulder, but the sincerity of his tone stopped her. It puzzled her how such a brainiac could believe in ghosts. They paid for and retrieved their lunches, which, unfortunately, smelled more appealing than they looked. The pizza was soggy with grease, and the side of vegetables looked well past their prime. Still, Zuri planned to scarf down every bite and then wash it down with the jug of two percent chocolate milk.

They walked across the lunchroom, zigzagging between tables, chairs, and boisterous students toward John and Edith. Zuri glimpsed the tall blonde girl she bumped in the hallway, leading a giggling pack of equally well-dressed and manicured girls. Zuri tried to move out of their way, but something impeded her. For a moment, she thought she collided with Luis, but the lad was several feet away. Even worse, she was shoved toward the oncoming girl mob. By who or what, she didn't know.

Zuri stumbled in front of the girls. Only her agile footwork from thousands of hours in the gym kept her from smashing into the teens and spilling her food all over them. Still, the damage was done. They glared at her like she was a cockroach they'd like to step on—but only if doing so wouldn't dirty the soles of their designer shoes.

"You again?" the tall girl said. "What's wrong? Can't see with that black eye, you black-eyed pea?"

As the crowd of girls laughed uproariously, Zuri kept her head down and had to run to catch up to Luis. She had never been called a black-eyed pea before and didn't like it.

"Come on, you don't want to mess with Miriam," he said. "She only goes from mean to meaner."

"Oh, look, the new girl has already hooked up with that nerd Luis," an overly feminine voice called after them.

The laughter that followed the remark rang like the cackle of hyenas. Students looked up from their lunches and paused conversations to observe the ruckus. Humiliated, Zuri, nevertheless, slowed. The urge to confront the bullies was almost too strong to resist. A shouting match, or even worse, a fight, might not be the capstone she wanted for her first day of school, but she swore if they said one more word…

Luis tugged on her upper arm, breaking her out of her downward spiral. He carefully balanced his lunch tray in one hand and continued pulling her along. "Ignore them, and they'll leave us alone."

With her head lowered to study the floor and not glimpse the expressions of the gawkers, Zuri followed Luis. Someone shouted a final jibe, but Zuri ignored the insult. They reached the table side by side, sat, and Luis made introductions. Edith was warm and friendly, while John came off as reserved in a snooty way. They were obviously an item, which Zuri chalked up to opposites attract.

"Miriam O'Dell can be a real bitch," Edith said with passion after the introductions. "She thinks just because she's rich and there's a statue of her great-great-great-grandfather, or whatever, in the town park, she can act like she owns the place."

Zuri already chewed on her pizza, which tasted better than she expected, given its sad appearance. She had hoped the nerdy kids wouldn't want to talk much, but apparently, Edith was as outgoing as Luis. Surprisingly, Zuri recognized the surname O'Dell. Occasionally, a tall college-age boy, blond with blue eyes now that she thought about it, came to Pinedale Fight School and hung out with Demarcus.

"Does she have a brother?" Zuri asked.

"Ryan," John said before taking another bite of an apple.

"He graduated last year," Edith added. "He goes to university in Raleigh. I'm not sure which one."

"Not a good one." Luis snickered, and John joined in. "He's a dimwit."

Zuri didn't recall Ryan O'Dell coming across as a dimwit, but she had only observed him interacting with Demarcus from afar. But Luis's remark solidified her belief that she couldn't ask him for help with algebra without risking being labeled a dimwit or worse.

"Hey, new girl," John said, overly serious once again.

Edith elbowed John in the side. "Her name is Zuri."

"Err...right. Sorry. Zuri, next time Fat Nick pushes you around, tell him you know how he died. Whisper that, and he'll leave you alone."

"Fat Nick pushed Zuri?" Luis clapped his hands and stared at Zuri. "You had your first encounter with a ghost. Did you see him? I didn't. He's a tricky one to spot despite being the size of a blimp."

"I didn't see anything," Zuri said.

Edith and John gazed at her as if they didn't quite believe what she said.

Edith nodded and said lightly. "Neither did I. But John can always spot Fat Nick. They have a special connection."

"On my first day here as a freshman, Fat Nick dumped me into the garbage can," John said. "And rolled the can around the lunchroom with me in it."

"How did Fat Nick die?" Zuri asked innocently, hoping to expose a tall tale.

"I don't know. I don't think anybody does," John said. "Not anymore."

Luis and Edith nodded sagely. All three teens exuded honesty. Zuri didn't know what to believe, but a ghost shoving her was far-fetched. She must have stumbled over something, maybe tripped over a chair leg, without realizing it in the moment.

Chapter 9

Fighting is Life

In the weeks that followed Zuri tried to buckle down at her academics while keeping her eyes peeled for ghosts and hitting the gym after school, sometimes for several hours. She didn't see any apparitions, or experience another strange incident, but she did make it to the gym every day. Of course, she had to walk Luis home before she could go there. She didn't want him being jumped by the Anderson brothers, and as Luis predicted, the bullies kept their distance whenever they crossed paths.

Zuri thought she'd find walking Luis home a hassle, a duty she had to perform, and never imagined she would enjoy it. At first, walking him home was a bother, cutting into her gym time, but as the days passed, she found herself looking forward to the event, listening to him speak at length about mathematics, chess, and his many other interests, which included building scale replicas of everything from the Eiffel Tower to the International Space Station out of ConnectSmithery STEM bricks.

In early October, a tropical storm parked off the coast brought torrential rain. On a particularly stormy Friday afternoon, Zuri surprised herself by asking Luis if she could come inside to see his model of London Bridge, which he had completed the night before. His eyes lit up at the question, and he even smiled, the rain beading off his weatherproof jacket forgotten. "Really? I mean, sure!"

Luis's enthusiasm was infectious. As he led her across the tidy yard past a fir tree and various shrubs, Zuri discovered she was curious to see his creation and wasn't only inviting herself inside to escape the downpour.

"Won't you miss out on the gym?" Luis asked as he opened a side door to the garage. "We have to leave our coats and shoes out here. Mom will go crazy if anything gets dirty inside."

Zuri glanced around the spacious, empty garage with enough room for two cars. Rain drummed against the roof, and the faint chemical scent of fertilizer came from a plastic bag near the door. "It's Friday. I can stay late at the gym. I've never been inside a garage this huge."

Luis stripped off his coat, which dripped water. "It doesn't seem that big when the cars are parked inside. I'm glad my sister is gone. I'd never hear the end of it if she knew I brought a..."

Trailing off, Luis blushed, and he smiled sheepishly.

Zuri set her backpack on the floor. "A girl home. Don't worry, Luis, I won't stay long. I wouldn't want your sister to get the wrong idea and think you have a girlfriend."

"I wouldn't mind." Luis blurted. "If you were my girlfriend."

Zuri set her soaked coat next to her backpack and gave him a playful sock on the shoulder. "Don't get your hopes up."

****

An hour later, Zuri dripped with sweat while working the heavy bag at the gym, determined to complete her routine despite the ample distractions. A crowd gathered around the ring to watch Demarcus spar in preparation for a fight on an undercard in a couple weeks in New York City at Madison Square Garden. It was the biggest fight of his career; victory would earn him a shot at the welterweight title.

Try as she might, Zuri couldn't find a rhythm to her punching. Demarcus was far too distracting. She knew that, in theory, he was too old for her and that he was married with a child on the way, but reality didn't keep her fantasies at bay. Glancing into the ring and glimpsing his muscular arms made her abdomen tighten and her cheeks burn. She wouldn't mind being held in those arms, staring into his gentle eyes, and kissing his full lips.

She considered giving up on her workout and joining those watching Demarcus spar, but she was afraid someone might notice her staring at the contender with what might be deemed puppy love, and Mason Rider was among the crowd. She was afraid if she ever crossed paths with him again, she might return his sucker punch with one of her own.

The sound of a glove smacking skin brought oohs and aahs from the bystanders. Zuri looked to the ring in time to watch Demarcus's sparring partner stumble across the canvas, clearly hurt, with the contender in hot pursuit. Two thunderous left hooks to the body later, Demarcus was in the corner, and his sparring partner was on a knee, catching his breath and collecting his wits. Mr. Tito jumped inside the ring and, after conferring with the fallen fighter, announced that sparring was over for the evening.

Even more impressed by Demarcus's body shots than by his body, Zuri practiced throwing left hooks into the heavy bag, imagining she was nailing Mason in the gut.

"Hey, Zuri," Mason said from behind as if summoned by her violent fantasy.

Zuri backed away from the heavy bag, giving herself enough room to throw a high kick. Her foot struck with a resounding whomp, sending the bag oscillating like a pendulum. Smirking, she faced Mason.

"Nice kick," he said. "But you'd generate more power on your hooks if—"

"What do you want?"

Mason shrugged. "Fine. Don't listen to my advice."

Zuri rolled her eyes. Mason might have done well at the amateur boxing tournament, but that didn't mean she wanted his advice regarding fighting. She'd already proven that she could beat him.

"Mr. Tito wants me to thank you for sparring with me," he said. "You taught me to keep my left up. That helped at the tournament."

Zuri sighed, noting that he failed to apologize for the sucker punch. "You're welcome."

"He also wants to see you in the office before you leave."

Zuri crossed her arms before her chest. "Okay. Is that it?"

"Nah," Mason smirked, looking her up and down. "Keep wearing those tight short shorts. Makes your ass look good."

How dare this jerk make any kind of comment about her body? It took all her restraint not to launch a high kick for his temple. She was tempted to threaten him with another ass whipping; instead, she took a calming breath and remembered Mr. Copeland's advice. "I'm going to tell Mr. Tito you aren't following the gym's rules if you keep harassing me."

"What?" he blustered, hands up in surrender. "I'm giving you a compliment."

She stared at him in silence until he muttered an apology and retreated. Zuri moved on to a free speed bag. The entire time, she was distracted with thoughts of what cesspools teenage boys were. Toby Alkorn tried to sexually assault her. Luckily, she knew how to fight him off. Now, Mason Rider thought he could harass her, sucker punch her, and after all that, flirt with her. They were just like her dad, monsters.

Unbelievable.

Finally, Zuri moved on to jumping rope, her thoughts fixating on Luis. How he was passionate about everything. How surprisingly awesome she found his one two hundredth scale replica of London Bridge. The model took up his room from nearly from wall to wall and floor to ceiling. He even disassembled his bed and slept in the hallway on the floor to make space. He talked her through the entire build process, from the design to the finishing touches. Most of it, she hadn't bothered trying to follow, instead simply listening to the pleasing sound of his voice. The whole endeavor was obsessive, but Zuri understood obsessive. Liked it. Loved it, even. That's how she was about mixed martial arts. That's why she would one day be a champion.

Closing in on her one-thousandth repetition with the jump rope, Zuri realized she wouldn't mind Luis checking out her butt, even remarking on it if they were alone, somewhere private. Zuri's feet tangled with the rope, and she nearly fell. Shaking her head at her foolishness, she returned the jump rope to the hook on the wall. Nine hundred ninety-nine hops would have to do for tonight.

Mr. Tito's office was even more stifling than the rest of the gym. The oldster sat sweating in the chair behind a rickety metal desk covered in paperwork.

"You wanted to see me, Mr. Tito?" she asked from the open doorway.

Tito looked up. "Zuri, yes. Come. Sit."

She entered, passing into the thick menthol and herbal aroma of pain relief cream, and sat on a folding metal chair in front of the desk. Nervously chewing her lower lip, she waited to hear how much the gym membership would cost. She was sure that's why she was summoned to the office.

"How does twenty dollars a month sound?" Tito asked.

Zuri's jaw dropped. "For a gym membership?"

"That's right. After Demarcus's fight, I can even help you brush up your boxing skills."

"Umm…Yeah. Yeah." That amount was far less than mother had budgeted. "That's great, Mr. Tito. Thanks!"

"In two weeks, we're arranging a watch party here on Thursday. For Demarcus's fight. You're welcome to come."

"You bet I'll come, Mr. Tito. I wouldn't miss it for anything."

****

On the Thursday of the watch party, Zuri found out she had an algebra exam the following day. She knew she should study, but she couldn't miss the fight even if it meant doing poorly on the test. She'd already asked Luis if he wanted to tag along to the watch party, and he had said yes. She wanted to share her obsession with him and must support Demarcus by cheering him on. Without his encouragement, she might never have entered Pinedale Fight School. In the end, it was an easy decision. She'd skip extra studying and hope the exam was easy.

Little did Zuri know that was one of the most fateful decisions of her young life.

Chapter 10

Visitation

The high from watching Demarcus win his big fight at Madison Square Garden carried Zuri through the weekend. One day, that would be her. Of course, she'd be fighting in the octagon like Malee Chaiyathorn, who had recently announced she'd signed a contract for her first title fight in November. Zuri felt like she would burst at the thought that Demarcus and her idol might soon become world champions in their respective combat sports.

Even Luis enjoyed watching the fight, although he had complained about the gym's typical broiling heat and oppressive humidity. The biggest flatscreen TV Zuri had ever seen in person sat on a cart under the gym rules on the back wall. After Demarcus knocked out his opponent in the fifth round, cheers erupted from the crowd of about forty packed into the space. Zuri enjoyed the vibe but could tell the hollering and boisterous banter was too much for Luis. After watching Demarcus have his hand raised by the referee with Mr. Tito at the fighter's shoulder, Zuri told Luis they could leave.

"Zuri, wait," Luis called as they passed a heavy bag.

Zuri glanced at Luis, who stood next to a heavy bag with his phone out. In the back of the gym, the crowd milled, and someone had turned on jazz music. "What?"

she asked.

"Can you punch the bag?"

"Why? I'm not here to work out."

"I want to calculate how hard you can punch."

She was tempted to say no, but she heard the keenness in his tone. "Sure. But I tell you, Luis, I already know I hit hard because I knock down my opponents."

"But do you know how many pounds per square inch you deliver?"

After allowing him to take measurements, Zuri punched the bag with as much force as she could muster. Luis recorded the blow on this phone. The bag swung precariously close to him, and he scrambled to avoid being buffeted.

"Get what you need?" Zuri asked.

"You bet I did."

They exited the gym into the chill night. A Hunter's Moon backlit the clouds and cast a ghostly radiance across the parking lot, reflecting off cars and small puddles from the rain earlier in the evening.

"Oh, man," Luis said. "It's almost ten. My mom is going to kill me. I can't be out this late on a school night."

"Did she call you?" Zuri asked. His agitation reminded her that she had an algebra quiz tomorrow—an exam she needed to ace if she expected her mother to pay for the gym. Blinking and shaking her head, Zuri pushed thoughts of the test from her mind. That was a worry for tomorrow. Now was the time to dream of a future where all that mattered was how skillfully she could punch, kick, and grapple.

"She left me about fifteen texts." Luis typed out a text and pressed send. "I told her I'm on my way. Do you think you can guide me while I work on calculating how hard you hit the bag?"

Silently, she took him by his upper arm and drew him close to her. She guided him down the street around puddles and potholes while he worked feverishly on his calculations, face alight in the glow of his phone. Once, they even scrambled to avoid road spray kicked up by a raised pickup truck. That annoyed Zuri, but Luis hardly seemed to notice.

Soon, her displeasure faded. It was hard to stay irritated or angry or pissed off in Luis's presence. Even when a cold wind picked up, causing the skeletal branches of nearby trees to clatter, Zuri felt warm on the inside, a heat that the ambient temperature, whether it be Arctic or tropical, could not affect.

When they were about two-thirds of the way to his house on a dark, damp avenue, Luis declared. "I got it! You hit that bag with six hundred and eighty-five pounds per square inch of force. It says on this website that the average pro boxer can hit at about seven hundred and seventy pounds per square inch."

"I could hit harder," Zuri said. "If I were warmed up."

"I know you could," Luis said. "Still, six hundred and eighty-five is pretty good for a sixteen-year-old girl."

Testiness flashed through Zuri at his remark. No, Luis wasn't perfect, but nevertheless, her infuriation was there and gone in an instant. Instead of pushing him away or crashing an elbow into the side of his head, Zuri pulled Luis tighter to her, and they meandered down the road, side-by-side, in no hurry to reach their destinations despite the cold and damp, school, tests, worried parents, or any other concern.

Zuri's lofty good spirit came crashing down at the end of algebra class on Monday when the teacher passed out the graded exams. Written on the top of the paper in bold red ink was a five over a ten next to an F. She footslogged to lunch in a haze, staring at the ground with hunched shoulders.

An F.

She was such an idiot.

An F.

Such an unbelievable idiot.

What was she going to do? Her grade was a B minus before the quiz. Now, what was it?

A C?

A D?

As soon as her mother saw the grade, her gym money was toast. Luckily, her mom wasn't one of those parents who checked their kid's grades online every week. No, she'd wait until the end of the month. Maybe she could raise her grade by then?

God. She was screwed.

"Zuri, hey." Luis intercepted her in the hallway, and they lined up in the queue to enter the lunchroom. "I heard Mr. Benson handed back the test from last Friday. How did you do?"

"Good. A solid B." Zuri had told Luis she planned to pull on an all-nighter after watching the Demarcus fight to be ready for the exam. Instead, she stayed up until midnight watching clips of The Jade Tiger and shadowboxing.

"That's great! I guess the all-nighter paid off," Luis said.

"Yeah." Zuri forced a smile.

"What's wrong?" Luis asked.

"I feel nauseated…I'm going to sit down with Edith and John."

"Oh, you don't want to eat? Gosh. John isn't here today. He has the flu. I hope you didn't catch that."

****

After school, Zuri sat at a study desk in the back of the school library, staring at an algebraic equation. The only problem was she had no idea how to solve for x. She should have asked Luis or Edith for help. She was already doing calculus as a sophomore. Instead, Zuri had told Edith, who had the same sixth period as Luis, to inform him not to wait for her after school. Edith, of course, wanted to know why. She knew Zuri protected Luis from the Anderson brothers.

"They won't bother him again," Zuri said dismissively.

Edith looked at her doubtfully. "What happened? Did he get on your nerves? Sometimes…sometimes I think Luis is too enthusiastic for his own good."

"No." Zuri shook her head. "I like that about him."

Edith set down her juice box and gave Zuri an encouraging smile. "Spill the tea. Before Luis gets here."

Zuri surprised herself by doing that after making Edith swear she wouldn't tell Luis a thing. Now, staring at the equation, $20 - 7x = 2x + 4$, she wished she had taken Edith up on her offer to help. But she had said, no, because she was afraid Edith would decide she was a complete and total moron.

"I really am a moron," Zuri murmured. "Can't do math. Can't accept help."

In disgust, Zuri threw her pencil onto the desk. The writing implement struck the desktop with a loud crack and rolled onto the carpeted floor. Crossing her arms before her chest, Zuri stewed. She wasn't getting anywhere. All she was accomplishing was making herself late to the gym. But that was the rub. If she didn't get a good grade in the stupid class, she'd never go to the gym again. It was so unfair. When would she ever need to know stupid algebra anyway?

Heaving a sigh, she whispered. "Get a hold of yourself."

She looked across the desk to her algebra book. All she needed to do was read a chapter or two. How bad could that be? Of course, whenever she tried to read the math book, she always found herself suddenly sleepy. Next to the book rested her phone with the promise of clips of Malee Chaiyathorn beating people to a pulp. She reached for the device. She'd watch a clip to get her blood flowing before tackling math.

Only her hand never made it to the phone. Her nose twitched—what was that putrid smell? And the cold? The library had been pleasantly warm when she entered. In her peripheral vision, she glimpsed the pencil she had tossed floating through the air, stopping to hover above the algebraic equation. The coldness radiated from around the pencil, which lowered to the paper and started writing.

Zuri's hand went to her chest. Her heart raced so hard she could feel the rapid thump, thump, thump in her palm. Before her very eyes, the pencil wrote the solution to the equation.

Very cool.

Chapter 11

Awakening

Zuri stared at the apparition levitating beside the study table. Icy cold radiated from the specter with such intensity goosebumps formed on her arms and what breath that left her mouth came out as steam. Humanoid in form, the phantom was short and petite, but smudgy like an out-of-focus photograph or a shape seen through fogged glass. In color, the ghost was dark gray, almost slate, reminiscent of thick mist during those early morning hours only illuminated by predawn light. An earthy smell hearkening of loam's moist potential and the moribund decay of the crypt drifted from the phantasmic anthropoid.

Zuri's flight-or-fight response told her to punch the intruder or run and never look back. Her heart thumped so violently that it felt like her bones vibrated against the palm she held to her chest. *This isn't real. Ghosts aren't real. This is my tired mind running amuck.*

But her breath really did steam from her mouth like she was outside on a cold winter's day, and the goosebumps were real. She might deny what she saw with her eyes, but that smell was like nothing she had ever experienced. How could she possibly imagine it? The aroma was beyond belief. The duality of it all—the sweetness of life with the rot of death intertwined as tightly as woven fabric—turned her stomach.

No. This is some kind of bullshit like when she tripped, or someone shoved her in the lunchroom, and John claimed a poltergeist named Fat Nick had pushed her. She was being hazed. This was a sick prank.

Steeling herself, she reached for the apparition. She didn't know how the prankster pulled off the illusion but planned to find out. The air became colder the closer her fingers came to the ghostly form, until the tips burned and tingled like she submerged her digits in ice water only a few degrees above freezing.

"Ahh." Zuri jerked her hand back and tried to rub warmth into her fingers. Gulping, she whispered words she never imagined speaking. "Are you a ghost?"

In response, the phantasm tapped the tip of the pencil against the paper.

"You want me to look at the equation?" Zuri glanced at the solution, unable to make sense of it. Pure honey combined with a bitter necrotic smell invaded her mouth with her next breath. She almost gagged. "How do I know if it's right?"

A door at the front of the library opened, then shut softly. Footfalls followed, steadily coming closer. The apparition dropped the pencil and withdrew back toward the stacks, becoming less distinct the closer it came to the books.

"Wait! What are you?" Zuri called. "Who are you?"

"Zuri," Luis whispered, still out of sight.

The apparition passed into the books, became shimmery, then dissipated like candle smoke caught on a blustery wind.

"Oh, my God," Zuri mumbled, glancing back and forth between the stacks where the phantom disappeared and the pencil resting on the desk.

Frost formed on the writing implement where the apparition had touched it.

****

Somewhere in the depths below Pinedale High, inside a murky chamber, an ancient enmity stirred. Only a few had ever heard of the chamber, and none believed in its existence. Most brushed aside the hideaway as the imaginings of an old man descending into dementia or a work of fictionalized history written to entertain the author and his descendants.

But the unbelievers fooled themselves. Deep beneath the school, the chamber was carved out of the earth, supported by beams and columns, finished with bricks for the walls and heavy flagstones for the floor. The chamber was moist and cool, a favored hangout for nightcrawlers and rats made unnaturally potent, some might say supernaturally so, by the infernal radiation that emanated from the idol resting atop a pedestal at the room's center.

It was within the idol that the malevolence swirled, causing the statuette to shake with ever increasing intensity. A sickly green aura, casting twisted, abysmal shadows, flared from cavities carved into the icon by its maker. Wherever that devilish light fell, nightcrawlers skittered for bolt holes, and rats shrieked while running for dear life. The demonic denizen locomoted for nearly a full minute but, thank God, still slept—for now.

****

Luis rounded a bookshelf and came into view. "Zuri, are you okay?" A smile lighted his face as he asked, "You look like you saw a ghost."

Zuri swallowed the lump in her throat. "I think…I

might have."

Luis's smile broadened as he approached the desk. "That's great. Finally! You've been here for almost two months. I was starting to think Fat Nick pushing you around at lunch would be your only encounter."

"I..." Zuri shut her eyes. At least the smell and coldness had dissipated as soon as the phantasm disappeared. Still, she felt chilled. "It was terrible."

"Seriously?" He knelt beside her, his expression puzzled and concerned. "What happened?"

Zuri pointed at the pencil. "Look."

Luis's brow furrowed. "Is that frost?"

"Yeah, I think so," she said and relayed her ghostly encounter.

"Damn." Luis stood and retrieved the chair from the other side of the table. He maneuvered the chair next to Zuri and sat. "That's intense." He glanced at the paper. "But...it wasn't all horrifying, right? The ghost helped you with algebra."

Zuri shrugged. "I don't even know if it's right."

He reached for the pencil but didn't take it. Instead, his fingers hovered centimeters above it. "The frost is gone, but the pencil is...radiating cold. I don't like it." Luis picked up the paper and used it to brush the pencil off the table. He set the paper on the desktop and studied the equation. "$20 - 7x = 2x + 4$. Okay, that's easy."

"Not for me," Zuri mumbled.

He glanced up at her. "We all have our strengths and weaknesses. The Anderson brothers pushed me around for years, but you handled them both without breaking a sweat."

"I guess you're right," Zuri said. "I just feel like such a dolt sometimes."

Luis studied the solution. "Okay. Good. Good. Yeah, x = 20/8 or 2.5." He looked up. "You're not a dolt, and neither is the ghost. This is correct."

Zuri crossed her arms over her abdomen. "The ghost was trying to help me, I guess."

Luis shrugged. "Apparently."

"How did you know I was here?" Zuri asked, already suspecting the answer.

"I begged Edith until she told me."

"Did she tell you why I need to study algebra?"

"Only that you were going to the library to study."

Zuri sighed. "I flunked the algebra test."

"What?" Luis's jaw went unhinged. "You said—"

"I lied. I'm sorry." Zuri stared at the mathematical formula written on the paper. "I didn't want you to think I'm an idiot."

"Zuri, I…" Luis sounded genuinely hurt. "I'd never think that about you. I can help you study. You need to keep your grades up, right, or your mom won't pay for the gym."

Zuri looked up and smiled self-consciously. She was embarrassed that she had underestimated his kind heart. In all honesty, she really was an idiot. How could she have ever thought he would look down on her? He wore his compassion on his sleeve, just like his enthusiasm. "Really?"

"Absolutely." He rubbed his hands together in evident excitement.

Zuri checked the time on her phone. "Great. I still have an hour before I need to hit the gym."

"We can make good progress in an hour. I promise."

"Can we move tables first?" she asked. "This one gives me the creeps."

"Of course. But not too far away. I want to get a glimpse of this ghost."

Zuri looked at him askance.

"Don't worry. I know how to handle poltergeists. I'll protect you."

Zuri bit her lower lip and then smiled. "Okay."

Chapter 12

Headspace

"No." Mr. Tito shook his head. "On the second hook, rotate your weight from the front foot to the back. Twist at the hips."

Zuri frowned. This was basic stuff. She knew how to throw a dominant hand hook and a nondominant hand hook. Her father had drilled it into her before deciding to nearly beat her mother to death, but now it was like she had forgotten how to control her body. Like the muscle memory built up from all the hours in the gym had miraculously deserted her. Making matters even worse, she was punching like a toddler while under the close inspection of Mr. Tito. He must think she was a complete neophyte, and the whooping she gave Mason Rider a fluke.

"Try again," Mr. Tito instructed.

Zuri wiped the sweat from her brow with her gloved hand. Jesus, the gym was hot and airless today. A few fans buzzed in the corners but did not impact the space's stuffiness.

She threw her dominant hand hook, rotating her weight from her back foot to her front. Her right hand smashed into the heavy bag with a resounding thud. Smoothly, she threw a left hook, shifting her weight from her lead foot to her trailing foot and rotating at the hips.

Her left hand crashed into the heavy bag—a solid blow.

Mr. Tito disagreed. "You threw the left hook *to* your opponent. You need to throw the hook *through* your opponent. Stand aside. Let me demonstrate."

Nodding, Zuri did as instructed. The old boxing coach stepped up to the heavy bag. First, he demonstrated the two hooks in slow motion, and then he fired off the punches with remarkable speed. Not just impressive speed for an oldster but with agility that would be the envy of a man half his age.

Zuri watched the demonstration without really seeing. Her mind turned inward to the F on the algebra quiz, then the ghostly visitation. Maybe she should be kneeling, praying to God Almighty or any other deity who might be listening in case the spirit visited her again. She needed all the help she could get to raise her algebra grade, that was for damn sure. Only, she wasn't too keen on another encounter with the specter.

Its stench had turned her stomach.

While in its presence, the taste of the air made bile rush up her throat.

The memory of the unearthly cold radiating from the phantom made Zuri shiver even in the gym's oppressive temperature.

"Zuri!" Mr. Tito glared crossly. "Come back to Earth's orbit."

Startled, Zuri blinked. "Sorry, Mr. Tito. I guess my mind wandered."

"You don't say?" he scoffed.

Zuri gulped. She was desperate to have him coach her—look at Demarcus's success under his tutelage—but she was fearful that he was unimpressed with her attitude. Dammit. Why couldn't the stupid algebra test happen at some other time? "I'm really sorry. I'm…"

Tito held up a hand for silence, and his expression softened. "No excuses, Zuri. You're not in the right headspace to train with me right now. What's wrong? Do you wanna talk about it?"

Zuri lowered her gaze to the floor. Disappointment in herself and angst at the world surged through her in a heady concoction. In frustration, she slammed her gloves against her hips and slouched as if the world weighed her down. Part of her didn't want to say anything to anyone. As much as she knew she might benefit from the ghost's help, she didn't want to think about it. The apparition was creepy as hell. She felt shame about the quiz and didn't want to expose herself to Tito's judgment. But.…but she felt obligated to say something. And it had to be the truth. The last thing she needed was to be caught in a lie.

"I flunked a math test."

"Ahhh."

Zuri looked up. Tito gazed at her sternly, but surprisingly, she didn't feel judged by him.

"Math was never my strongest subject," he said.

Zuri couldn't contain herself. "It's stupid! When will I ever need to know algebra?"

The oldster chuckled. "I felt the same at your age. But you know…" He turned his gaze to the office in the back. "Every time I have to do the accounting, I wish I had spent more time studying math when I was younger."

"But that's not algebra," Zuri grumbled. "Is it?"

He gave her shoulder a grandfatherly pat. "No, it's not. Maybe you'll never need to know algebra as an adult. Maybe you will. But remember this. In any math class, you learn more than how to solve math problems. You're learning how to think. You're practicing the thought processes you'll use to resolve real-world problems you will face in life. I think we're done for today. Go home. Study."

How could he be sending her home? She was a fighter. Not a mathematician. How would she become a champion if she wasn't in the gym? "But—"

"Zuri." Tito's tone broached no argument. "You'll have fantastic grades if you apply half the effort to your schoolwork as you do to your fighting. Go home. Study. The gym will still be here tomorrow."

"Seriously?" she said, unaware of her whining tone. "I've been studying extra since the test, honest. With…with my friend Luis every day after school before I come to the gym."

"Luis is good at mathematics?"

"He's a genius! He doesn't do high school math. He takes online courses from a university in Raleigh."

"Ahhh. Yes, I've read about him in the paper. He's a good friend for you to have. I bet he spends hours working on math problems every day. Is he a decent tutor?"

Zuri nodded. "Yes, definitely."

"You're learning algebra from him?"

Zuri nodded enthusiastically, hoping Mr. Tito would change his mind. That he wouldn't send her away, and he would continue training her. She'd double down. Push aside all her problems. And focus on the here and now. Connect with her body. Allow her muscles to take over and execute from memory so ingrained it was almost instinctual.

Mr. Tito nodded and smiled. "My advice, Zuri, is to

spend more time studying with Luis."

Zuri's eyes widened, and she was about to make an aggrieved retort, but Mr. Tito held up a hand for silence. Although she felt like she would burst at the seams, Zuri kept silent.

"Don't worry about today. Don't worry about spending a little less time in the gym for a few weeks. I will train you, Zuri. You have the raw material to be a great fighter. You just need some refinement. But I can only help you if you're with me one hundred percent while I'm training you. Get your head on straight. Pass your class. Then we'll talk."

Zuri wanted to argue. But she knew better. "Yes, Mr. Tito."

****

Zuri readied to leave the gym in a funk. Angry at herself. Angry at Mr. Tito. And feeling convinced she was too stupid to pass algebra no matter how much help she had from Luis or Edith, or the unnerving ghost, or whoever. What did it matter anyway if Mr. Tito didn't train her? As soon as Mom saw her grades, her gym money would be up in smoke. Not in the right headspace? What does that even mean?

Throwing her backpack over her shoulder, Zuri marched from the gym, keeping her head down. Luckily, the gym wasn't packed yet, but she feared some patrons might have overheard Mr. Tito lecturing her. She didn't want to glimpse their critical stares.

As she neared the exit, she saw Mr. Copeland sitting on a bench, busily working his phone. She was ready to escape without speaking to him, but he briefly glanced up. She knew he spotted her, even though his gaze quickly returned to the screen. Sighing under her breath,

Zuri walked over to greet the counselor. She felt compelled to be polite since she owed him for helping her out of the jam with the SRO.

"Hi, Mr. Copeland," Zuri said politely and attempted to smile brightly. She was almost sure the expression came across as brittle.

"Hey, Zuri." Mr. Copeland glanced up from the phone. "I'm signing this petition. Something I'd usually never do, but my wife insists."

"What petition?" she asked, feigning curiosity.

"Something to do with this new advice columnist at The Pinedale Gazette." Mr. Copeland carefully typed with fingers the size of bratwurst. "I guess the author is writing under a pen name. The advice is so good, people want to know the author's real name."

"Advice columnist." Lightheadedness assailed Zuri, and the gym seemed to spin. "A petition."

Mr. Copeland glanced up from his phone. "Zuri, is something wrong?"

She shook her head and blinked, trying to clear the fog of fear and confusion. The room stopped spinning, but she still felt woozy. *Big Jake will learn about this.*

"Zuri?"

Big Jake will know where we live.

The counselor's expression became concerned. "Are you okay?"

"I'm okay," she said. "I need to study."

Zuri bolted for the door without waiting for him to answer.

Big Jake will come. He will come.

Chapter 13

Conflicted

Outside, the sky was lighter than when Zuri usually left to jog the approximately three miles home. Despite the dark clouds overhead, rain didn't fall from the sky, and there was nary a breeze. If it wasn't for her inner turmoil, it would be the most pleasant run home she had in ages.

Zuri was about to set off across the parking lot when a red sports car, engine purring, whipped into the lot. The vehicle sped across the asphalt to pull into an empty slot in front of Pinedale Fight School. Zuri knew who the car belonged to, the part-time college student, sometimes boxer, and full-time rich boy Ryan O'Dell, brother to the nasty bully Miriam. She was about to leave without acknowledging him. It was not like they were friends or even on speaking terms, but she spotted Demarcus riding shotgun and immediately felt a warm flush.

It was the first time she had glimpsed the contender since the referee had raised his hand in victory at Madison Square Garden. Shyly smiling, Zuri waved and was disappointed when Demarcus didn't notice her because he was speaking animatedly to Ryan. She knew that was silly. He was married with a baby on the way. Why would he notice her? He probably thought she was too young for him. Intellectually, Zuri understood that was undoubtedly true, but her body screamed at her otherwise.

Feeling truly awkward, Zuri was about to slink away before the young men took notice of her. The sports car engine turned off, and the door opened. Zuri kept moving, refusing to look back, hoping to be on her way without being noticed.

"Zuri!" Demarcus called. "How you doing, girl?"

Tensing, Zuri stopped and turned to face the handsome boxer. Demarcus stood on the pavement opposite the car's red hood. He looked like he had been in a fight, his left cheek swollen and discolored, and his upper lip puffy. His eyes, however, were as compassionate as ever, and even bruised and battered, his beautiful physicality showed through, making Zuri's abdomen clench and her heart rate hasten.

"Hi," Zuri said, mind racing for something to say that wouldn't make her seem like an idiot. "I watched the fight."

"Yeah, Ryan told me you were at the watch party with your friend...what's his name?"

As if summoned by the mention of his name, Ryan opened the driver-side door and got out with a smirk plastered on his face that, along with his blond hair, reminded Zuri of Toby Alkorn. Her pleasant, if awkward, ardor shriveled up like a raisin. Fighting to keep her body from sagging, Zuri replied. "Yeah, Luis."

Demarcus's smile broadened. "You'll have to introduce him to me if he's ever around at the gym again."

"Sure," Zuri said, although now she wondered if she should keep those aspects of her life separate. The gym and school. The gym and Luis. The gym and the unsettling phantom.

"I'll catch you around, Zuri," Demarcus said. "I'll be back training regularly in another week or two."

Zuri said farewell to Demarcus and exchanged nods with Ryan. She couldn't help giving him the stink eye when the blond man turned away. Ryan seemed innocuous enough for an entitled rich boy, but then again, so had Toby. Despite him being on friendly terms with Demarcus, there was something about Ryan she didn't like, although she couldn't put her finger on what. *Don't think about that rich white boy. Don't think about him or Demarcus.*

Zuri quickly fell into a rhythm on the jog home, her backpack bouncing against her shoulders in time with her footfall. She ruminated on the ghost and the petition to reveal her mother's name. She couldn't shake the feeling that both things could bring the world crashing down around her, crushing her beneath tons of emotional and physical detritus.

To escape the dread brought on by those thoughts, Zuri kept swinging her contemplations back to Demarcus despite her earlier intention not to think about him. Compared to her ghostly visitation and her trepidation that Big Jake would come for her mother with murder on his mind, thoughts of Demarcus were lovely distractions. How spectacular he was in the ring. How he was such a nice guy, always kind. And, of course, twice as gorgeous as any human has the right to be. Just thinking about him made her feel all giddy and excited like no one else. Not even Luis.

Zuri shook her head surprised by where her mind wandered. *Luis is just a friend. Just a friend.*

****

After a simple dinner of linguine bathed in olive oil with garlic and broccoli, Zuri and her mother tidied up the kitchen. Zuri dutifully scrubbed the pan used to sauté the garlic and broccoli with a bright pink sponge. The water was warm against her hands, and soap suds coated her skin. Amari cleared the table, making the trek to the dishwasher loaded with dishes and utensils. With the money coming in from Amari's reporting gig, they were gradually purchasing more cookware and eating instant ramen less often.

"Do you know about the petition?" Zuri rinsed the dish soap from the pan with hot water.

"Petition?" Amari set the dirty dishes on the counter and opened the dishwasher.

After rinsing the soap from her hands, Zuri grabbed a towel and dried the pan. "The online petition demanding The Pinedale Gazette reveals the identity of the new stupendously popular advice columnist."

Utensils clinked together as Amari put them in the dishwasher. "Oh, that petition." Amari laughed. "That's going nowhere, Zuri. I have nothing to worry about. The paper won't reveal my identity."

Zuri placed the dry pan on a dish rack. "How can you be sure?"

Amari faced her daughter and smiled. "It's in my employment contract."

Zuri turned away from her mother and reached for the pot used to cook the pasta. "If Dad—"

Amari took Zuri by the shoulders and wrapped her arms around her daughter from behind. "I've told you before, dear one, we don't have to live in fear of him anymore. If he was still hunting us, he would've found us long ago. Still, I've taken precautions. Do not worry yourself. Do not."

****

After tidying up and showering the sweat and grime from the gym off her body, Zuri retreated to her spartan bedroom, intending to study algebra as Mr. Tito instructed her. On the bed, covered in a faded blue blanket she had had for as long as she could remember, Zuri did study.

For about twenty minutes.

Unfortunately, the entire time her restless mind obsessed over to Big Jake.

That he would come.

That he would knock on their door.

That he would use his hands as murder weapons.

Zuri gave up on studying, turning to the comfort of watching clips of The Jade Tiger knock out her opponents in the octagon with kicks, punches, spinning elbows, and even a flying knee. Oh, what would Zuri give to be half as good as Malee one day? The answer was simple. She'd give anything. At least, that's what her adolescent mind told her.

Zuri touched her idol's smiling face on the phone screen after a brutal knockout of her opponent. "Soon you'll be world champion."

Then Zuri was up shadowboxing in her tiny room. She couldn't practice flying knees in the cramped space, but that didn't stop her from throwing punches in rapid combinations and various kicks. If she wanted to be a champion, one day, she had to grind. Grind. Grind. So what if Mr. Tito didn't train her? She had a fire in her belly, blazing with desire. Whatever it takes. Grind. She'd find a different trainer somewhere. Grind.

When she finally crawled into bed, she was slick

with sweat and feeling good, if sleepy. For the first time in days, her mind was a blank slate, and she fell asleep quickly. At first, her slumber was dreamless and restful, but all good things come to an end.

Screams came from the front of the duplex, startling Zuri awake. One voice belonged to her mother. The other was deep, gruff, and instantly recognizable—Big Jake!

"No!" Zuri scrambled out of bed, bolted from her room, and raced down the short hallway into the living room. "Stop! Please! Daddy, no!"

The space was in shambles. What little furniture they had overturned and broken. In the center of the space, Big Jake straddled Amari, who seemed as lifeless as a dead fish, methodically destroying her bloody face with his mammoth fists.

Sobbing, Zuri rushed to her parents and grabbed her father by his thick right arm. "Daddy, stop! Please."

He didn't stop. Instead, he did something he had never done before. Big Jake punched Zuri in the face hard enough that she saw stars.

Zuri woke up writhing and hyperventilating on her narrow bed, the blanket damp with sweat wrapped around her body like a python squeezing the life from its prey.

Chapter 14

Action Plan

Zuri did manage to fall asleep, and stayed in slumberland, though her time in that land remained restless. The next morning, her alarm buzzed too early and failed to drag her into consciousness. In the end, Amari opened her bedroom door and turned on the overhead light.

"Zuri, wake up! Your alarm has been going off for at least ten minutes."

Opening tired eyes, Zuri moaned, casting a half-squint, half-glare at her mother and then at the alarm clock. Now that she was aware of the blare, she found the sound intolerable. With impressive lethargy, she pawed at the bedside table until her fingers groped the alarm clock and found the snooze button.

The alarm clock went off five minutes later. The irritating beep woke her up this time, and she forced herself to swing her legs off the bed. After turning off the alarm, she remained on the bed's edge, reliving the dream. She could still hear the meat-grinding impact of Big Jake's fists against her mother's bloody face, each loud, squelching smack like raw T-bone being tossed onto a counter.

Her breath caught in her throat after a crash from the front of the duplex sounded loud as a bomb exploding. It couldn't be him. It couldn't be Big Jake.

"Sorry. I'm making eggs and dropped the pan." Amari's voice was muffled by the distance and the closed door.

Zuri sighed and glanced at her bedding—still damp from sweat. She'd have to wash it. And speaking of washing…she sniffed her shoulder, catching the ripe odor of BO. She needed to shower before going to school unless she wanted to be labeled a skunk.

Idly, without consciously considering her action, Zuri touched her cheek where Big Jake had struck her during the phantasmagoria. She winced when her fingers brushed her cheek. *What the…no, that's impossible.*

Suddenly full of vigor, Zuri rushed to the bathroom where the fan still droned, having been left on by Amari after she showered. Zuri leaned over the sink, staring at her reflection in the mirror. From the tenderness she experienced, she expected to see a bruise or a knot on her cheek, but her smooth skin was unmarred. She touched her cheek and took a sharp intake of breath when a stab of pain lanced through her cheekbone. Frowning, she shook her head.

Zuri stripped and started the shower, considering how she might confront her mother again regarding the petition in light of the dream, dare she say premonition, regarding Big Jake.

In the dining area, Amari set two plates full of steaming scrambled eggs on the table. She glanced to the hallway leading to the bedrooms and bathroom when she heard the shower start. Odd. Zuri rarely, if ever, showered in the morning. Amari checked the time on her watch. She needed to get a move on or risk being late for work. The delicate conversation she wanted to have with her daughter would need to wait for another time. Shrugging, Amari sat and started eating. The eggs were excellent—fluffy and seasoned to perfection.

The shower did wonders for Zuri's demeanor. She felt fully alive like the deadly pall draped over her had sloughed off. When she touched her cheek again, she experienced no pain, not even the mildest twinge. Breakfast's delicious scent beckoned her to the dining area, where she found the scrambled eggs waiting for her. Mother had already gone to work. Zuri sat and wolfed down the food—heavenly.

****

The lunchroom resounded with the boisterous gossip and confabs of the student body. In the back of the room, Zuri sat with her friends beneath the banner displaying the school's mascot, a curling green python. As Zuri told them about her ghostly encounter, no one touched their food, not even John, who usually ate heartily despite his cadaverous build. "This ghost..." he said, eyes narrowed. "...solved an algebraic equation?"

She nodded.

"Correctly, too," Luis said. "Showed every step."

John and Edith exchanged a glance. The mousy girl shrugged, and the gaunt-faced boy slunk in his chair, shaking his head. "I've never heard of a ghost helping anyone." John retrieved his ham sandwich from his lunchbox. "The ones who interact with the living are bullies or tricksters."

"You don't believe me?" Zuri asked, irritated by his dismissive tone.

John coughed like he was choking on his food, and his cheeks reddened. Edith slammed a hand against his back, and the boy settled down. "Of course, we believe

85

you," Edith said. "Don't we, John?"

The gaunt boy nodded in agreement, but his eyes said otherwise. Zuri crossed her arms before her chest and leaned back in her chair. John might only be playing skeptic, but Zuri hated being made to feel like she was less than truthful.

"There's irrefutable evidence," Luis chimed in. "The pencil. It was covered in frost." He held up his right hand and wiggled his fingers. "Like...like where your fingers would grip it while writing."

John swallowed a mouthful of ham sandwich. "And where is this pencil, Luis?"

Luis shook his head dismissively. "I threw it on the ground. It was strange. Radiating cold."

"We have to take your word for it." John smirked and took another bite of his sandwich.

"And Zuri's," Luis said, voice rising.

John raised a doubtful eyebrow as he chewed.

Edith socked him in the arm. "John, why are you being such a jerk!"

John threw his girlfriend a hurt glance and swallowed. "I'm just saying it's a little weird." He pointed at Zuri with the hand holding the half-eaten ham sandwich. "She goes from not seeing a single ghost to seeing one no one has ever seen? A ghost who does algebra. I mean, come on. You can't tell me that's not lowkey sus."

"I saw the ghost, John," Zuri said. "Part of me wishes I hadn't, but I did." Life was much simpler when she lived without ghosts, premonitions, or anything else remotely otherworldly. Back when all her problems—well, okay, most of her problems—could be solved with her fists. Inspiration struck her, and she dug into her backpack, pulled out the scratch paper she had used in the library, and slid it across the table to Edith and John. "That's not my handwriting or Luis's."

Edith inspected the fluid, insanely neat script and nodded. "Neither of you write this neatly. It's pretty."

John rolled his eyes. "This proves nothing."

"You think we're liars," Luis said.

"This wouldn't be the first time you pulled a prank at my expense," John said, his gaunt cheeks flushing bright red.

"That was a year ago," Luis said. "I didn't know…I didn't know he'd do that. Besides…they threatened…" Luis's voice dropped, whispering, "…to give me a dynamite wedgie."

"What's this all about?" Zuri asked.

Neither boy replied. Instead, they glared at each other across the table like gunfighters at a standoff. Edith broke the silence. "Dumbo Jock gave John a swirly, and he blames Luis."

"Dumbo Jock is another ghost?" Zuri queried.

"He's a hulking brute who sometimes haunts the boy's locker room during PE. He must've been a football player or something like that in life," Luis mumbled. "I think he died in a car crash. He looks…pretty gnarly."

"And he gives swirlies to anyone who goes inside the locker room during PE," John said, his voice rife with accusation. "I didn't know about Dumbo Jock. Luis begged me to go into the locker room to retrieve his English Lit homework from the top of a locker he couldn't reach. Some football player had stashed it there. There wasn't any homework. Luis lied. Lied so I'd get a swirlie from Dumbo Jock!"

"I didn't know!" Luis shouted. "It was a year ago.

Get over it."

It was Edith's turn to roll her eyes. She leaned across the table toward Zuri. "Boys. Duuuuumb."

Zuri couldn't suppress a giggle. "Yeah."

"The only ghost I know about that haunts the library is The Librarian," Edith said. "An old lady wearing a skirt with granny glasses perched on her nose and hair in a bun. She goes around the stacks, moving books. The only problem is I don't think she can see very well. She places the books out of order. You're certain the apparition you saw wasn't her?"

Zuri shook her head. "I don't think so. My impression…my impression is the ghost isn't old. I don't know if that makes any sense."

Edith smiled. "It's okay. I know what you mean. I have an idea. There's a book called The Compendium in a locked room in the library. It has descriptions of all the ghosts seen in school. My friend Chloe might be able to get us access, but it will take time to set up."

"That's a good idea," Luis said.

The boys had stopped glaring at each other and followed the conversation with interest.

"Only if the librarian doesn't find out," John said between bites of ham sandwich.

Luis groaned. "Mrs. Binder is the worst."

"She isn't that bad and she won't find out," Edith said. "What do you say, Zuri? Do you want to look through The Compendium?"

Zuri chewed on her bottom lip. She wanted to know more about the ghost. She wasn't sure why, but despite the unease the encounter left her with, she was also drawn to the phantom. Like they were kindred spirits, somehow. She needed to know more about the specter if only to sate her curiosity.

"Yeah," Zuri said. "I want to look through The Compendium."

Chapter 15

Showdown

After school, Zuri and Luis met up in the library to study. At Luis's insistence, they worked at the same table where she'd experienced the paranormal encounter. Zuri tried to concentrate as Luis reviewed the problems she missed on the test, but thoughts of Big Jake bludgeoning her mother to death and her ambivalence regarding her desire to encounter the ghost for a second time kept cawing in her mind like a murder of crows.

"What's wrong?" Luis asked, tapping the tip of his pencil against the marked-up test—*tick, tick, tick.*

Blinking, Zuri strained to pull herself back to the here and now, but still the ghastly thoughts squawked. Were the corvids circling inside her skull harbingers of the future or denizens of a tired mind? "Sorry, my mind wandered."

Luis gave her an exasperated look. "You need to pay attention. These are the questions you missed. You'll flunk your next test if you don't learn how to solve these. The problems you'll be solving will be harder than these, and the skills you need to solve these, you will also need to solve those."

Tick, tick, tick. God, that was annoying. If Luis didn't stop with the pencil, she might have to do something drastic. "I'm sorry. Okay? I have a lot on my mind. Not just the test."

Zuri placed her hand on his hand, which held the pencil. His skin was soft, smooth, and warm—an intellectual's hands. Not a fighter's hands or a laborer's. Her father had been both. Huge palms and knuckles full of calluses. There was something comforting about Luis's hands. At one time, she would've thought him a weakling. But she knew that he wasn't. His mind was a weapon as honed as any razor-edged blade. And his hands…he used his hands to build wonderous creations as opposed to using them as weapons. His expression softened, and he looked at her with yearning in his eyes.

"Can you stop that?" she said. "It's annoying."

"Oh, sorry." Luis dropped his gaze to her hand, holding his. "I can get fidgety when I'm nervous."

"Why are you nervous?" Zuri asked, tenderly squeezing his hand before letting go.

Luis shifted uncomfortably. "I'm not. I don't know. Are you ready to study?"

They worked together side-by-side, with their shoulders brushing, and even once, their heads coming gently together, which elicited giggling from both of them. Zuri discovered the dark messengers on black wings retreated to the back of her mind. She still heard the crows' cries, but the din was distant, announcing worries that could be addressed later. Now, she was with Luis and, to her surprise, found herself learning to solve algebraic equations. Moreover, she experienced that inner warmth, like the coziness of a glowing hearth, staving off anything that might chill her—ill thoughts, turbulent emotions, and the ambient temperature.

Zuri felt safe. Even as Luis corrected her mistakes, and there were many, she never felt judged as she plodded through the first and then the second algebra problem. And there was comfort, more than she would ever have imagined possible, that she didn't need to fear that he would ever become physical with her like Toby Alkorn or beat her like Big Jake did to her mother.

After they finished the second problem and were about to move on to the third, movement in the stacks caught Zuri's attention. She immediately tensed and stared into the shelves of books, fearing she'd catch sight of the apparition. But no, it was only a small girl with hackneyed hair and coke bottle glasses that were too large for her face reshelving books. She was so slight she could be mistaken for eleven or twelve, but there was a jaded, world-weary air to her demeanor that indicated she was indeed a teenager.

"That's Chloe," Luis whispered.

"Should we ask to see The Compendium?" Zuri asked.

Luis shook his head. "Nah. Mrs. Binder is around, and Chloe is a real goody-goody. If we ask her, she'll go tattle to Mrs. Binder right away. We need to let Edith talk to her. Do her thing."

Zuri nodded, and they worked one more problem before leaving the library for the gym and home.

****

Zuri arrived at the duplex ready for a hot shower, soaking wet from sweat and a brief squall on her jog home. To her surprise, Amari sat prim and proper at the dining room table, with her phone on the tabletop before her. She had yet to change out of her work clothes, which was unusual. Zuri was already on guard as she took off her shoes and unslung her damp backpack.

"Hi, Mom. I'm going to shower." She headed for the

hallway, carrying her pack in her right arm.

"Not yet, Zuri." Amari patted the chair next to her. "We have something to discuss first."

Zuri's jaw clenched. Forcing a smile, she faced her mother, gazing at the phone. She half expected to see her grades displayed on the screen, but the phone was locked and the display blank. "I'm cold." She didn't need to feign shivering.

"Not so cold you can't speak with your mother for five minutes." Amari picked up her phone, pointing the screen at her face, using her biometrics to unlock the device. "Sit."

Klaxons blared, shrill and irritating through Zuri's skull. This had to be about her algebra grade. She quickly reviewed all her grades in her mind. Solid Bs and an A in physical education, of course. Mother could only take issue with algebra. This wasn't the ideal time to have a showdown regarding her C minus, but then again, there never would be a perfect moment. Heaving a sigh, Zuri crossed the room, dropped her school bag on the floor, and flopped down in the chair next to her mother.

Zuri crossed her arms before her chest. "Is this about my algebra grade?"

Amari raised an eyebrow. "Oh, you are aware of your poor grade. Yet, you seem to spend as much time at the gym as always. I thought I made it clear that I would not pay for your gym membership if you did not maintain acceptable grades, Zuri. A C minus. An F on your last exam. What is going on?"

Amari set the phone on the table; the screen displayed the teen's grades.

"I haven't been spending as much time at the gym," Zuri said, voice rising. "I've been—"

"It doesn't seem that way to me."

"Are you even going to listen to me?"

"I am listening."

"You interrupted me," Zuri snapped.

Amari took a deep breath, collecting herself. "I apologize. I will try to listen better. Please continue."

Zuri didn't want to continue. She didn't want to have anything to do with this conversation, but Mother controlled the purse strings. It was so unfair. "I have been studying. With Luis. Every day after school. I swear."

Amari's eyes narrowed. "What about the night of the watch party? That was the evening before your test. You were out late, as I recall. Did you study that evening?"

Groaning, Zuri dropped her gaze to the table. "No. I didn't. I should have."

"A little late for that realization." Amari tapped the screen, indicating the F.

"I know." Zuri grabbed her backpack off the floor and set it on her lap. "But I'm studying. I really am. You have to believe me."

"Regardless of whether I believe you, Zuri, you are not holding up your end of the bargain. I pay for the gym as long as you maintain good grades. That is the deal."

Zuri opened the backpack and pulled out the test and the scratch paper she had worked problems on with Luis. "Look. I did this after school with Luis. In the library. He's helping me. I'll raise the grade. I promise." Inspiration struck Zuri at that instant. "I've been distracted. About your new job. You writing for the paper. What if Father finds out? I've had dreams. Flashbacks. Sometimes it's hard to concentrate."

Amari's expression wilted. "Oh, Zuri." She took her

daughter's hand and squeezed. "Why didn't you tell me? I knew you were worried, but…" she sighed. "I didn't know you were having PTSD."

PTSD meant counselors. Zuri didn't want to deal with that. Not now. Not ever. She lightened her tone. "It's not that bad, but sometimes it makes it hard to concentrate. But it's getting better now. Luis is really helping me a lot. Mr. Tito even told me not to spend as much time at the gym. To spend more time studying. I have been, Mom. Honest."

Amari stared at the ceiling for a minute. "Okay. Okay. I must admit Luis and Mr. Tito have been good influences on you. Walk me through these problems Luis helped you with."

Walk through the problems?

Great…despite doubting her ability, Zuri showed Amari step-by-step how to solve the algebraic equations, only stumbling in her explanations twice. Mother was impressed, and before Zuri left the table for the shower, she had negotiated another two months of gym payments with the expectation that she would raise her grade to at least a B minus by the end of those two months for payments to continue.

Chapter 16

Connection

Knowing she was on thin ice, Zuri made a beeline for the library after school. Two months. That's all she had to raise her algebra grade. Last night, two months seemed like plenty of time after she had successfully explained the solutions to the three algebraic equations to Mother. Now, sitting alone in the library, looking at the other two questions she missed, two months did not seem nearly long enough.

She fished the cell phone out of her backpack and checked the time. Frowning, she placed the phone on the table. Luis was ten minutes late. That was totally unlike him. "Where are you, Luis?" she murmured.

Gotta grind. Zuri buckled down, attempting to make sense of the two remaining problems. All she accomplished was making her head throb. Why in the world did she need to waste her time studying this? It was so stupid and unfair. She shook her head to clear the downward spiral of dismal thoughts. Being a crybaby about her situation would only guarantee losing the gym money. Instead of trying to work the last three problems, she turned her attention to the three she'd already solved with Luis's assistance. At the very least, she could review the solutions to ensure she understood every step.

Zuri was pleased to find that was a task she was up

to, even if she had to fight to keep her mind from wandering. After about ten minutes, she reviewed the first two problems to her satisfaction. She understood every step—at least, she thought she did, maybe. A niggling voice whispered in the back of her consciousness: *if you truly understood the problems, you'd be able to solve the other two without Luis's help.*

She rechecked the time. Nearly twenty minutes late? What was with Luis? She typed out a text.

—I'll be in the library for another thirty minutes.—

Zuri almost placed her phone on the table. Almost. Friday night was Malee Chaiyathorn's title fight. The lure of The Jade Tiger was powerful. A siren's song beckoning her to throw away her dreams for a shot of dopamine. Just one clip. A reward for reviewing the problems all by herself. It would only take two minutes, and then she could look at the remaining questions with fresh eyes.

As she typed The Jade Tiger's name in the search bar, a sepulchral stench wafted from nearby, and her breath frosted. The biting cold made goosebumps prickle her flesh, and the phone slipped from her grasp, striking the table with a dull thump. Centimeter by centimeter, Zuri twisted her neck until she faced the stacks. Levitating before the row of books was the slate gray apparition, radiating cold and boneyard stink. Fear pulsed through Zuri, along with recognition. Like she knew this ghost. Knew the ghost intimately, almost as well as she knew herself. The ambivalence of her feelings and the impossibility of the specter being a kindred spirit were puzzles that piqued the teen's curiosity. Also, she needed help if she was going to raise her algebra grade, and, well, Luis had ghosted her.

"Are…are you here to help me with math?" Zuri asked tremulously.

The phantom might've nodded; Zuri wasn't sure. The apparition was still indistinct. A featureless artist's impression of the human form. Nevertheless, the ghost floated toward her, the coldness and reek becoming more intense. Once again, she could taste a rotten flavor on her tongue. It was enough to make her want to retch, almost. She sensed that the disgusting taste, the noisome odor, and the cold were not as strong as during her first encounter.

Levitating beside Zuri, the spectral entity reached its nebulous arm for the pencil resting on the table beside the test. Zuri battled the desire to cower at the very least, or even better, to sprint from the library and never look back. Fingers like wisps of smoke curled around the writing implement, frost forming where they touched. The pencil rose from the table, and the apparition moved closer as if leaning over the test.

"I…I need to…work on these two." Zuri pointed to the two problems she had missed, errantly brushing her elbow against the phantasm. Coldness made her flesh tingle beneath her sweatshirt, but it was not the searing frostbite she had previously experienced. Even stranger, there was a flash of imagery in her mind's eye. Pale arms raised defensively as a bowie knife slashed and stabbed. Each time the knife fell, terrible pain lanced through Zuri's hands and forearms. The images only lasted a second, flickering out as quickly as they came. But it was enough. Zuri gaped at the ghost and whispered. "I've dreamed about you."

Lambent light shimmered inside the nebulous form, starting near the center, at the core. The luminosity grew in intensity, shafts piercing the slate cloak. Zuri glimpsed a pale, nigh translucent young girl in a high-collared dress through the enigmatic shawl. Then, a door banged from the front of the library, followed by Mrs. Binder's shrill voice.

"No running, Mr. Torres."

The radiance faded like the last beams of sunlight, cut off by dark clouds and a far horizon. The gray mist swirled, blotting out the girl's face. At the same time, the phantom withdrew toward the stacks.

"No, wait!" Zuri cried, reaching for the phantasm, the innocent young girl. "Don't go!"

The ghost hovered next to the shelving, and for the briefest of instances, Zuri believed she might stay a little longer. But that was not to be. With a poof the shade dissipated through the shelving and books, like smoke from a blown out candelabrum.

****

In the sanctum below the school, the ancient enmity shuddered like a monstrous creature waking from a long and restless hibernation. The icon containing the rancorous presence shook upon the plinth. The rats made fat and potent by the radiation from the idol paused in their activity, listening, sniffing the air, and on the lookout for the deadly green light. Even the nightcrawlers burrowed deeper or tucked in further into hideaways, driven by something more primordial than the instinct to survive.

The shaking stopped. The rats continued their business, and the nightcrawlers slowed their burrowing or edged out of bolt holes. Although they feared the diabolical manifestation contained within the statuette, they were driven mad with lust for the power it granted them. To bathe in that sublime radiation for one more second, for one more electrical pulse along nerves, was worth the risk of death.

Slowly, a consciousness awoke within the malevolent aura. The consciousness was muddled, nascent, malformed.

Where am I?

The thought would have echoed in its skull had it still possessed one.

My body...what happened to my body?

Existential terror gripped the wayward spirit, and a terrible ululation sprang from the icon. The banshee wail rebounded through the chamber. Rats convulsed, and blood poured from their ears. The weaker rodents, those who had enjoyed the bounty of the radiation for the shortest amount of time or nearest to the end of their unnatural lifespan, died in agony. Their corpses grist for nightcrawlers and the surviving rodentia.

But as all good things must come to an end, so must all the horrors, even if what terrifies us seems to linger and linger and linger. Memory seeped and spurted into the consciousness. Recollection and abysmal purpose. The dark magic as black as any devilry wrought on the living world. The obsession. Spells woven over years. And the sacrifice. The virginal ichor of his descendent. All to protect what he had created. What he had paid for in sweat and blood.

His legacy.

The legacy of George O'Dell—entrepreneur, leading citizen, philanthropist, sorcerer, and filicide.

Good Old George. He is I, and I am him.

But then he experienced the most terrible realization of his existence, both from before and after death. The keystone of all his work was loose. Threatening to ruin everything.

The idol shrieked a single name: "Rrrrrrooooooosssse!"

Chapter 17

Ambush

"No!" Zuri stared at the shelving where the ghost had disappeared. "I want to help you. I need your help."

Of course, she didn't know if the apparition needed or wanted help. But that seemed like a safe assumption, given the nightmares. The bowie knife rising and falling, wielded by the cruel killer in the white suit. In the second, he had been chanting something. The only problem was the words were in a foreign tongue she couldn't recognize or pronounce. The demise of whoever the man in the white suit attacked was written in blood. Maybe the victim wasn't Zuri's spectral visitor. Didn't all ghosts appear pale and nearly translucent?

The girl had certainly looked white, petite, and as pale as the thin arms of the victim in the dream implied. Generally, Zuri found all white people looked pallid. And in all honesty, she didn't know if the person being slain in the phantasmagoria was a girl, a young boy, or even a slight woman.

"Zuri!" Luis called, disturbing her rumination.

She looked at him, anxious to talk about her second ghostly encounter and to be tutored. But she immediately backburnered those subjects when she spied him, speed walking and looking harried with a thin trickle of blood running from the corner of his mouth down his chin.

She stood so quickly she nearly overturned her chair. "Luis, what happened?"

His eyes were moist and bloodshot like he'd been crying. Reaching the table, he leaned against it, breathing deeply to catch his breath.

"You're bleeding." Zuri glanced around for something to wipe away the blood. "What happened?"

Luis swiped the blood with the back of his hand, wincing. "The Anderson brothers jumped me in the bathroom."

"What? You can't be serious. I'll...I'll..." Beat them. Kill them. No, she wasn't Big Jake. She wasn't. "I'll teach them a lesson." She wasn't sure what lesson yet, but she'd figure that out. "Where are they?"

Luis dabbed his lips and grimaced. "I think they're out in the hall."

Hands clenching into fists, Zuri strode past her friend. "Stay here. I'll take care of this."

"No, Zuri, it's okay. I don't think they'll come inside the library. They know Mrs. Binder is here."

A hand on her shoulder tried to pull her back. Zuri spun, glaring at Luis. As he stared at her with rheumy eyes and trembling lips, she hated him and could have punched him right in his pudgy midsection. She detested him for not understanding that bullies had to be taught hard lessons. She despised him even more for not understanding her. Standing up to bullies, no matter what was central to her identity.

"Consider the consequences of being suspended," he warned.

Her expression softened, her anger at Luis gone faster than it had emerged. "The consequences of not standing up to bullies are worse. They need to understand that if they mess with you, I'm coming for them, and I won't stop."

Luis slumped against the table again and gulped. "Don't do anything drastic?"

"Drastic? Of course not." Zuri winked at him. "I'm only going to talk to them."

But, of course, that was a lie. She didn't know what she would do to the brothers, but it would involve more than harsh words.

Zuri quickly strode through the stacks, breaking into a jog when she reached the front of the library. From the circulation desk, Mrs. Binder shrilly chided her for running. She slowed but still could've passed as an Olympic speed walker. She spotted the Anderson brothers through the glass doors. They saw her at virtually the same time. The bigger one's eyes and mouth went wide as she burst through the doors.

"You didn't say she would be here!" he yelped as he broke into a run down the hallway.

"Shit!" The smaller brother took off in the same direction.

Zuri loped after them. They couldn't outrun her. She could keep this pace for miles and still go three rounds in the octagon afterward. They came to an intersection where heading straight led to the lunchroom, and hooking a right, went to the front of the building, near the office, and outside to where the brothers undoubtedly had their scooters stowed. With a burst of speed, she headed them off. Having a tussle in front of the administrators seemed like a bad idea, as did allowing the brothers access to their scooters. The last thing she wanted was dodging a hunk of metal swung at her head.

The brothers, as bright red as tomatoes from

exertion, slid over the linoleum, shoes squeaking. They took the only path left, racing toward the lunchroom and through the double doors. Smirking, Zuri followed. They were hers now. There were only two ways out of the lunchroom: the double doors leading back into the hallway and the door in the back opening onto the expansive sports fields behind the school. Either location was a fine place for a rumble.

Zuri slithered into the lunchroom before the double doors clanked shut behind the brothers. They were about a quarter of the way across the space, heading for the back door. The larger boy was starting to fall behind his brother, who, for his part, did not slow his pace despite his lagging sibling's pleas. So much for familial loyalty.

Zuri picked up her pace, planning to intercept the boys before they escaped the lunchroom since the area appeared deserted. They'd have a nice long and private discussion. That's when, out of nowhere, a morbidly obese man or boy dressed in ill-fitting shorts and a T-shirt that failed to hide his bulk appeared before Zuri. She was moving too fast—and the figure was too close for her to prevent a collision. She slammed into him, rebounding and landing hard enough on her tailbone to make her wince.

The huge figure hovered over her with a malevolent glint in deep-set eyes and drool running down his chin. He breathed in great huffing puffs, spewing bad breath that stank like roadkill left to decay in one-hundred-degree heat. From between thick, dangling legs, Zuri saw the Anderson brothers were halfway across the lunchroom now. They were going to escape because Fat Nick blocked her path.

"I can see you," Zuri whispered.

The ghost reached for her with mammoth, greasy hands.

"I know how you died," Zuri said. "Do you want me to tell you?"

Nick froze except for his eyes. Those widened until they looked like they would roll right out of their sockets.

"Stop those boys. Make them understand they don't want to mess with my friends or me again. Do that, and I won't tell you how you died."

Nick nodded once, triple chins wobbling. In a blink, he was gone, only to reappear beside the bigger of the Andersons. Nick's bulk crashed into him, sending him sprawling across the floor like a hockey puck. Then, the ghost dematerialized, reappearing in front of the other boy before he reached the back door. He must've seen Fat Nick because he veered away from the phantom. But Nick caught him in hands the size of hams and dumped him squealing into a garbage can. Judging by the squelching sound, the can hadn't been emptied since the last lunch period.

Nodding with satisfaction, Zuri left the lunchroom. She had made her point more resoundingly than she could have with her fists.

Chapter 18

Eye-opening

"Zuri, what did you do?" Luis gasped as he peered into the lunchroom through the vertical rectangular window built-in to the door. Both Anderson brothers were stuffed inside the garbage can and struggling to extricate themselves. "Oh, no. You promised not to fight."

Zuri glanced into the lunchroom, unable to keep a smirk from her face. Fat Nick was already gone, but she doubted the Anderson brothers would dare lay a finger on Luis again. "I didn't touch them."

"But…" Luis fell silent. From nearby in the hallway came whistling. "Hank is coming. We better get out of here unless you want to explain how they ended up in the garbage can."

A thud resounded inside the lunchroom. The garbage can overturned, spilling the Andersons, half-eaten lunches, leaking milk jugs, and other detritus across the floor.

"You're right." Zuri giggled and pushed Luis down the hallway. "Run."

****

When they arrived at the library entrance, Luis was out of breath and sweat glistened across his brow. He also looked like he'd been socked in the face, his lower lip swelling on the left side. The bleeding, however, had stopped.

"We better grab our stuff and get you home," Zuri said as she inspected her friend's wound with a critical and knowing gaze. "You need to ice your lip. It's starting to swell."

Luis's eyes widened. "My mom is going to kill me if she thinks I've been in a fight."

"Please, you were jumped in the bathroom." Zuri took hold of the door handle but didn't pull the door open. "Tell her the truth."

"She'll want answers. She'll call the school." Luis wrung his hands. "That will lead back to whatever happened in the lunchroom and your role in it."

With a roll of her eyes, Zuri opened the door. "You don't have to worry about what happened in the lunchroom, Luis. Let's get our stuff all quiet like…unless you want to explain to Mrs. Binder why you have a fat lip."

Luis emphatically shook his head in the negative and followed Zuri inside the library. Mrs. Binder eyeballed them sternly from her perch on a stool behind the computer at the circulation desk, where she scanned the books' barcodes.

Zuri positioned herself between her friend and the librarian, flashing her most winning smile. "Hello, Mrs. Binder."

"Miss Williams. Mr. Torres. I will tolerate no more rowdiness from the two of you. Running in the library is unacceptable." The teens slowed to a halt. A sure way to anger the librarian was to stay on the move while being lectured. Zuri made sure she stood in front of Luis. "I certainly expected better from a scholar like you, Mr.

Torres."

"I apologize, Mrs. Binder," Luis said. "It won't happen again."

"And you, Miss Williams." Mrs. Binder leaned forward and frowned. "I'd hate to have to conclude that you are a bad influence on Mr. Torres."

A bad influence? Anger flashed. *A bad influence?* How dare that old bat say that? What an entitled...*Calm down. Calm down. Be the bigger person.*

"She's not..." Zuri kicked Luis in the shin with her heel to silence him. He took the hint.

"I don't mean to be a bad influence on Luis. I'll do better," Zuri said, even though the words turned her stomach.

Mrs. Binder leaned back on the stool, giving Zuri an appraising look. Her lips twitched upward in a brief smile quickly replaced by a straight-lipped neutral expression. "You do that, Miss Williams, you do that."

The librarian went back to scanning books, and the teens ambled at a scholarly pace to the back of the library, where their school supplies were stashed on the study table. Luis grabbed his backpack as Zuri collected her stuff. She paused over the test, squinting.

"Luis?" Zuri picked up the test. "Did you solve this problem?"

"No." He shook his head. "I didn't even look at it."

"This looks like the ghost's handwriting," Zuri said.

Luis dropped his backpack. "Let me see." He took the paper from Zuri and sat in a chair, leaning over the test. "You're right. That is the ghost's handwriting. Let me see if the answer is correct."

Zuri inspected the pencil on the table next to the test paper. Not seeing any frost on the writing implement, she picked it up, only to immediately wince due to the cold burning her digits and drop the pencil. The pencil clattered to the table, rolled to the edge, and stopped.

Luis glanced up. "What? Oh, cold?"

His gaze flicked to the pencil, then back to Zuri.

She massaged her chilled fingers. "Super cold."

Luis reached for the pencil but stopped short of picking it up. Instead, he held his hand a few inches above the writing implement.

"Careful," Zuri said.

"It's not radiating cold." He edged his hand closer to the pencil. "Not like last time."

Zuri held up her reddened fingertips. "I don't know. It felt cold when I touched it."

Luis reached closer until his fingers were centimeters from the pencil. "I still don't feel anything. Did you see the ghost?"

"She showed up before you and disappeared when Mrs. Binder told you not to run."

"She?" Luis picked up the pencil and held the writing implement out to Zuri. "It's a little cold but not freezing."

Tentatively, Zuri tapped the pencil with a finger. "Strange. You saw my fingers. I was getting frostbite."

Luis nodded. "Agreed. Given what happened to your fingers, I'd expect the pencil to be colder than it is."

"I don't want the pencil," Zuri said.

Luis shrugged. "I'll hold onto it." He picked up his backpack and slid the pencil into a back pocket. "Are you going tell me about your second encounter?"

"Shouldn't we be going?" Zuri whispered. "I thought you were worried about me having to explain what happened to the Andersons."

Luis grimaced. "You're right. Let me finish checking your ghostly friend's work, and we can skedaddle. You can give me the deets on the way home."

"Of course." Zuri nodded.

The teen boy focused on the algebra problem and solution, murmuring. "Simplify completely i(5−i)." His finger moved along the lines of the apparition's elegant script. "Good. Okay." He nodded in the affirmative. "Equals 1+5i." He looked up at Zuri. "It's correct. Have you had a chance to study the solution?"

"No, she…the ghost, I mean, must have come back when we were gone and solved it."

"Huh." Luis looked around the library. "I really want to meet this ghost. Let's go. I can walk you through the solution on the way home after you tell me all about your ethereal tutor and…" his voice dropped to a whisper. "…what happened in the lunchroom."

****

They exited the school by a side door to avoid passing the office just in case the Andersons were there, attempting to explain how they ended up in a garbage can and fingering Zuri. The day was clear, if a little blustery, with the sun providing enough warmth to beat back the worst of the wind's chill. Across an access road was the harvested field littered with the yellow desiccated remains of corn stalks. Beyond the field stood the forest, trees swaying in the wind. A few red and gold leaves clung stubbornly to the branches of the many deciduous trees but most already blanketed the forest floor.

"Still want to walk through the woods?" Luis asked.

Zuri looked at him quizzically.

"After seeing the ghosts. Do you want to still want

to walk through the woods? Remember what I told you? People who enter the woods don't come out."

"I remember," Zuri said lightly. "On the first day of school after I saved you from the Anderson brothers."

Luis guffawed. "That was the best walk to school ever!"

When Zuri glimpsed the trees, she only felt darkness, like a sable shawl draped over her soul. She knew there was no way she wanted to travel the woods, no matter how desperately they beckoned to her in a singsong: *Come play beneath our branches and cavort through our fallen leaves.*

"Tell me about the ghost from the library," Luis said.

Come play beneath our branches and cavort through our fallen leaves. You will find. You will find. That you will never want to leave.

Zuri shook her head and looked at Luis. "What?"

"The ghost from the library. Tell me about it."

After a final glance at the forest, Zuri tore her attention back to her friend and the walk home. The trees didn't really call her. That was her imagination…but she had only started believing in ghosts a few days ago…no, trees did not sing. Period. Full stop.

Taking a deep breath, Zuri told Luis about her encounter with the phantasm in the library and her nightmare featuring the man in white as they walked, and to her relief, the woodland's call lessened with every footstep until the singsong was nothing but an unpleasant and slightly whimsical memory.

"Wow. You really think you dreamed about the ghost that you later saw in the library?" Luis said. "That is weird. And this man in white…"

Luis shook his head.

"Recognize him?" Zuri asked.

"No, but we need to tell Edith and John about the dream. Your latest paranormal encounter. Everything."

Zuri frowned. "John thinks I'm a liar."

"They might know something. This whole dream thing isn't good, Zuri. We need to get to the bottom of it."

Zuri grunted noncommittally.

Luis glanced at her. "I'm serious."

"I am seriously undecided. I don't like being called a liar."

"And the lunchroom?" Luis asked to change the subject.

The memory of the brothers stuffed into the trashcan made Zuri smile. After she recounted what happened, Luis's jaw went unhinged. "No way! That's awesome. I'm glad you didn't beat them up. Wow. Your description of Fat Nick...that's exactly how John describes him. There's no way he can call you a liar now."

Chapter 19

Building Trust

Zuri was eminently pleased with John's gobsmacked expression after she described Fat Nick to him and Edith during lunch the next day. The gaunt lad's mouth gaped wide enough that masticated hunks of ham sandwich fell onto the table, which was admittedly disgusting.

"Ewww," Edith said, looking away.

"I was right," Luis said, undisturbed by the disgorged food. "Zuri accurately described Fat Nick."

Zuri had described the obese poltergeist in great detail, which, chewed-up sandwich aside, wasn't conducive to having much of an appetite—at least, for her and Edith. The boys didn't have that issue. Luis had already devoured half his cheese pizza, which smelled enticing in an overly greasy kind of way, and well, John's food littered the table.

John went red in the face, brushing the munched-on ham and bread into the stainless steel container he used to transport his sandwich. "Sorry," he murmured to his girlfriend.

"I'm in the same boat as Luis," Edith said. "I've seen flashes of Fat Nick, but I've never had a good look at him." She shuddered. "I'm glad I haven't, honestly. Your description matches what John has shared with me." She glared pointedly at her boyfriend. "More than once. Even after I told him I didn't want to hear it."

Zuri's hunger won out over her revulsion at the recollection of Nick's appearance and John's antics. She picked up the room-temperature pizza, grease running over her fingers in rivulets, and took a bite.

John glanced between the mousy girl and Zuri, mildly shamefaced. "Agreed. The description is accurate."

Zuri swallowed the bite of cheese pizza, thinking school lunch had rarely tasted so delicious. "I told you I wasn't lying."

"For the record, I still think...ouch!"

Edith elbowed John in the side and turned back to the group.

"That hurt," he complained.

"For the record," Edith said sweetly. "John no longer thinks you lied about ghosts or anything else. Right, John?"

John's face became even redder, the color spreading to his neck, and he shot his girlfriend a dark look. "I'm sorry I ever doubted you."

The gaunt boy didn't sound sincere, but Zuri decided not to call him out. John was still a skeptic, but she had won this round. No need to rub his face in defeat.

"Tell them about your second encounter in the library and the dream," Luis prompted.

Zuri dropped her gaze to the table, and appetite going the way of the dinosaurs, tossed her quarter-eaten pizza onto the institutional tray. The salad, consisting solely of sad-looking iceberg lettuce drizzled in what was supposed to be ranch dressing but looked decidedly blue, did not inspire ravenousness. Her second encounter with the phantasm was unsettling enough, but recalling the dream was so chilling that goosebumps rose on her arms, and she shivered.

Luis took her hand comfortingly in his. His fingers were greasy. "I can recount what happened for you."

Zuri lifted her gaze and shook her head. "No, I can do it."

Nodding encouragement, Luis withdrew his hand. Zuri placed her hands in her lap after wiping off the grease with a napkin. After brief consideration, she related her second encounter with the apparition in the library. Edith listened with rapt attention, never blinking. Even John appeared enthralled, leaning forward and not once taking a bite of his sandwich.

"Your instincts were right," Edith said. "That definitely doesn't sound like The Librarian. Way too young."

John nodded. "Agreed." He added thoughtfully, "What about this dream you had?"

Zuri felt like a zip tie was cinched around her throat. For an interminable instant, she feared she couldn't breathe, and panic set in. In that liminal spell between seconds, images flashed in her mind's eye—the man in white, stabbing and slashing with the blood-coated bowie knife, only to transform into Big Jake, scarlet-stained fists rising and falling to a melody of juicy smacks and squelches. But the moment passed, and Zuri swallowed the lump in her throat. After taking a deep breath, she haltingly spilled the tea.

As Zuri spoke, Edith gasped and placed a hand in front of her gaping mouth. John's eyes narrowed, and his lips drooped into a frown. When Zuri's voice cracked and she fell silent, Luis gently encouraged her to continue until she finally finished the retelling.

"Oh, my God, Zuri," Edith said. "That dream sounds terrible."

John nodded in agreement. "Terrible and not a good thing. Not a good thing at all."

"What does that mean?" Zuri demanded.

John blinked, taken aback by her vehemence. "I…I don't know."

Edith spoke up. "I've never heard about someone…someone having a dream and being absolutely convinced it was connected to a ghost."

"What do you mean?" Zuri looked around the table. "People at this school must dream about ghosts all the time. Right?"

"I don't," Luis said and added quickly. "That's probably because I only dream about math."

John chuckled but turned somber after Edith glared at him.

"Of course, people have dreams about ghosts," Edith said. "But…I've never heard someone talking about feeling so connected to a ghost in their dreams."

John nodded. "Believe me, I've dreamed about Dumbo Jock, but my connection with him ends with him giving me a swirly. This whole thing about you experiencing how the girl died. That's not normal."

Zuri looked to Luis, who shrugged. "I told you it's concerning."

"Believe me, I'm concerned," Zuri said dryly and turned to the couple. "Can't we ask someone—like a ghost?"

"Don't waste your breath," John scoffed. "The ghosts around here have their own agenda. Mostly, that is either bullying people or screwing with their minds.

117

That's something you need to consider. Maybe the ghost is messing with you. In that dream, you're sure you didn't understand the language?"

Zuri shook her head.

"I wonder…" Edith bit her lower lip "…you said it was like this man in white was chanting. What if he was casting a spell?"

"That's something we could research," John said, nodding. "There has to be something we can find about demonic languages or spell craft."

"What about The Compendium?" Luis asked.

Edith smiled. "Good news on that. Chloe can get us access during lunchtime on Friday. Zuri and I will look at the book. All you boys need to do is distract Mrs. Binder."

"Great," John grumbled, and Luis sighed.

"In the meantime, maybe you should avoid the library," Edith told Zuri. "Until we have a better idea—"

"No." Zuri shook her head. "The ghost. No, not a ghost, the little girl needs my help. I'm going to help her."

Her friends tried to dissuade her, even Luis, but Zuri remained firm in her intention to return to the library after school. The bell announced the end of the lunch period while Edith continued pleading with Zuri not to be foolish and put herself at risk.

The friends rose from the table, Edith clearly distressed.

"Don't worry," Luis said. "I'll be with Zuri. I've got her back."

Edith crossed her arms before her chest and glowered at Luis. "You better have her back, Luis

Torres, because if anything happens to Zuri, I will never forgive you." She turned her glower on Zuri, the intensity of her gaze enough to melt ice. "Or you."

****

Zuri sat alone in the back of the library with her marked-up algebra test on the study table, along with her math book and current homework. In her hand, she held her cell phone with the message "She is here," ready to send to Luis, who was stationed at a nearby study table that was out of sight around the corner. With any luck, he was far enough away the apprehensive apparition would make an appearance.

Five minutes ticked by. Nothing. Not a hint of graveyard stink or abysmal cold. Half groaning and half sighing, Zuri set down her phone and flipped the algebra book open to the page with today's homework, which included ten problems she didn't know how to solve. She paid attention in class. She really did, but nothing seemed to stick. Everything was in one ear and out the other without leaving a trace in her consciousness. Why couldn't she absorb the information like a sponge? Almost as an afterthought, Zuri took out her marked up test and placed it next to the algebra book—she still needed help solving the problem.

Don't death spiral, girl. Reread the pages we went over in class and try to do homework. Besides, she could always call Luis over to help her if the ghost girl didn't show up in the next ten minutes. Young girl to help or not, Zuri still needed to raise her math grade.

Zuri surprised herself by reading a page and a half before she yawned for the first time. That must be a new record. Usually, she was yawning by the second sentence. What wasn't surprising was that she didn't understand anything she read. Sure, she understood the words, even the sentences. Her reading comprehension was fine. But she couldn't make heads or tails of the math, which might as well be written in an alien language.

Warm light, like the rays of the setting sun, spilled across the page. Zuri looked up and sharply drew in her breath. Floating beside the table was the girl, unobscured by the gray mist from the waist up. Below the waist, the fog swirled, as expansive as a hoop ballroom gown. The warm light radiated from the girl much like the cold had discharged from the slate-gray apparition. Despite the light, her pallor was so pale she was almost translucent.

Zuri took her cell phone and hit send. The ghost watched, eyes narrowing with suspicion. The phone buzzed. It occurred to her that the ghostly girl might understand that the phone was a communication device. For all she knew, the girl might be familiar with cell phones.

"I told my friend you're here."

The ghost's eyes widened, and she started withdrawing toward the stacks.

"Wait. I can tell him not to come. Will you stay then?"

The girl stopped and nodded at once.

Zuri quickly typed out a message.

——*stay where you're at. I will try to gain her trust.*——

She hit send and placed the phone screen facing down on the table.

Chapter 20

Help

"I told him not to come," Zuri told the spectral girl. "It's just you and me."

Assuming he gets the text. Assuming he reads the text. Assuming he does as he's told.

Zuri pushed aside her doubts, hoping she hadn't made one assumption too many, and gave the girl her friendliest smile. It was the same grin she sometimes gave sparring partners in the gyms and back alleys she had frequented over the years before clobbering them, but the girl didn't know that—hopefully. She dreamed about the girl, maybe the girl had visions of her fighting or watching Big Jake nearly beat her mother to death. The latter was exceptionally unappealing. Some things were better kept buried in the past, and that was one of them.

The girl grinned in return, a slightly strained expression that showed no teeth. Nevertheless, it seemed like a step in the right direction, especially when she floated to the table. As the girl neared, Zuri felt a chill in the air, not as powerful as before, but enough to make her shiver, and she forced herself not to pull away. *Gain her trust. Gain her trust.*

Not retreating was easier thought than done when Zuri caught a whiff of boneyard stink. This time, she scooted back in the chair before stopping herself. Fortunately, like the coldness emanating from the phantasmal girl, the stench was not nearly as intense as during their previous encounter. She could tolerate it.

The girl seemed oblivious to Zuri's reaction to the odor, already considering the exam with an analytical gaze. She picked up the pencil, and after glancing at Zuri to ensure the teen paid attention, started working the problem.

****

Luis was enjoying some light reading when the phone buzzed, announcing the text from Zuri. If you can call Sir Isaac Newton's *The Principia: Mathematical Principles of Natural Philosophy* light. Luis liked going directly to the source material so he could draw his own conclusions from the works of great minds unsullied by the assumptions and ideas of lesser academics.

He finished reading the sentence he was on, bookmarked the page, and set the venerable tome on the study table. After confirming the text was indeed from his friend, girlfriend, maybe—no, but he could always dream—quietly, as a mouse he liked to think, he stood from the chair and crept along the wall, with phone in hand. It was all he could do to scurry along in silence and not break into an all-out sprint. He was so darn excited to finally meet the mathematically inclined ghost he could burst.

He had many questions. Too many questions. So many that he had made a list. He should have reviewed the list instead of reading. That was stupid. As a rule, Luis didn't like doing anything foolish and hated feeling stupid. Still, he had the list committed to memory.

The number one question: did she know Sir Isaac

Newton in life?

He tried to stop midstride and only managed to stumble, which made a little bit of noise, a mild thud. That wouldn't be enough to scare off the ghost girl, would it? Nah, Luis told himself, no way. He stopped because he'd forgotten the plan in his excitement.

He was supposed to reply to Zuri's message. He slowly typed out a message on his phone.

—Coming—

Geez, that must've taken him thirty seconds, at least. Luis was properly jealous of whirlwind phone jabbers who could type out five-paragraph essays in seconds. He was also envious of people who could text and walk at the same time. But the envy was tempered by the suspicion that texting while walking increased your chances of being run over by an automobile or running into something. He'd look up the statistics on that. He loved statistics. He loved anything to do with numbers, honestly. That's when he realized he was daydreaming instead of moving. *God, you sent the text. Now, get a move on.*

Just as Luis reached the wall's terminus, where all he needed to do was turn the corner to the left to gaze upon his beautiful, strong girlfriend—okay, not girlfriend—and the ghost, his phone buzzed. Luis slowed but didn't stop scampering. He knew he should check the text. That was part of the plan. Check any text that came…just in case he wasn't supposed to barge in on Zuri and the ghost. But boy, did he want to see the ghost. And ask questions! But Luis was a planner. He liked to plan and stick to the plan to the extent possible. That's how he built those massive models in his room. He came up with a design, and he followed it through to the end.

In his experience, deviation from the blueprint led to unsatisfactory results.

Luis stopped and checked the text.

——*stay where you're at. I will try to gain her trust.*——

"What?" Luis whispered and nearly tossed his phone on the floor, which was totally unlike him. He didn't toss his phone, like ever, and the only times he occasionally felt the urge to was when his sister teased or bullied him.

It took him a moment to realize that he was feeling something he rarely did in association with anything to do with Zuri. Irritation. Well, he might not have the opportunity to question the ghostly girl, but he intended to get an eyeful of her. That was a certainty.

I'm a spy. I'm a secret agent. Luis sidled along the wall, stopping right at the edge, and stuck his head out far enough to catch sight of Zuri and the ghost. His girlfriend—no, no, thinking like that will get him in trouble—his friend had her back to him. Floating next to the table was a pale girl in what might be called a Victorian-era blouse with a high collar from the waist up. From the waist down, the girl was a swirly slate grey fog.

That's when Luis decided to deviate from the plan. He didn't consider sneaking a glimpse of the ghost a deviation...that...that was just sating his curiosity. Snapping a photo of the ghost was an alteration, an improvisation. But how could he resist? The photo would provide indisputable evidence of the ghost for John and Edith. Of course, the ghost might not show up in a photo. Not all did. Well, there was only one way to find out.

After double-checking that his phone was entirely in

silent mode, the last thing he needed was a camera click to give him away, Luis edged his phone out until he saw Zuri and, to his satisfaction, the ghost on the screen. After taking a moment to adjust the angle for the optimal composition, Luis took the picture. Never one to linger after pilfering a cookie from the jar, Luis scampered quietly back to the study table and *The Principia: Mathematical Principles of Natural Philosophy.*

****

Zuri packed up her things after the ghost had walked her through the final test question and helped her with her homework. Luis was an excellent tutor, he really was, but the ghost was better. After studying with Luis, Zuri always felt her head was left spinning like she'd been spun around on a merry-go-round pushed by a three-hundred-pound linebacker. But after studying with the spirit, Zuri understood how to work all the equations. Not only that, she reckoned she could apply what she learned to solve similar problems.

Overall, the experience brought a smile to her face. There was one exception, though. One oddity. Something that made the experience annoyingly askew, like a picture on the wall off by a fraction of a centimeter from level, but noticeable nonetheless. The girl never spoke. Not once. Not one word of explanation was spoken or written for that matter. All the instruction was given with taps of the pencil to paper, stern, or on occasion, exasperated looks, and effusive pointing. Every time Zuri asked a question, she was met with silence, a critical gaze, and some gesture informing her to look at the math.

After they had finished working all the problems, Zuri had deigned to ask the phantasm's name. The girl had stared at her silently, with a mournful expression, floated back to the stacks, and faded to wispy fog before disappearing altogether. But she had waved. Zuri clung to that parting gesture. Maybe, the wave meant the ghost would return tomorrow. She hoped so. She needed help with her algebra, and she was confident the girl needed her help with something. She was anxious to discover what that something was.

Chapter 21

The Compendium

Initially, Zuri was annoyed when Luis showed her the image of her and the ghost girl. He had deviated from the plan! A plan they had both wholeheartedly agreed to. But as they strode through the emptying school hallways toward the library, Zuri couldn't help feeling pleased that Luis had a little bit of a bad boy in him. That he was willing to bend the rules if not outright break them. She liked that, and the picture had gone over wonderfully with John and Edith. The gaunt boy couldn't doubt the existence of the ghostly mathematician now, oh no.

"Zuri. Zuri?"

Luis waved a hand in front of her face, catching her attention. Uh, oh. What had he been talking about? She'd only been listening to his voice, which possessed a delightful timbre. He said something about Isaac Newton—a book by him, maybe? It had to be a book. If Luis wasn't doing math or building models, he was reading.

"What's up?" Zuri asked.

Luis frowned. "Did you listen to anything I said?"

"Newton. You were reading a book by him," Zuri replied and was relieved when Luis's expression softened.

"Yeah, *The Principia* is a great read," he said. "But

I asked if I could meet the ghost today."

This again? He had only asked her about fifty times already. "I'll ask. Okay? That's all I can do. It's early days yet. I want her to trust me. I don't want to scare her off by moving too fast."

Luis scraped the sole of his shoe against the linoleum, making a loud, annoying squeak. "All right. You promise to ask, though, right?"

"Yes, Luis, I'll ask."

They arrived at the library's entrance, and Luis darted forward to open the door for her, smiling. Zuri returned the smile and suppressed a giggle. She had noticed lately Luis putting in extra effort to be a gentleman. She wasn't sure what to make of it, suspecting that he was attempting to woo her. His efforts were cute, but beyond that, Zuri wasn't sure how she felt. Like everything in her life, her feelings for Luis were complicated. He was charming, thoughtful, and smarter than any boy she had ever kissed, but she feared they didn't have enough in common to succeed as a couple. She was an athlete. He was a super nerd.

To their surprise, they encountered no one other than Miriam O'Dell, who was checking out a pile of books as they entered the library. Even more surprising, Mrs. Binder smiled at the rich girl, not a snarky or mean smirk, mind you, but a genuine grin. Zuri grimaced at the scene in aversion. Luis was one of the library's most frequent and conscientious users, but she had never seen the librarian treat him with anything but barely contained disdain.

The friends strode quickly toward the stacks, hoping to avoid the moneyed white girl by mutual and unspoken agreement. But of course, Miriam was finishing up at the checkout counter and wasn't one to let the new girl and the school's super nerd walk by without comment.

"Look at the lovebirds," Miriam said mockingly, not bothering to keep her voice down. Mrs. Binder didn't even raise an eyebrow. "I heard you took Luis on a date, new girl. I guess you like it a little rough? Tell me, who took the beating at the gym, you or the nerd?"

"Miriam, be respectful," Binder chided, but the rebuke was only half-hearted.

Zuri clenched her hands into fists, sorely tempted to show Miriam how good she was at handing out beatings. But Luis grabbed her by the arm and gave a gentle tug. Zuri allowed him to lead her into the stacks.

Miriam watched them retreat, lips pouty. "What a cute couple."

Zuri was tempted to at least make a retort, but Luis whispered. "Be the bigger person. Don't engage. That only gives her what she wants. Attention."

Once they had withdrawn into the stacks a ways Zuri vented her frustration like a volcano letting off steam. "I can't believe it. She talks to us like that, and Mrs. Binder doesn't say a word. What the hell?"

"Keep your voice down," Luis said. "Binder might give Miriam a pass, but you know she won't give us one."

"That's my point exactly," Zuri replied but kept her voice down this time. There was only one way Miriam knew about her and Luis attending the watch party together at Pinedale Fight School. "I'm going to have a discussion with Ryan O'Dell next time I see him."

"Why?" Luis asked, sounding genuinely puzzled.

"Because I don't like him gossiping to his bitchy sister about us behind my back," Zuri scoffed.

They hooked right at a break in the shelving, taking a path between the books to the study table Zuri used. The table was unoccupied, as usual, which was something of a relief. After stumbling upon Miriam, it would be their luck to find it being used. Luis paused beside the table as Zuri set her backpack down and started getting herself situated.

"You know," Luis said. "You're thinking about this Miriam situation the wrong way. You need to reframe it. She has nothing better to do than gossip with her brother about us. I mean, we are like nobodies in the school's social strata, and she's at the pinnacle. When you think about it that way, you realize that despite everything, she probably doesn't feel good about herself. It's sad."

Zuri dropped her algebra book onto the table, making a loud thud. "That's really thoughtful, Luis, but it doesn't change the fact that she's a bully, and you know how I feel about bullies."

Luis shrugged. "I hate you getting worked up over nothing. That's what she wants. To wind you up."

"I'm wound up. Please leave me alone." Zuri removed pencils from the backpack and set them on the table.

"You promise to ask...if she'll see me?" Luis asked.

Zuri flashed a flirtatious smile. "Luis Torres, I'm starting to think you have a crush on a ghost."

Pink tinged Luis's cheeks. "You know that's not who I have a crush on."

The words were delivered with such fervor that Zuri flinched as though slapped. She let out the breath she had been holding when Luis turned his back on her and walked away, nearly but not quite stomping. To say the least, she didn't have a clue how to respond to what he said. But it was the butterflies flitting through her abdomen at his demonstration of passion that confused her the most.

****

During lunch on Friday, Luis and John pretended to browse the books near the front of the library by the circulation desk so they could keep tabs on Mrs. Binder and Chloe, who were both busy sorting through books. Their mission was to distract Mrs. Binder while Zuri and Edith gained access to The Compendium.

"The ghost came," Luis told John, glad to have something to distract him from his nervousness. "But she wasn't willing to see me…for a second time."

"Did you ever consider maybe she wants to keep the ghost for herself?" The gaunt boy checked the time on his wristwatch. "Two minutes."

Luis shook his head. "What do you mean?"

John shrugged. "Most ghosts talk. At least a little bit. Even Dumbo Jock said swirlie, ssswwiiiirrrlllie. You'd think a ghost conversant in sophomore algebra could also string a few words together in English or some other language."

Luis ran a finger along the spines of books. "I guess that makes sense. But Zuri wouldn't lie about that."

Luis saw John's knowing smirk in his peripheral vision, and he didn't like it one bit. So what if he had a crush on Zuri? It was better than continuing to pine after Edith while she was dating his best friend. That was the height of sad dorkiness. Having unrequited love for Zuri was a step up. *Edith thinks you're an asshole. She's only with you because she likes the idea of having a boyfriend. She'd dump you in a second if she thought someone she liked would have her.*

John's watch buzzed. "It's time."

Luis pushed his angst aside; he had a job to do. "We got this."

Side-by-side, the boys marched to the circulation desk straight to Mrs. Binder. They arrived precisely when the library door opened to admit Zuri and Edith. Luis grinned. He liked precision…no, actually, he loved it.

Mrs. Binder gazed at the lads over a pair of garish lime green reading glasses encrusted with faux jewels from her perch atop a stool. She smelled faintly of potpourri, far from Luis's favorite scent.

"What can I help you boys with?" Binder asked.

"We are here on chess club business, Mrs. Binder," Luis said in his most polite and scholarly tone. "We hope that you can help us find these titles…"

****

Zuri listened to the exchange at the circulation desk from her location at the computer beside Edith.

"I'm surprised you don't know where these titles are between the two of you," Mrs. Binder said, rising from the stool. "No worries. I am always happy to help you boys bring another state championship to Pinedale High, and I know exactly where these are. Follow me."

After telling Chloe to mind the circulation desk, the librarian led the boys into the stacks, not paying any heed to the two girls going through the motions of looking up books on the computer near the library's entrance. Little did Mrs. Binder know that the volumes the boys wanted would not be where she expected and that their list of books was voluminous indeed.

"Hurry," Chloe called from behind the desk. Her voice was as high-pitched as a twittering songbird. "I don't want to get caught."

Edith quickly logged off the computer, and the girls scampered to Chloe's side. The blonde girl was truly waiflike with colossal coke bottle glasses that were far too large for her face. Her sense of fashion seemed to come directly from Mrs. Binder: librarian chic. She even stared at the girls disapprovingly. Her glare lingered extra-long on Zuri. But when Chloe held up the key dangling from a keychain shaped like an open book, she smiled mischievously. Also, she was suffused with one of the latest perfumes trending on social media, a pleasing scent reminiscent of the tropics.

"Follow me."

The student librarian guided them past carts and shelving leaden with books and along the back wall displaying numerous posters stating the benefits of reading to a locked door. The lock surrendered to the key, and Chloe pushed the heavy door open with an assist from Zuri. The three girls scampered inside, and Edith turned on the lights. Zuri pushed the door shut with a click.

The illumination revealed a trifling room, not much more than a closet, with only a small table along the far wall. On the table sat a three-ring binder, and not a particularly thick one at that. On the binder's cover, slipped in behind the plastic sheeting, was a white sheet of paper with big block letters centered on it stating, "The Compendium."

Zuri blinked and glanced around the room in confusion, looking for anything besides the table and binder.

"That's The Compendium?" she said incredulously.

Chapter 22

Trust

Chloe touched the binder, lightly brushing her fingertips over the cover. "Not what you expected? Totally relatable. I expected a dusty old tome. They make a new print out every five years. The previous edition is shredded and incinerated."

Zuri blinked. "I don't know what I expected. I just know I didn't expect a three-ring binder."

"John and I had the same reaction," Edith said and rolled her eyes. "And you know how John is. He saw the binder and was immediately spouting off how The Compendium is a bunch of bullshit."

"I can imagine," Zuri replied, looking between the two girls. "Should we get started?"

"Definitely. I do not want to get caught." Chloe opened the binder and started flipping through the pages. "Based on Edith's description of the ghost, I found two possible candidates."

****

"This is odd." Mrs. Binder stared at the section of shelving at the darkest back corner of the library where the books on chess should be but were conspicuously absent. "All the books on your list are missing."

The librarian crossed her right arm around her midsection and chewed on the tip of her left thumb. Luis and John were familiar with this habit, which meant she was either deep in thought or ready to explode. Luis suspected that deep thoughts were harbingers of Mrs. Binder erupting like a volcano.

"Perhaps The Librarian has been at work?" Luis said helpfully.

Mrs. Binder snorted. "That old ninny. Maybe. She rarely bothers with this section of the library, though...the history section is her favorite to rearrange." Binder shook her head in loathing, causing the jewel-encrusted reading glasses around her neck by a thin golden lanyard to sway. "She's through that section once a week, at least. She's a menace."

****

The first ghost Chloe offered up was Beatrice "Eat Your Heart Out" Hedgegrove, who, according to the entry, attended Pinedale High from 1919 to 1922. She was the top student in her class year after year until she choked to death on an artichoke heart during the lunch period on May 12, 1922. Accompanying the entry was a faded photograph of a severe young woman in a high-collar dress very similar to the one worn by the mathematically inclined ghost.

"Too old," Zuri said. "Beatrice was seventeen at her time of death. The ghost girl is eleven or twelve."

"You're sure?" Edith said. "Sometimes...sometimes a ghost's features are fuzzy. It was hard to tell her age in Luis's photo."

"Yeah," Chloe chimed in. "I saw the photo. You can't tell the age by that."

"She's eleven or twelve years old," Zuri replied firmly.

"Okay." Chloe turned the pages past ghosts with

names such as Hangman Dan, Bludgeoned Bill, and Electric Susan. "Next up is Maureen Hopper."

The distinct chime of a phone alert broke the relative silence and positively startled Chloe. The page she had been turning, featuring a ghost named Milton "One Eye" Quaid, tore nearly in two. "Crap."

"Why isn't your phone on silent?" Chloe snapped at Edith. "I hope no one consults this before the next edition."

"Sorry." Edith retrieved her phone from her backpack. "It's only on so John can message me in case..." Edith's gaze goes to the phone screen. "... Mrs. Binder is heading back early."

Zuri didn't believe someone could be any paler than Chloe without being a ghost. But somehow, the girl managed to go even whiter, as if every ounce of blood drained from her face and neck. Behind her coke bottle glasses, her eyes bugged out like a fly's. "I have to go," Chloe twittered, wringing her hands. "Stay here. I'll come back when it's safe for you to come out."

Chloe darted to the door and heaved it open.

"Wait," Zuri said. "What page is...Maureen's entry on?"

But it was too late. The door closed behind Chloe.

"Don't worry," Edith said. "Chloe messaged me yesterday with the relevant page numbers."

"What do we do about this?" Zuri indicated the torn page, frowning. Apparently, Milton "One Eye" Quaid died in 1935 after taking an arrow through his left eye during an archery contest that was part of physical education in those days. Archery was scratched from the school's physical education program after the accident. Nowadays, Milton, with an arrow protruding from his eye, could be seen marching around the baseball field, which in 1935 had been an archery range. "Anything?"

"Hmmm…" Edith rummaged around her backpack. "I think I have some tape. Here we go."

Edith held up a roll of scotch tape. Working together, the girls carefully taped Milton's entry. It was far from as good as new, but someone might not notice the shabby page if they were flipping to a specific listing.

"What page?" Zuri asked as Edith returned the tape to her backpack.

"Forty-six." Zuri carefully flipped through the pages, noting the numbers in the top right-hand corners. She tried not to focus on the details of any listing. Many of the deaths were rather odd, if not bizarre, and gruesome enough to result in gnarly looking phantoms. She didn't need any more seedlings for her waking and sleeping phantasmagorias, thank you very much.

****

Mrs. Binder stormed between the stacks, heading to the front of the library. "Something is suspicious. Very suspicious, indeed."

"I hope you don't suspect us of anything?' Luis asked, nearly running to keep up with the irate librarian.

It had been their ill fortune that The Librarian, preceded by a chill draft smelling faintly of musty books, had materialized in the photography section only a handful of shelves away from where Mrs. Binder had frantically searched for the missing chess books. Upon spying the elderly and, undoubtedly, mentally declined bibliophile, Mrs. Binder had questioned her in a stern, no-nonsense tone.

"Have you been rearranging the books on chess strategy?"

Luis's stomach did a backflip when the old ninny stopped rearranging the photography books, looked Mrs. Binder straight in the eye, shook her head once in the negative, and then returned to her wayward task.

Binder turned her death glower on the boys. "Are you boys up to something? I did see Miss Eddington and Miss Williams…"

With that, she had whirled away and marched toward the front of the library.

"I thought she ignored everyone?" Luis mouthed, pointing at The Librarian.

John shrugged, and the teens scampered after Binder.

In the present, Binder mused. "Should I suspect you of something, Mr. Torres? Don't bother answering. You've changed since you started associating with Miss Williams."

Binder impugning Zuri so incensed Luis that he was about to do something totally out of character. He was ready to backtalk a member of the faculty, but John socked him in the shoulder and held a finger to his lips for silence. Luis literally had to bite his tongue to keep from spouting off. After several seconds, his recklessness passed, and he was beset by the dread that Chloe wouldn't be at the circulation desk. If she wasn't there, they were dead meat. Binder would undoubtedly scour the library for her missing assistant so she could harangue the poor girl about not minding the desk, as she had been instructed.

Luis's heart rate must have cut in half when he saw Chloe, white as a corpse on a morgue slab, studiously scanning books behind the counter. Little did Mrs. Binder know, the volumes on chess Luis and John had asked after were tucked inside Chloe's voluminous backpack.

****

Page forty-six contained the entry for Maureen "The Jumper" Hopper, who in 1975 was already considered a math prodigy at the tender age of thirteen. She had a bright future, with colleges and universities nationwide already interested in enrolling her in their mathematics programs. Unfortunately, the girl had been relentlessly bullied and had ended her life by leaping off the school's roof onto lethally sharp ornamental fencing. On clear nights, her spirit could be found atop the school building, gazing at the stars, perhaps looking for patterns in the twinkling lights.

"Maureen seems promising," Edith remarked.

Before Zuri could reply, the bell announcing five minutes until the end of lunch sounded. Edith looked up from The Compendium, eyes wide and gritting her teeth.

"Where is Chloe?" she said tremulously. "I've never been late for class before."

"Seriously?" Zuri asked, not nearly as worried about being late as her compatriot.

Edith nodded. "Not once. Not even in kindergarten." She laughed nervously. "Please, tell me this isn't all for nothing?"

Zuri sighed. "I hate to tell you this, but my ghost is a white girl."

"Could you be mistaken?"

"Edith, look at my skin. My father is white, and my mom is black. I'm black. Believe me, I know the difference between a white girl and a black girl."

Chapter 23

Good Old George

Edith was stressed, pacing back and forth and muttering about being late for class. After several failed attempts to calm the mousy girl, Zuri turned her attention to The Compendium. At first, her perusal of Maureen "The Jumper" Hopper's listing was meant to distract her from Edith's obsessive-compulsive behavior. But the description of how a Pinedale science teacher, Mr. Anton Beaker, befriended Maureen piqued her interest.

Mr. Beaker was the faculty advisor for the short-lived astronomy club. On a clear night in 1978, Mr. Beaker supervised the two-person club's expedition to the school's roof to set up a powerful amateur telescope. Shortly after dusk fell, the amateur stargazers were joined by the phantasmal Maureen. The students had been friends with Maureen in life and found her appearance upsetting, especially when the spirit didn't acknowledge their presence, being enthralled by the night sky.

The paranormal encounter ended the astronomy club in its infancy, but Mr. Beaker, who had known Maureen as a top pupil, did not find her spectral form upsetting in the least. She was the first spirit he had encountered at the school. Up until that point, he had believed all the talk about ghosts was the faculty and students hazing him. Intrigued by what Maureen saw in the night sky, Beaker returned to the roof night after night. He attempted to converse with Maureen, but she ignored him. After a week of this, Anton brought books on astronomy, which he left with the ghost girl. When he returned the next night, she thanked him for the books and requested more.

"I will bring you more books," Anton said. "But I must ask. What do you see in the night sky that captivates you?"

The science teacher reckoned that if he knew what mesmerized this spirit, he might use that knowledge to capture the attention of his living pupils.

Without moving her gaze from the black expanse overhead, Maureen replied. "My vision pierces the veil of time. I can see the birth of stars in the cauldron of creation. I have no words for how beautiful it is."

"Zuri!" Edith's voice came from behind her. "We have to go."

Blinking, Zuri looked up from the page and turned toward the room's entrance. Edith and Chloe stood in the doorway, both harried and cross.

Chloe stomped her foot. "Now! Binder will be in the bathroom for less than five minutes. Don't ask me how she's so fast."

Zuri carefully closed The Compendium and followed the girls out of the small room. After Chloe locked the door and returned the key to a drawer at the front counter, they practically ran from the library. Edith and Chloe whispered about their distress at being late for class, but Zuri did not share their anxiety. She turned over the tale of Maureen Hopper and Anton Beaker in her mind.

****

After school, Zuri relayed the story of Mr. Beaker and Maureen Hopper to Luis as they traversed the crowded hallways ripe with the latest scented deodorants and perfumes toward the library. Her friend listened intently, smiling as the retelling neared its end.

"I was thinking," Zuri said. "Maybe you can—"

Luis interrupted, his tone overflowing with enthusiasm. "All my math homework from the university is on my laptop. I'll log onto it, so you can show it to the ghost."

"Exactly." Zuri threw an arm companionably over Luis's shoulder. "Maybe she'll start talking. Algebra is easy for her, but I bet whatever you're studying might prove a challenge."

"Yeah, maybe she'll agree to meet me!" Luis leaned his head against her shoulder, eliciting a few sidelong looks from passersby.

Flustered and not wanting Luis to get the wrong idea, Zuri removed her arm from his shoulder and hurried ahead to reclaim her personal space.

"Wait up," Luis called after her.

They found Mrs. Binder at her usual spot in the library, minding the circulation desk. "Mr. Torres, those books on chess strategy you are interested in have mysteriously returned to the stacks."

"Thank you, Mrs. Binder," Luis replied politely. "I'll be sure to look them over."

"You do that, Mr. Torres, you do that." Binder glowered at Zuri over her jewel-encrusted reading glasses. "Miss Williams."

Zuri froze, absolutely certain Mrs. Binder was about to call her out for sneaking a peek at The Compendium.

But the librarian simply stared at her, waiting for a reply.

"Thank you for keeping the library open after school so we can study here," Zuri said disarmingly.

Binder's mouth formed a small o. She removed the glasses, allowing them to sway by the golden lanyard, and her expression softened almost into a smile. "Miss Williams, you are very welcome. It is nice to be appreciated. Please, go study."

Zuri and Luis didn't need to be told twice and scurried away. Once they were a safe distance from the librarian, Luis said, "How did you charm her?"

"I guess everyone likes to feel appreciated," Zuri replied.

****

Zuri waited for the ghost girl at the usual table next to the stacks in the back of the library. Her algebra book and latest homework sheet were arrayed on the table with the addition of Luis's laptop, displaying mathematical problems far beyond anything Zuri had ever encountered, which he called real analysis. Real or not, looking at the squiggly lines, graphs, and numerous variables was enough to give her a headache. Mr. Tito might be right that learning to work algebra equations would help her solve real-life problems. That might even be true about what was on the laptop screen, but she hoped to never face real-world issues as complex as those equations. She preferred simple problems. Problems that could be resolved with her fists or a spinning back kick. The screen darkened, a harbinger of the laptop locking, so Zuri hit the spacebar, and the screen brightened.

Of course, helping the ghost girl might prove to be as convoluted as real analysis. Zuri hoped not. Her latest algebra homework was already too complicated for her to do without serious tutoring from her spectral friend and, more than likely, follow-up with Luis. It didn't help that this evening was Malee Chaiyathorn's title fight. Instead of concentrating on the algebra class lecture, Zuri had daydreamed about taking on her idol in the cage. Malee would certainly win the championship tonight. Maybe Zuri would one day fight her for a belt.

Zuri would be eighteen in two years, the minimum age to fight as a pro in the U.S. That would make Malee only twenty-five. It could happen. She could meet her hero in the octagon! Win or lose that would be a dream come true, the greatest honor she could imagine. She was about to reach for her phone to watch clips of The Jade Tiger when a chill draft smelling faintly of the grave emanated from the stacks. Zuri gazed at the ghost, who again appeared like a young and very serious-minded white girl in a high collared dress from the waist up. From the waist down, the phantom was a swirling, gray mist shaped like a hoop skirt.

"Hello." Zuri smiled and waved to the girl. "Can you help me with my algebra homework?"

The girl nodded and floated to the desk. This time, Zuri hardly noticed the cold emitting from the ghost and caught a floral bouquet scent intermixed with the stink of decay. The girl reached for the algebra book but stopped and stared at the laptop screen.

"Does that interest you?" Zuri pointed to the screen.

The girl nodded once, obviously riveted by the mathematical formulas.

Zuri swallowed. It was time to roll the dice. "This is my friend's homework. Would you like to meet him? He'd like to meet you."

Never once blinking nor taking her gaze from the formulas, the ghost nodded in the affirmative.

"Great. I'll use my phone to message him…"

****

Deep below Pinedale High in a hidden subbasement, the maleficent presence known in life as Good Old George roared its boiling anger. The lurid sound was so cacophonous it would have been heard far and wide had it been trumpeted above ground. Instead, the furious ululation reverberated around the chamber with frightful, some might say, supernatural intensity. As it was, only rodents and nightcrawlers were subjected to the din. The rats in the chamber, and there were many, loitering like sunbathers in the dread icon's radiation, died with blood leaking from their eyes and ears. The nightcrawlers slithering and scuttling on the walls, ceiling, and floor vibrated until they exploded with soft pops that could not be heard over the shriek.

He was Good Old George, and he would not allow his good works to be undone by a wayward child, by his own flesh and blood, by Rose.

George reached out of the statuette containing his essence. It was difficult because his spirit was bound to the idol by magic, both ancient and evil. But magic was often a test of sheer will, and George, despite all his faults, never lacked willpower in life or death. In spurts, shimmering, sickly green tendrils leaked from the figurine. The tendrils wound through the air and down to the floor, consuming what little life force lingered in the dead and dying rats littering the chamber. Their vital energies weren't enough to sate George's hunger, but it would have to be enough for the task at hand. Failure was not an option George was willing to accept.

The green tendrils coalesced into a giant, twinkling clawed hand that rose into the air and passed through the ceiling.

Chapter 24

An Encounter too Close

Luis figured he would pop like an overinflated balloon if Zuri didn't text him right now—like this instant. He paced back and forth with his phone clutched in his hand, oblivious to everything around him, even Sir Isaac Newton's *Principia*, open on a nearby table. In the back of his mind, he knew this was odd behavior for him. Unlike Zuri, who was always full of nervous, kinetic energy, Luis always found it easy to focus his verve on mental pursuits, usually math related. Being unable to sit still was not his style.

But the story of Mr. Beaker and Maureen Hopper filled him with hope that today, he'd meet the mathematically inclined spirit. If the ghost girl was truly a math prodigy, she'd be powerless to resist the honey pot he and Zuri had prepared. He wouldn't be able to walk past an open laptop full of real analysis to perform without at least taking a crack at solving the equations, and neither would a dead mathematician.

Plus, if he met this ghostly mathematician, really saw her, and communicated with her, he would finally connect with a phantom. Unlike John, who had seen numerous shades and had interactions, albeit undesirable ones, with Fat Nick and Dumbo Jock, Luis had nary an encounter with any specters, despite what he told Zuri.

Yes, he glimpsed ghosts now and then, but he'd never truly experienced a haunting. Sometimes, he felt guilty for leading Zuri to believe he was a paranormal expert. Whenever he felt that way, like his prevarication went too far, he always told himself that he could handle ghosts. But the truth of it was, his expertise added up to zilch.

When Luis's phone buzzed, he hopped into the air like he'd been zapped by static electricity and nearly fumbled the device. That was just like him—butterfingers all his life. Using face ID to unlock the phone, he checked the message that was indeed from Zuri and summoned him to meet the ghost.

Barely able to contain his enthusiam, Luis nevertheless forced himself to walk—okay, speed walk. It wouldn't do to scare the ghost off like what happened the first time. Near the end of the wall and the left turn that would give him a view of beautiful Zuri—he hoped she was standing so he could surreptitiously admire her firm and shapely butt—and the ghost girl, there came a wordless scream that he recognized as his friend.

"What the…" Luis broke into a run.

He rounded the corner, his jaw went unhinged, and he stuttered to a stop. *Buck up, Luis, buck up.* Paranormal expert or not, he wasn't about to allow Zuri to face down whatever that was alone.

****

A cold as piercing as an arctic gale-force wind blasted up Zuri's body. It was like being dipped feet first into ice water. The uncomfortable sensation startled her, and she nearly glanced at the floor, but the ethereal girl's stunned expression captured her attention.

"What's wrong?" Zuri asked the split second before

the girl started shimmering. The swirling fog of her dress spread up her torso, distorting her form. Simultaneously, the eerie cold spread up Zuri's legs with disquieting speed.

Like the glacial cold, a sickly green radiance emanated from below the table. The ghost's mouth spread wide in what could only be called a silent scream. Unable to sit still, Zuri leaped from the chair, knocking it over in the process. Beneath the table, a lustrous green thing—a spider, maybe—emerged from the floor, proceeded by the chill and reek of a graveyard. The blurry monstrosity grasped at the ghostly girl with wraithlike legs...no, immense clawed fingers. A giant, phantasmal hand pulled the ghost girl down through the floor.

Zuri knew a bully when she saw one and reacted as she had been trained to, having been taught by her father, Mr. Tito, and those like them. She threw a straight right hand into the back of the spectral hand. Her fist passed through the unearthly material, and burning pain lanced through her hand and up her arm. Screaming more from the shock of the pain than the actual hurt, Zuri stumbled backward and fell over the overturned chair, landing on her rump with a jarring thud.

The ghost girl's traumatized features turned nebulous as the green mist spread up her neck and over her face. The clawed hand tightened around her, only to grasp at smoke, slate haze seeping through the sickly green digits. With a whoosh, the mist rushed toward the stacks and dissipated amongst the books.

The spectral claws swayed side to side like a predator attempting to sight prey, finally turning upon Zuri. Her mind and body screamed at her to run, but her right arm hurt so much that the pain was nearly paralytic. As the glowing hand stalked toward her, she knew she couldn't escape.

From behind her came pounding feet and Luis's scream. "Go back to whence you came, spectral fiend!"

Something flew past her head, almost grazing her ear. A phone, she realized, hurled toward the monstrous hand. The handheld device passed into the semitransparent appendage, struck the floor, and the screen lit up, suffusing the hand with bright light that outshone the green. Halting its advance, the clawed hand shuttered as if struck and sank into the floor like a submarine diving into the ocean.

Luis scrambled up beside Zuri. "Are you okay? What was that?"

Before Zuri could reply, Mrs. Binder's voice came from the stacks. "Mr. Torres, Miss Williams, what is all this racket?"

****

In his sanctum, George wailed. The rats feasting on the carcasses of their fallen brethren became the next victims of the malevolent spirit's rage. The rodentia collapsed upon their meals with blood spouting from their orifices. The soft pops of exploding nightcrawlers came from around the chamber, the dirge of their demise drowned out by George's scream.

"Rooose! Rrrrroooooooose!" He hurled the name like an epitaph, a deadly hex.

To think everything he had striven for, sacrificed for, killed for could be undone by an ungrateful child, by his own daughter, would be unfathomable if it wasn't happening. Didn't she realize he had given her a place of highest honor? To aid him in protecting his legacy, the

O'Dell family fortune forevermore? Why was she such an unappreciative little floozy? She was too smart, that was why. Always with her nose in the books. Always studying mathematics, not just the arithmetic required for accounting either. All kinds of advanced mathematics. The stuff of science and engineering. He should've put a stop to her bookish and mathematical inclinations long ago. Insisted that she partook in womanly pursuits like needlework, music, and reciting insipid poetry. Yes, that girl had always been too shrewd for her own good. Too clever for the family's good. That's why he chose her. That, and he knew for certain that she was a virgin. The spell had called for virginal blood, after all.

George was angry at himself for failing to capture his wayward daughter, but as his rage peaked and subsided to a simmer, he realized he had touched the girl's familiar, this Zuri. Zuri Williams. And that touch brought him knowledge—more knowledge than he had ever possessed of this girl, this unwomanly fighting girl. He knew her dreams and fears.

In the ephemera of the unfeminine lass, George saw a potential ally, more accurately, a rube. Now, if he could only get a message to Big Jake Williams. But first, he needed to feed and regain his strength, as his failed attempt to capture his daughter had cost him dearly. He slowed the descent of his spectral hand through the building, sending out ghostly feelers through the school's superstructure, gobbling up the life force of the tiny inhabitants the tendrils brushed up against.

****

"A ghost?" Mrs. Binder glanced speculatively between Luis and Zuri. "You saw a ghost and screamed

151

at it to go back from whence it came?"

Luis nodded. "Yes, Mrs. Binder. Honestly, I think there were two ghosts."

The burning pain had subsided from her hand and arm, and Zuri tried to rub warmth back into the limb, which was as cold as all get out. Next time, Zuri promised to throw her phone at the spectral hand instead of punching it. Throwing the punch had been stupid after receiving mild frostbite during her first meeting with the ghost girl.

Binder's judgmental gaze rested on Zuri. "Two ghosts?"

At this point, Zuri decided telling the unvarnished truth was the best option. The librarian had caught them with their proverbial pants down and there weren't any legitimate reasons to lie. They could tell Binder all about the ghostly encounter while leaving out the illicit operation to gain access to The Compendium.

Binder listened intently as Zuri recounted the affray between the ghost and phantasmal hand. All the while, Zuri continued massaging her right arm and flexing her hand. When the tale was told, her appendage started to feel normal again.

"That is positively harrowing." Binder crossed her arms over her chest. "I'll overlook the fact that you both have phones in the library. You know those aren't allowed in school. No, Mr. Torres, don't touch anything, and Miss Williams, don't bother with the chair just yet. Both of you remain where you are. I need to take a picture of this."

From somewhere on her person, Zuri couldn't tell where, the librarian produced a cell phone and quickly took a snap. The device disappeared as quickly as it was retrieved.

"I will need to report this haunting to the principal." Binder raised a hand for the teens to remain silent. "Don't fret. You aren't in trouble—yet, anyway. This is standard procedure when new ghosts are discovered, especially ones that might be dangerous to students."

Chapter 25

The Gnawing Cold

As soon as Mrs. Binder finished taking the photos of the haunting's aftermath, Luis darted past Zuri and snatched his phone off the floor. He yelped and dropped the device as if stung by a bee. The phone plummeted, a frosty sheen on its surface glinting, almost imperceptible in the poor light.

"Awww! Cold!" The yelp from Luis elicited an arched eyebrow from Mrs. Binder.

Zuri wasn't surprised to learn that the cell phone was cold enough to burn. From the tips of her fingers up to her elbow, her arm stung like a painful yet recovering sunburn. After shaking his smarting hand for a few seconds, Luis bunched up the corner of his shirt and knelt beside the device.

"One moment, Mr. Torres." Mrs. Binder squatted beside Luis and placed her jewel-encrusted reading glasses on the tip of her nose. "Allow me to inspect the device more closely before touching it again, please."

The librarian leaned precariously over the device, so far Zuri was certain she would topple forward and do a faceplant, but Binder possessed the balance of a yogi.

"I believe this is frost on your phone, Mr. Torres." Binder fished her phone out from somewhere on her person. Once again, Zuri couldn't tell from where. The librarian was, apparently, a yogi as well as an amateur magician.

"Seriously?" Luis lowered his head to the floor and stared across the device. "Oh, I see it. Just like the pencil."

Binder took several close-up photos of the phone. "Pencil? This isn't your first encounter with these ghosts? Hmmm?"

Luis glanced at Zuri, his eyes wide. Zuri spoke before her friend, who was unskilled at the art of prevarication and white lies, said anything that might give away too much.

"This is our first brush with the clawed hand, but I've had a run-in with the ghost girl before," Zuri said and launched into an explanation of her first encounter with the ghost and how the specter had left her pencil coated with frost. She salted the tale with hints at the apparition's mathematical ability, hoping the scholastic tangent would impress the librarian.

Binder stared over her glasses, her eyes narrowed, to slivers at both teens. "A mathematically inclined ghost. Fascinating. This will all go into my report. Mr. Torres, your phone. Is it still too cold to the touch?"

"I don't know," Luis said. "Should I try to pick it up again?"

"I'm certainly not foolish enough to touch it, nor do I suspect is Miss Williams," Binder said. "You were about to pick it up using your shirt."

"Do you think it's safe?" Luis asked the librarian.

"Use your shirt, and you will probably be fine," Binder replied.

Luis glanced nervously at Zuri.

Zuri shrugged. "The pencil wasn't cold after a bit."

But Zuri wondered if that would be true for the phone. The phone had passed into the sickly green hand, which she suspected was more potent than the ghost girl, at least in some respects. On inspection of her right hand, she didn't see any redness, like when she had brushed up against the tween, but the coldness that had shot through her arm when she punched the spectral hand was far more frigid and draining. Yes, that was it. She felt drained after her limb passed into the green aura, and the coldness lingered like an old soft tissue injury that never seemed to fully recover.

Zuri kept those thoughts to herself. Part of her wanted to trust Mrs. Binder, but she had a natural distrust of authority outside of the boxing gym. She had seen people like her be screwed over and even killed by those with authority on the news. Sometimes, it seemed like a weekly occurrence. Combine that with her experience in Badger Hollow, of being told she should leave town after being assaulted, and Zuri took a dim view of anyone in authority. On top of that, the librarian had done nothing to ingratiate herself with Zuri or her friends. There was no way she would reveal anything extra to Binder. Trust and respect were a two-way street. The librarian needed to show her a little bit of both before Zuri would do the same.

Luis tentatively picked up the cell phone using the corner of his shirt. "Not cold." He tapped his fingers on the device, and the screen lit up. "Phew. Looks like it works too."

Zuri let out a soft sigh, relieved her friend didn't scald himself a second time.

Binder stood. "Mr. Torres. Miss Williams. Eyes on me. I will need to include all of this in my official report to the principal. Your names will be included. Now, I want you to both think very carefully about your encounters with these ghosts." Binder paused to give her words a chance to sink in. "I hope you are telling me everything. I'd hate to think you might have forgotten something. Something that could prove vital for the safety of the school's students and faculty."

The lie came easily to Zuri, well-watered and fertilized by all the reports of young black men and women done wrong and even killed by those with power. "That's everything, Mrs. Binder. I can't think of anything else." She looked at Luis, hoping he'd follow her lead. "Can you think of anything, Luis?"

"Ummm…nothing pertinent," Luis said.

****

Zuri's right fist smashed the heavy bag hanging from a tall, rectangular metal frame bolted to the floor, and she winced, burning discomfort shooting from her fingertips up her forearm. The bag swayed, and the support structure creaked. Zuri speculatively eyed the equipment. She hadn't hit the bag that hard, had she? Shaking her head, she shook out her arm. The pain was mild in the scheme of things, especially for a fighter, but it was an aftereffect of striking the sickly green hand, which made it disconcerting.

After dealing with Mrs. Binder, Zuri and Luis had decided that the chance of the ghost girl returning that afternoon was nil and that they didn't want to remain in the library any longer. At Luis's insistence, they moved to the seating area near the front office to review Zuri's algebra homework. That had worked out fine and dandy until Mrs. Binder came storming up the hall with paperwork clutched to her chest about fifteen minutes later. She had paused at the entrance to the office to give the teens a long, and Zuri had thought, prejudicial stare. After that, they decided it was best to skedaddle before they were called into the principal's office or worse. The entire time, Zuri's forearm itched like her skin had been burned raw by icy cold, but by the time she had parted ways with Luis to head to the fight school, the hurt had subsided.

Zuri struck the heavy bag again and was rewarded with the burning sensation lancing up her forearm. But that was not all she was rewarded with. The blow was mighty, causing the bag to skyrocket toward the top of the groaning support structure, stop short of impacting a steel bar, and swing back at her. She danced aside to avoid being plowed into by the bag and stared at her fist in puzzlement. *How in the world...*

"Holy shit! Remind me never to piss you off."

Zuri looked up from her aching hand to find Ryan O'Dell watching her and the swaying heavy bag. Fury pulsed through her, hot as magma.

"Actually, you already pissed me off." Zuri pointed a gloved hand to the empty ring. "Want to spar? One round. Come on, let's do it."

Ryan held his hands up beside his head, palms out. "No way. I've never seen anyone do that to a one-hundred-pound heavy bag. You'd knock my head off. And...ahhh...what have I done to piss you off? I want to make sure I never do it again."

Zuri stepped around the still oscillating bag to get right up in his face. "You gossiped to your sister about me being at the watch party with Luis."

Ryan dropped his hands to his sides and laughed. "You're mad about that?"

It was all Zuri could do not to punch him in his stupid face. As it was, she was so angry she was tongue-tied, only nodding in response to the query.

"I wasn't gossiping," he said.

Zuri's eyes bulged until they felt like they would roll right out of their sockets and splatter on the floor like broken eggs.

Ryan backed up. "I promise. It just came up, I guess. Miriam knew I was at the watch party and asked about it...I said you were there with a boy...what did you say his name is? Louie? I don't even know his name."

"Hey, Ryan! Hey, Zuri!" Demarcus called from the gym's entrance.

They both turned to bask in the contender's radiant smile as he entered. Zuri's inferno of anger spluttered and died down to red embers at the sight of the handsome fighter. Flustered, as always, by his presence, she waved a gloved hand and murmured a shy hello.

"Demarcus!" Ryan boomed, then, in a normal voice to Zuri. "Got to go. Training with the future champ. Don't worry. I won't utter your name to my sister ever again." As he turned away, he pointed to the heavy bag that still gently moved back and forth like a pendulum. "That was a hell of a punch."

After confronting Ryan, Zuri threw a final right hand into the heavy bag. She still had some discomfort, but it was only slight. She couldn't decide if it was because she purposely pulled her punch or if she was genuinely recovering from striking the spectral hand. Regardless, Zuri switched to practicing kicks and shadowboxing but didn't keep that up for long as she couldn't get into a rhythm. Deciding she was too wound up by Ryan's presence and distracted by her attraction to

Demarcus to put in more quality training, she quit the gym early. She could use the extra hours at home to study algebra by herself, and Luis had offered to tutor her more via video chat. She might take him up on that. Plus, she didn't want to tire herself out too much. She planned to stay up late to learn the results of The Jade Tiger's title fight.

Fantasizing about Malee Chaiyathorn's impending victory and her own future conquests, Zuri felt great on the run home despite the cold breeze and drizzle, like she could sprint a marathon and go three rounds in the octagon against anyone on the planet. That was up until about halfway when her right forearm started aching from a bone-deep chill that she couldn't shake off or massage away.

Little did she know that at that exact moment, Good Old George expanded his awareness beyond the confines of his sanctum and even the school grounds. George was reaching, reaching, reaching.

Chapter 26

Dreams and Nightmares

The sun drifted below the San Gabriel Mountains that gloomy day, and the only sign of its passage was a marked decrease in ambient luminosity. Big Jake sat in a small, nondescript hatchback, barely large enough to contain his bulk, and watched the entrance to the dive bar across the street. Oldies softly buzzed from the hatch's wonky radio and heat blasted from the vents to fend off the winter chill. Damn car was too old to have a hook-up for his phone, or he'd be listening to his own tunes. Jake checked the time on the dash, 5:33 p.m. Now that the sun was down, his target, a small-time dealer who had been shorting the bosses for months, would leave the bar in twenty minutes or less.

He shifted uncomfortably, trying and failing to find a position to put his lower back at ease. He hated jobs like this. Jobs where he needed to stake out a location and wait and wait. Hell on his back. Always put him in a foul mood. Made him a little rougher than necessary. Jake didn't mind being rough per se, but punching little men with his full force behind the blow had consequences. It made little men dead, and worse, sometimes tweaked his back.

Worst of all was the lack of sun. Not a lick of it all day. He lived in L.A. for the sun, and on days like this, he thought he might be better off in Phoenix. But then he'd need to establish himself all over again. He had street cred in L.A. which made his job easier. That made getting paid easier, both in cash and the narcotics he needed to keep his back pain manageable. Ah, well, he'd have to dream of summer.

And that's when something strange happened. The face of his estranged wife flashed before his eyes, blotting out the dull reality of the ramshackle bar on the cold street leading to nowhere, but an early grave with her glorious radiance—there and then gone. A vision of Amari as he hadn't seen her since her college days, dressed for work at a news outlet.

Jake shook his head, snorting like an enraged bull.

She was successful.

Big Jake remembered all the times she had emasculated him. How she failed to support him when he hurt his back, ending his pro fighting career.

She was happy.

Jake clenched his massive, gnarled fists. He couldn't wait to get to work. That always made him feel better.

****

At eleven p.m., Zuri was hyped up to the point that she didn't think she'd get a wink of sleep all night. She bounced around her room on her toes, throwing punches and launching kicks in rapid combinations, the gnawing cold in her right forearm gone and forgotten. Malee had won by knockout.

From accounts Zuri had scoured from the internet, a fearsome high kick had put the champion to sleep in the third round. Zuri could hardly wait for clips of the fight to be posted so she could study every second of footage with a critical eye, especially the knockout. She wanted to compare her high kick technique to Chaiyathorn's. Such a blow had knocked out Toby Alkorn, after all.

Zuri executed a spinning back kick, another Jade Tiger special. Some fighters claimed the technique was the most potent strike in all the martial arts when delivered properly. Misjudging her space by millimeters, Zuri caught the edge of the bedpost with the ball of her foot. The bed scraped over the floor, and the headboard thumped against the wall.

"Shoot!" She cried, hopping on her good foot and grimacing.

"Go to bed, Zuri," Amari called tiredly from the bedroom across the hall. "I'm trying to sleep."

"Sorry!"

Zuri had no intention of sleeping anytime soon, but she knew better than to keep her mother awake. She flung herself onto the bed, which caused a racket.

"Zuri!" Amari's voice cracked like a whip, the tiredness gone and replaced with irritation.

Zuri gritted her teeth. "Sorry, Mom. I didn't mean to."

"You're going to wake our neighbor and landlord."

The comment deflated Zuri a little. More than once, during their years on the run from Big Jake, neighbors in dingy apartment complexes or patrons at roach motels had complained, often stridently, about the rambunctious—the complainers usually described her as out of control—black girl. One time, the police were called, pounding on the apartment door shortly after midnight. Being rudely disturbed in the middle of the night to be lectured by two hulking men with badges on their chests and guns on their hips taught Zuri two things. First, she didn't want to be on the wrong side of the law, of men with their guns and tasers and handcuffs and badges. People like that could do anything they wanted to someone like her.

Second, she had decided from that night on, it was better to quiet down after being warned not to wake the neighbors. Zuri grabbed her phone from the bedside table and checked for clips of The Jade Tiger's fight. Nada. She checked the time, eleven twenty—shouldn't be long now. Still, what was she going to do in the meantime? The energy surging through her body made her skin tingle and she needed to move—to grind, to grind, to grind. But the memory of the lawmen reminded her that wasn't the brightest idea at the moment. Instead, she put her head in her pillow and screamed, knowing from experience that muffled the sound enough not to land her in more trouble. After a minute, she felt more in control of her exuberance.

Sitting up in bed, she heaved a heavy sigh at a loss of what to do. Check for clips of the fight again? Maybe in five minutes. But those would be the longest five minutes of her life if she didn't find something to do. Doom scroll? Not in the mood. She glimpsed her backpack, leaning against a bedside table, in her peripheral vision. Inside the bag was her algebra book. What better way to drain her excess vigor than to crack that open and read a page or two? She had placed a video call to Luis early in the evening and, surprisingly, had made real progress in her understanding of the algebraic concepts, namely polynomials.

****

While his alienated daughter studied algebra and quickly surrendered to sleep without watching a single clip of The Jade Tiger's watershed victory, two thousand five hundred miles away, Big Jake sat in his recliner downing painkillers with a fifth of whiskey. He daydreamed of a time when his back didn't kill him every day, when he could always count on seeing a smile on his daughter's face after he complimented her for performing an overhand right or a takedown to near perfection. But those weren't the only thoughts running rampant through his gray matter. It was the vision of Amari, his wife, finding success that enraged him and made it impossible to sleep. Amari, who had undermined him, stole his daughter from him, and left him to rot when he needed her support the most.

She didn't deserve success.

She deserved to be dead for what she had done to him.

He swallowed two more painkillers and chased the pills with a swig of whiskey. Setting the bottle on a side table, Jake winced and flexed his stiff hand. The knuckles were raw and cracked, seeping blood. His middle knuckle, the largest and most gnarled, had started to swell. Jake threw his head back in the chair, knowing he should ice his hand to take care of his preferred weapon if nothing else. But he was afraid to move. Scared that if he left his chair, he'd see his wife again, not as the lost, downtrodden soul as she should be, but as a proud and confident woman. A woman of ability. An affluent woman. Everything she didn't deserve to be without him.

"A dream," Jake said to the blank eighty-inch flatscreen TV affixed to the wall across from him. Usually, after a job, he'd watch fights he had recorded, fantasizing about how he would defeat the fighters in the octagon or the boxing ring. But tonight…tonight he was too disturbed and furious even for that. "A goddamn dream."

He took another long swig of whiskey and slammed the bottle against the table, hard enough to chip the glass. He'd given up searching for Amari and Zuri two years ago and wasn't about to pick up the search again. Oh, he could find them. He was sure of that. He had connections now, but those meant responsibilities: little men to break and debts to collect.

****

Zuri thrashed against the crushing weight of a man straddling her. A featureless silhouette backlit by an eerie green glow that felt as heavy as a school bus. Even though the man was all dark shadows, the bowie knife wasn't. Uncanny light glinted along its razor edge. As the knife slashed down, Zuri threw her arms before her face and neck in a futile attempt to protect herself. The blade carved her forearm. A hot flash of pain. By some trick of the weird lambency, she saw the countenance of her attacker reflected along the steel.

"Daddy, no!" she screamed.

Chapter 27

A Warning

On Saturday morning, Zuri woke to stinging pain running up and down her forearms. Her breath caught in her throat. Was this something to do with the phantasmal hand? No, that wasn't right. It was only her right arm that had been affected by the ghostly hand. This was both arms. And the coldness was gone. The teen gasped, memories of the nightmare flooding back.

"A dream. That's all," she murmured, but her throbbing arms declared otherwise.

Pushing herself to a sitting position, she swung her legs off the bed and placed her feet on the floor. It wasn't real. It was a dream. A nightmare. That was all. Her father hadn't attacked her with a bowie knife.

Blinking her gummy eyes into focus, she inspected her arms. "Oh, my God!"

Her forearms were marred by crisscrossing scars. She clenched her eyes shut, willing, whatever this was, nightmare or waking dream, to end. When she opened her eyes, the disfigurements were gone, leaving behind no trace of trauma. But the pain remained in the form of dull throbbing in her forearms.

She concentrated on getting her breathing under control, reminding herself over and over again that whatever she was experiencing wasn't real. She was undermined by a soft voice whispering in the back of her mind: how could she discern reality from the phantasmagorical in a world where ghosts were real? Maybe she experienced a paranormal phenomenon. She couldn't write it off as a dream if that were true.

Clenching her fists in her lap, Zuri reminded herself that she was better than this. She wasn't a victim. She was a fighter. She wasn't afraid of bullies. Bullies feared her because she would stand up to them and give them a fight they would remember. That was true for Big Jake and the killer in white. The inner tough talk worked, and slowly, her breathing came under control. Her heart still raced, but it no longer felt like it would dash out of her chest.

She almost went back to sleep but then remembered the best thing that happened last night—The Jade Tiger had won her title fight. This time, her pulse quickened for all the right reasons. She sat up in bed and reached for the phone on the bedside table. How did she not watch clips of her hero's victory last night? That's when she glimpsed the overturned algebra book open on the floor. Oh yes, she had fallen asleep, studying math. She wished her memories of what she had read were as crystal clear as her father attacking her with a knife.

Opening the phone's web browser, she entered Chaiyathorn title fight into the search bar. Dozens of results filled the screen, including highlight videos. Zuri tapped the first video, feet drumming against the floor. She was rewarded with a clip of Malee Chaiyathorn, all one hundred ten pounds of her, delivering a perfect high kick to the chin of her unsuspecting opponent after distracting the equally petite fighter with a blisteringly fast jab.

"Ahhh!" Zuri ululated in excitement, literally bouncing up and down on the bed.

Springing to her feet, she threw a left jab, followed by a high kick in rapid succession. She'd be practicing this combination in the gym today and tomorrow and the next day and the next. For weeks. For months! She threw the combination again and her right foot came down from the kick on top of the algebra book. Coming back into Earth orbit, shoulders slumping, Zuri stared at the textbook. She wouldn't be practicing at the gym if she didn't raise her grade.

****

Zuri split her time between the gym and studying math over the weekend, and her hard work paid off with algebra class proceeding far better than she could have ever dreamed. As Mr. Benson lectured the class about the homework given last Friday and concepts built upon that foundation, Zuri discovered, to her delight, that she did have a basic understanding of polynomials. It was a challenging concept, and today's homework would be tough, but understanding flickered in her mind instead of pitch-black nothingness.

With five minutes or less left in the period, Mr. Benson made an announcement that put a damper on Zuri's day. "Next Friday is the test for this section."

Most of what the teacher said next was lost in a chorus of groans and boos, but Zuri heard fifteen percent of your final grade for the semester. She crossed her arms on the desktop and laid her head on her arms. She was being tossed into the deep end, and it was time to swim or drown.

Water gushed down her throat.

****

Luis intercepted Zuri on the way to lunch, as usual. His quiet demeanor was out of the ordinary—not the thoughtful nature of it because Luis was always thoughtful even while boisterous and enthusiastic to the point of bursting. Something was clearly on her friend's mind, something troubling.

They queued in the line before the double doors to the lunchroom behind a group of football players, loudly reliving on-field glories. A tall, broad-shouldered blond boy glanced toward Zuri and Luis, his gaze lingering on her long enough to indicate that he was checking her out. Zuri knew boys found her attractive and didn't mind, but it didn't excite her the way it used to. Maybe it was the fact the boy was tall, muscular, and blond—a carbon copy of Toby Alkorn except for the eyes. This boy's orbs were green, like chips of dark jade, while Toby's were startling blue. Honestly, though, she'd much rather have Luis admiring her than the football player. She met his gaze and rolled her eyes. He turned his attention back to his teammates, and the moment passed.

"Thanks for helping me with my algebra homework last night."

Uncharacteristically, Luis only nodded, obviously distracted by his thoughts.

"What's bothering you? Something's up."

Luis glanced at her. "It's the hand. And your dream. Edith and John…they found something out."

Zuri stiffened. She hadn't told Luis about her latest dream from Friday where her father attacked her and didn't want to be reminded of it. The line shuffled forward, and they passed into the lunchroom. Fat Nick floated alongside the lunch queue, his spritely, almost aerobatic movement incongruous with his enormous, flabby bulk overflowing his ill-fitting clothes. When he spotted Zuri, his beady eyes widened, and he descended through the floor and out of sight. Her lips twitched upward into a pleased smirk. Good. The school's bullies are on notice.

"What did they find out?" Zuri asked.

"I don't know. It's not good."

They hiked across the noisy and crowded lunchroom to join Edith and John at their usual table. The couple immediately set in on Zuri before she even sat down.

"You need to stop going to the library after school," Edith said.

"Yeah, that green hand thing attacking the ghost girl," John said. "That's bad juju. You don't want any part of that. We don't."

"Evil juju." Edith's eyes were watery. "What the hand did to you and the ghost wasn't innocent. It was malicious."

Feeling ambushed, Zuri set her tray on the table and sat. She was about to respond, but Luis spoke first.

"This is getting serious, Zuri," Luis said. "The school administration is going to get involved."

Zuri scoffed. "Is that what all you goodie goodies are worried about? Being sent to the principal's office? What about the ghost girl? What about her? She's in trouble. She needs our help. If you don't want to help her—fine! But don't stand in my way."

"No, being sent to the principal's office is not what this is about," John said snidely. "But I, for one, don't want to be sent there. For any reason. If I get in trouble, my dad would kill me."

"Abusive, is he?" Zuri asked pointedly.

"Taking away my Internet access for a week or more

is abuse," John said.

Edith and Luis agreed that losing Internet access was a harsh punishment. Zuri bit her tongue to keep from making a nasty rejoinder.

"John found a lead on the man in white from your dream," Edith said.

John nodded and started in on his peanut butter and jelly sandwich.

Zuri leaned back in her chair. "What did you find out?"

John swallowed. "What he might have been saying."

"It's bad, Zuri," Edith added.

Chapter 28

Buckle Down

Zuri waited for her friends to tell her what they had learned, which was so terrible that she had no choice but to give up on her mission to aid the ghost girl. Edith and Luis stared at John, who tore into his peanut butter and jelly sandwich with gusto. Everyone else had neglected to touch their lunch, but it seemed nothing, including bad juju, could stifle his appetite for long.

"Well?" Edith heaved an exasperated sigh. "Are you going to show her or just keep eating your sandwich?" The mousy girl glanced at Zuri. "I swear, sometimes all he does is eat and eat and eat."

"I can see that." Zuri turned her head so she didn't have to watch John stuff the remaining third of the sandwich into his already full mouth.

Luis snickered and looked away, catching Zuri's eyes and grinning. It was amazing how, in some aspects, Luis was entirely different from any boy she'd ever known, but when it came to the patently grotesque, he was as lowbrow as every other male troglodyte she knew.

"Disgusting," she mouthed, which made Luis shake with laughter, and he almost fell out of his chair. Only Zuri catching him by the shoulder kept him from crashing to the floor.

"Hey, I'm a growing boy," John said, words coming out mushy. Only by breaking the laws of physics did the goo of white bread, peanut butter, and purple jam not fall from his mouth to splatter over the table.

"Keep your mouth shut," Edith said, "until you're done eating and get out your computer."

John tried to completely close his mouth, but even if he could defy the fundamental principles of the universe with the amount of food he could cram inside his orifice without any dribbling out, he couldn't manage that. Some laws, it turned out, were immutable even in a haunted school. John swallowed some of the gnashed-up sandwich, causing his throat to bulge precariously.

"Remind me why I'm dating you?" Edith murmured.

John leaned over and retrieved his laptop from his backpack, chewing the sandwich mush the entire time. Setting the computer on the table, the gaunt lad swallowed again and another huge lump descended slowly down his throat. He opened the laptop and his fingers danced over the keyboard. Spinning the computer around, so the rest of the table could see the screen, John almost unsealed his grinding mouth to speak.

After a monumental gulp, John spoke. Only a smattering of jam and peanut butter stained his teeth. "Check this out. You said this mysterious man in white had a bowie knife, right?"

Zuri nodded.

"Wiccanary.com to the rescue."

The webpage was full of paragraphs written in a fanciful font that was difficult to read. In the top right-hand corner was a black-and-white graphic of a pentagram. Floating above the pentagram were two flickering candles. John quickly scrolled down the page, too fast for Zuri to read anything.

"At first, I tried searching on the killer's description. I thought maybe I'd find something about a demon. But then…" John glanced around the table with a knowing and annoying smirk. Centered on the page was an audio player. Below the play button was a caption that read demonic spell sound sample. "I realized maybe the bowie knife is the key. I mean, why a bowie knife? Why not a steak knife or any other sharp knife? A bowie knife is pretty distinct. I started searching on that and voilà."

"What is it?" Zuri asked. "Demonic spell sound sample? Are you saying the man in white was casting a spell in my dream?"

"That's what we're about to find out," Edith cut in. "Play the recording. Either she will recognize it or not."

"Okay. Okay," John grumbled. "Ruin my lead-up."

He turned the volume up on his laptop and played the audio file. A woman's voice emitted from the speakers. The recording was scratchy and even cut in and out, but over the lunchroom's din, Zuri made out the harsh, slightly sibilant chant, transporting her back to the nightmare: the dark room, the man in white barely illuminated by the palest of moonlight, and the dreadful glimmer along his bloody blade as he stabbed and stabbed and stabbed.

"Zuri."

A hand rested on her shoulder and gently shook. "Zuri!"

It was Luis. Zuri blinked and shook her head, slowly rising from the daze.

"What happened?" Edith stared at her wide-eyed. "You spaced out."

"She recognized the recording, obviously," John said smugly.

Zuri removed Luis's hand from her shoulder, gently squeezing before releasing him. "John's right. I recognized it. That's the same language. The same chant...spell from the dream."

John and Edith exchanged a glance. Edith looked ready to cry, but her boyfriend leaned forward, eyes full of glee.

"Seal my legacy, seal my legacy, seal my legacy in blood," John chanted. "The blood of my descendent. My descendent. My virginal descendent. With this sacrifice, with this sacrifice, protect my legacy for all time. Protect for all time, protect for all time, my legacy, my name, all my earthly works. All my earthly works. For this Mammon I gladly give my child. My virgin child." John leaned back in his chair and grabbed a red apple from his lunchbox, holding it up. "The witch repeats the spell until the deed is done. Let me see." He glanced at the screen. "It has to be repeated at least three times."

John bit into the apple with a loud crunch, juice running over his lips and down his chin.

Zuri felt sick to her stomach. "The ghost is the daughter of the man in white? He killed his own daughter?"

"I told you this is serious," Luis said.

"Evil juju," John said as he chewed.

"That's why you need to stay out of the library," Edith entreated. "If the ghost in the library and the green hand that attacked you are related to the dreams..." she shook her head.

"Who is this...what was the name?" Zuri asked.

John swallowed. "Mammon. It's another name for

the devil or a demon."

"Specifically, one related to the sin of greed," Luis added.

"Promise us...promise me." Edith stared intensely at Zuri. "You're done with the library. Done with trying to help the ghost." She turned her gaze on Luis. "That goes for both of you."

Luis shifted uncomfortably in his chair and nodded. Zuri had no intention of giving up on the ghost girl. With or without her friends' help, she planned to do everything in her power to help the ghost. She had watched her mother nearly be beaten to death by Big Jake. In all the intervening years, they had needed helping hands. The help they had received was far and few between, but when it came in the form of a job, a break on rent, or training at a gym gratis, it had always been priceless.

She could never turn her back on another sister in need. What was an abuser other than a bully? Zuri knew how to handle live bullies. She figured she could find a way to handle a dead one too. She intended to pay forward all the help she and her mother had received over the years with interest.

"Sure. Sure." She nodded. "I won't go back to the library or try to help the girl. Like you said, it's bad juju."

****

How?

That question consumed George, fueling his barely contained anger. He'd rage if he could, but even that required energy. Vitality that he must conserve. If Rose attempted to escape the school again, and he was certain she would, being as willful in death as she was in life, he must be ready to stop her. To fail in that...it was unthinkable. His legacy, his fortune, his name, his works were meant to exist forevermore. To never fade. To never crumble, unlike Ozymandias and the many megalomaniacs before him.

How had his dupe, his brawny champion, resisted his summons? George had touched Big Jake, caressed the strongman's soul and found a kindred spirit. A fellow misogynist. A man who needed to put his women in their place. How had Jake resisted the call?

As importantly, did George dare attempt to contact Jake again? George wasn't one to suffer failure twice, and doing so might leave him too weak to prevent Rose from escaping the school should she try again. Oh, and he knew she would try again. She would try and try and try until either she escaped, or he slammed shut the door of her prison.

But first, he needed to recapture Rose. Her familiar, this Zuri, was the key. George was confident in that. He had touched her, after all, and now knew her intimately. All he needed to do was contemplate what would trigger to pull to cause the desired result.

****

Zuri laid out her math homework on the study table in the library and stared at the stacks where the ghost girl usually appeared. "I'm here to help you," she whispered.

From inside her backpack, her phone buzzed, likely announcing a text message. Zuri retrieved the device and opened it using her thumbprint. As she suspected, it was a message from Luis asking where she was. They were supposed to head to his house to study together before she went to the gym. Zuri considered lying to him, making up a story about already heading to the gym, but she found she didn't want to lie again—not to him.

—*I'm in the library. You coming?*—

Chapter 29

Tests

As soon as Zuri sent the text to Luis, she regretted it. What if he started obsessively texting or calling her to tell her to get the heck out of the library? She didn't want to have to deal with that. She needed to have her pencil up and head down, studying, grinding.

And what if he did come? That was an even worse outcome. Because it would put him in danger. Grave risk. Maybe even life and death peril. That wasn't something Luis needed in his life.

She should know.

She watched her father beat her mother nearly to death, listened to the wet crunch of his fists against her face, and smelled her blood. Zuri hadn't understood how much fluid could leak out of a human body until that night in the kitchen, listening to her father rage and her mother whimper. No, Luis didn't need to learn the true meaning of danger or the thinness of the embarkation line between the living and the dead.

Why had she texted Luis? Why was she trying to draw him into this paranormal web? She didn't understand the risk and doubted that he did. She'd text him again, tell him not to come. But she hesitated with her thumbs above the phone's pop-up keyboard. The truth was, she didn't want to do this alone. As hard as it was to admit, she needed someone in her corner. Someone she could trust. And what if the ghost didn't come? Who would help her study if not Luis? She couldn't lose her gym money. The gym was her lifeline.

But those weren't reasons to put Luis in jeopardy. She was typing out a message, telling him not to bother coming when his text came.

——*I knew you wouldn't give up on the ghost girl. I'll be right there and don't tell me not to come.*——

Zuri hung her head in defeat, knowing nothing she could say would prevent Luis from coming. Emotions she didn't understand roiled inside her, sending her to the verge of tears. She placed the phone on the table and massaged her temples with her left hand.

She wouldn't cry.

That wasn't her.

She was a fighter.

The entire time, Zuri was being watched.

****

Rose floated through the stacks as incorporeal as interstellar dust drifting between stars. Even in this form, she could read, observe, and vicariously live. It was a bitter draft. One that would fill her with yearning for all that had been denied her, with hatred for the living, and the desire for cold vengeance on her father if she allowed it.

That hateful man.

That monster.

But she didn't dwell on those things, or at least, she tried not to. It wasn't easy, but she did her best to occupy her time and take pleasure in what she could. Reading was a great joy, especially the math books. The only problem was that she had read every one in the library, most more than once, and she understood the math—all of it, and that understanding made her pine for more. Even the logic of mathematics could lead to dissatisfaction, which, in turn, led to dark thoughts, to the death spiral of eternal dismay.

That's when she would turn to romances. Often, any romance would do. She had been only twelve when her life was cut short, but she liked boys and wanted their attention, especially from the good-looking ones. As an O'Dell scion, Rose would've had no shortage of suitors. After all, young men of the finest breeding from Raleigh to distant New York City were tripping over themselves to woe her elder sisters. Had been tripping over themselves, Rose reminded herself. Like everyone else she had known, her sisters and their suitors were long buried. And, of course, that was the problem with romances in the end. Eventually, the stories of love, loss, redemption, and usually love in the end—Rose preferred the tales ending with happily ever after—reminded her of exactly what she had been denied. Love. Companionship. Family. Children. A life well lived. And the death spiral of dismay, unending, forevermore, until the end of all things, started again.

That's when she'd start reading anything. She had read everything. She knew exactly how many books Pinedale High's library contained: 13,572. She'd read all of them at least once; nearly half she read two times or more. She didn't care to read the other books more than once. The fact of the matter was she was running out of things to distract herself. When she did, she'd face the perpetuity of despair. She suspected that was precisely what her father desired.

It was to distract herself that she first coalesced from

the firmament into a vaguely humanoid apparition to help a black girl with mathematics. It was only when the girl, when Zuri, touched her that Rose knew she had encountered the very person she needed to achieve her goal. Not to have what had been denied her or to exact revenge on her father, but to finally rest in peace. Zuri could help her achieve that. How exactly, Rose didn't know, but she knew in every particle of her being that the black girl could help her and would.

Watching Zuri now, even knowing that her father might be surveilling the library, Rose was tempted to go to the girl and help her with math. It was the least she could do for the person she was sure would eventually help her be at peace. But she had to be cautious. Her father had almost captured her and dragged her back to his sanctum beneath the school, a cold, dark place populated only by grotesquely mutated rats, bloated nightcrawlers, and worst of all, his malefic spirit. If Rose had a body, she'd shudder at just the thought.

Maybe Rose had been a fool to approach Zuri in the first place. Up until now, she's been free to roam the library for close to by her count one hundred years without her father knowing. For all that time, she had approached no one, only observing and reading. Only after she contacted the living, did he know she had escaped his prison, only bound to that dreadful shrine by the most tenuous of threads. She didn't understand exactly what bound her, not in a literal sense, but she could feel the tug, always pulling her down. The further she moved from the library, the stronger the downward force became. That's why she could count on one hand the number of times she had dared float beyond the archive's four walls.

Father would stop at nothing to imprison her again now that he knew she was no longer confined to his altar. She didn't know why he had killed her or what purpose she served in his malevolent plot, but she knew that returning to the sanctum would mean an eternity of torment. It meant bathing in his hatred for every millisecond of every day, of every week, of every month, and of every year until the end of time. It was a fate worse than death. She would know, after all, because she knew that she was no longer among the living.

Still, she hesitated to coalesce, to take on a form that could interact directly with the living, because she feared her father would detect her and attempt to recapture her. Instead of emerging from the ether, Rose watched and bided her time. The black girl wasn't the most dedicated student, not in Rose's opinion. She was easily distracted by the thin rectangular device that she always kept close at hand. From her reconnaissance over the years, Rose knew this relatively new-fangled device was called a phone and wasn't allowed on school grounds. The rule, however, wasn't strictly enforced. Right now, for instance, the girl watched images play out on the small rectangular screen of two women dressed scantily in skin-tight undergarments locked in combat: kicking, punching, and grappling. The face of one combatant was smeared with blood. Rose couldn't watch without feeling revolted. At times like this, she wondered what the world was coming to. What the women engaged in was decidedly unwomanly.

Rose turned her attention to browsing the books, even though none in the immediate vicinity piqued her interest. Honestly, anything was better than watching those two young women go at each other like wildcats.

And to think Zuri partook in such activity, wanted to do it in front of cheering crowds, earn a living beating up other girls, and being beaten up herself. How sordid. *Keep an open mind, Rose. Times have changed.*

"Zuri, I thought you were studying!"

A male voice, whispering and teasing. Rose stopped reading about Kant's categorical imperative midsentence and returned her full attention to the living. It was the mathematician boy, the one who looked Mexican. Bigoted thoughts and emotions surged through Rose. She had never liked Mexicans in life. Not one bit. But she knew from reading the books and observing life in the library that things had changed from her day. And that much of her ill will for Mexicans and other minorities came from her father, the very man who killed her in the middle of the night. If she could look at Zuri and see a person who was more than the hired help around the house, she could consider Luis as something other than a dumb and dirty seasonal laborer. For one thing, Luis was highly proficient at mathematics, perhaps not as skilled as she was, but few were. Bottling up a lifetime of bigotry and racist tropes, Rose watched the students with interest and jealousy for the intimacy they shared and the advanced mathematics Luis studied.

The first thing Luis did before helping Zuri with her simplistic algebra assignment was open his laptop to display dozens of formulas upon its screen. It was a symphony of mathematics, but a clangorous one because Rose didn't fully comprehend all the notes. She could. She knew she could, without an iota of doubt, but first, she needed to fill in the gaps in her knowledge.

As Zuri and Luis studied, their heads close together and speaking softly, Rose drifted out from the stacks without really meaning to. She floated closer to the table to better view the numerological marvels on the laptop's screen. She needed more information, more understanding, more knowledge. Whatever this mathematics was called, it was amazing and discerning it would unlock wonders beyond Rose's complete comprehension.

For some reason, Zuri and Luis stopped whispering about algebra and looked up toward the stacks. The black girl smiled welcomingly, while Luis gaped. No, they weren't staring at her, were they? Oh, well, this was embarrassing and alarming. She had emerged from the firmament, coalescing into a humanoid form without intending to.

Chapter 30

Meet the Family

Both teens stared at Rose. The mathematician's eyes going so wide he almost looked like a toad. No, Rose chided herself, she would not think of him in disparaging terms. It would be hard, but it was something that she must to do. Otherwise, she knew she would be unable to see him as other than subhuman. She could do better. She could be less racist in death than she had been in life.

Zuri broke the silence. "This is Luis. He is the friend I told you about. The one who wants to meet you. You almost met the other day, before..."

Rose nodded and almost dissolved back into the empyrean filament. She didn't need to be reminded that her father might watch her. If she had a heart, it would've raced. If she could perspire, sweat would bead on her brow. Instead, she was left with a sense of unease permeating the spiritual matrix that formulated her thoughts and emotions. But just as curiosity killed the cat, inquisitiveness would be Rose's undoing. She must understand the mathematics. It was an imperative as categorical as the moral laws expounded by Kant.

Rose glided forward, focused on the laptop screen with all the wondrous equations. She could understand them, she knew, and master them—master them all, and more and more.

The mathematician slid the laptop toward her. "Do you know how to use this?"

He must mean the computer. Rose shook her head in the negative.

"You use this." He indicated a rectangular, depressed section of the device below the letters of the alphabet. He placed his finger on it, and an arrow on the screen started to move. "See? I can move the webpage up and down. You place the pointer on this bar on the far right. Press down on the trackpad and move the pointer up and down. Easy. Do you understand?"

Rose felt confident that she understood how to manipulate the computer in theory, but she wasn't certain that she would find it easy in practice. Nevertheless, she nodded.

"Have at it," Luis said. "I think you'll find real analysis incredibly fascinating. I know I do."

Luis turned back to the algebra homework splayed across the table.

"Are you sure she'll be able to figure out the computer?" Zuri whispered.

"I don't know." Luis turned back to Rose. "If you need help with the computer or anything…just ask. Okay?"

Inadvertently, Rose's right hand went to her throat, fingers brushing the high collar of her dress. She forced herself to keep smiling despite the words cutting through her like mystical bullets. But it wasn't Luis's fault that his words were barbs hooking into her ephemera. He didn't know. How could he? Neither of them did.

While Zuri and Luis studied, Rose considered the real analysis, quickly drowning her sorrows in a boiling cauldron of mathematical insight. Occasionally, she would do something, she wasn't entirely sure what, to disrupt the beautiful formulas on the laptop's screen. Fortunately, Luis was solicitous, often checking in on her in between explaining algebraic solutions to Zuri. Rose would think Luis was a wizard if she didn't know better. Every time she did something to interrupt her studies, he quickly brought back the formulas with a few flicks of a finger on the trackpad. He wasn't the best-looking boy she had ever encountered, not by a long shot, but he was a generous and gentle soul, and she began to appreciate what Zuri saw in him.

Too soon, an hour or more had flown by, and Zuri announced, "We need to stop. My brain is full. I need to go to the gym."

Luis was disappointed but conceded they had made good progress. Rose, though, was devastated. She still had many gaps in her knowledge to fill. Part of her wanted to take the laptop from the table and float to the ceiling to continue her education without them, but that would be rude beyond reproach, and she wasn't a trickster. Instead, she hung her head and floated back from the table to allow Luis room to collect his things without brushing up against her.

"Did you find the real analysis interesting?" the mathematician asked.

Glancing up, Rose nodded.

An enthusiastic smile split Luis's face. "Great! I'll bring a printout tomorrow that covers all the basics of real analysis. You'll love it. Believe me."

Rose smiled wider than she had in one hundred years or more. She could have kissed him on the cheek, but she knew the living found the touch of the deceased disturbing.

****

Zuri's week passed quickly between studying, trying to figure out how to aid the ghost girl, and hitting the gym. Before she knew it, Thursday rolled around, and the test was tomorrow. But unlike previously, this time, she felt prepared—well, sort of ready.

Maybe.

At least, that's what she kept telling herself and attempting to visualize. That's what she did before a fight. She pre-visualized success: standing in the middle of the octagon with her hand raised after knocking out her adversary with a high kick to their chin. When she was really in the zone, she could feel the concussion of her foot smashing into her opponent's face, hear the roar of the crowd, and smell blood and sweat and the referee's aftershave.

Sometimes, she even saw her mother cheering uproariously in the front row. But it wasn't as easy to imagine earning an exceptional grade on the test. Dreaming up images of studying with Luis and taking the test was relatively easy, but every time she received the test back, the grade was always less than stellar.

Zuri fretted about her preparedness on her way to the library after school. Was she ready? Was she grinding enough to ace the test, or was she fooling herself? Her trepidation increased when Luis didn't intercept her in the crowded hallways as usual. That was odd. He had been properly enthusiastic in the lunch line, whispering how the ghostly mathematician had devoured the introductory material on real analysis.

"Based on what I've seen of her work, she has had insights it took me months to realize," Luis said in a hushed tone. "I wish...I wish she would talk. That's strange, right? Her not talking. I don't think I've ever seen her write a word. Only math formulas."

"Maybe she's shy," Zuri had replied, but she couldn't disagree with him. It was strange, but then, again, she didn't recall Fat Nick uttering a word, and presumably, the only word Dumbo Jock said was, "Swirlie, Swwwwiiirrrlie."

Entering the library, Zuri wished she had spent more time carefully reading entries in The Compendium. Maybe then, she would have insight as to whether they should expect the ghost to speak. They could always ask Edith and John, but they had kept their continued contact with the ghost a secret from their friends.

"Miss Williams, how are you this fine afternoon? Any plans for Thanksgiving?" Mrs. Binder chirped from her perch behind the circulation desk.

Startled from her thoughts, Zuri only managed a distracted reply. "Thanksgiving? No plans, no."

Since the incident with the ghost girl and the gnarly green hand, the librarian's demeanor had thawed considerably. Binder was solicitous, almost pleasant. It was mildly unnerving, to be honest. She had reported the encounter to the school administration, but Luis's fear that they would end up in the principal's office had been misplaced. They had each been summoned to the counselor's office separately for questioning by Mr. Copeland. Zuri and Copeland had mainly discussed boxing after briefly speaking about the paranormal episode. Even Luis had to admit his visit to the counselor's office was a non-event.

"Well, I hope you have a good holiday," Binder said, smiling. "I'm out all next week. Going to visit family in St. Louis."

While the librarian spoke, Zuri's phone vibrated inside her backpack, making a faint yet distinct thumping noise. Zuri was certain she was about to be called out for having a phone on school grounds, but for once, Binder took no notice. After replying to the librarian with the bare minimum of pleasantries, the teen retreated between the stacks.

Zuri shrugged off her backpack at the study table and retrieved her phone. As she suspected, it was a text from Luis.

——*John and Edith know we're still seeing the ghost girl. They're threatening to tell the principal about your dreams. Trying to convince them not to.*——

"I have the test tomorrow!" Zuri slammed the phone onto the desk. "It's okay. It's okay. You got this, girl." She glanced at the shelving from where the ghostly girl always emerged. "I hope you're around and willing to help."

There wasn't even the faintest indication of the spirit's presence, not a wintery chill, the reek of decay, or a luminous glimmer. Frowning and heaving a sigh, Zuri pulled the algebra book out of her backpack and got down to reviewing polynomials. She quickly lost herself in her studies and wasn't sure how long she had been at it when she detected the odor of rotten meat in the air. It wasn't strong, but it was enough to turn her stomach and inform her that a ghost was nearby.

Let it be the ghost girl. It probably wasn't the dead librarian haunting the stacks. That ghost always smelled like musty old books, but it could be a different ghost like the vile green hand. Pulse thrumming, Zuri turned toward the stacks, glimpsing wispy grey mist seeping between the books, swirling over the shelving, and emerging slowly to form a nebulous cloud. That fog transformed into a vaguely humanoid shape shot through with golden radiance that burned away the excess mist until the apparitional girl levitated, fully formed before the shelving. As before, from the waist up, she wore a dress; from the waist down, she was swirling mist shaped like a hoop skirt.

Zuri smiled. "Hi. Can you help me?"

After the ghost nodded, they got down to work.

****

Nearly two hours later, Zuri left the library feeling like she'd do well on a math test for the first time in her life. But she also left disconcerted. As Luis had observed, the ghost never spoke and only wrote mathematical equations. Most of her communication was done with body language alone: emphatic hand gestures, repeated pointing, and glares stern enough to put Mrs. Binder to shame. Zuri was met with uncanny silence and a wave when she said goodbye.

The school's usually noisy hallways were also eerily quiet except for Hank's soft whistling as he mopped the floors. Zuri tried to avoid the janitor as she was still creeped out he knew her name on the first day of school. She failed to avoid him. He had a peculiar way of always being right where you were.

Hank looked up, leaning against the mop handle. "You're here late."

"I have a test tomorrow." Zuri rushed by him and outside into the sable evening.

Zuri pulled her phone out of her backpack as she walked down the sidewalk. In the distance, the forest behind the school across the cornfield stood like an army of skeletons. A breeze stirring her hair made the branches clatter like bags of quaking bones.

"Huh." Luis had left her several text messages. The first two stated that he had convinced Edith and John not to out them to the school authorities yet—that was a relief. But it was the third missive that piqued her curiosity.

——*Call me tonight. Seriously, call me.*——

Stopping under a streetlamp, Zuri called her friend.

"Zuri." Luis's voice piped from the speaker.

"What's up?" The wind gusted, causing her to shiver, so she started walking. "Listen, it's cold. I'm going to run to the gym."

"You're not at the gym yet?"

"No, the ghost girl is a great teacher, considering she doesn't talk. Now, what's up?"

"Do you want to come over for Thanksgiving? You and your mom."

Chapter 31

Encoding Messages

Lying in bed, Zuri entered the Thanksgiving holiday buoyed by her stellar grade on the math test. Her mother would continue paying for the gym, for now at least. She'd have to keep up the extra studying, but that no longer made her brim with dread. Doing homework with Luis and the ghost girl was…well, pleasant. Sure, she left study sessions with an exhausted mind, drowning in figures and formulas, but she reset at the gym. Of course, nothing mathematical came easy for her. But the hard work, the grinding, was paying off.

The only bad part of the holiday weekend was that Pinedale Fight School was shut down until Monday. What was a girl to do for four whole days without a heavy bag to work? Shopping was out of the question. Mother was making a decent salary, and they were doing better financially than they had in years, but money was still tight. Besides, the Black Friday and Cyber Monday ads she stumbled upon while searching for clips of The Jade Tiger didn't interest her. All she needed was access to a fight gym, and she already had that. Well, she would on Monday…maybe if the weather cooperated, she would work on her stamina by putting in extra miles on the road.

But that was for tomorrow. Footfall came from the

kitchen and dining area, probably Mother setting out the ingredients needed to make a homemade pumpkin pie to bring to Luis's. Zuri looked forward to seeing him and meeting his mother and sister. To think, only a few months ago, she wouldn't have glanced at Luis twice. How quickly things change. Of course, back then, she didn't believe in ghosts or anything remotely supernatural. Now the paranormal preoccupied her waking and unconscious mind.

Zuri checked the time on her phone—God, only seven forty-seven! She had hoped to sleep in a little more than that. It was a hard commodity to come by, given her anxiety over the test and desperate desire to help the ghost. Horrible nightmares hadn't afflicted her for several days, but that didn't mean she had been sleeping well, even after acing the exam. Last night, she'd spent hours staring at the dark ceiling, yearning for slumberland while dogged by thoughts of the ghost girl and fear for Luis's wellbeing.

Why didn't the girl speak? Every time Zuri or Luis tried to converse with the spirit, she responded with body language alone—the tap of a finger against the tabletop, an expression of categorical exasperation, or she'd ignore them. And yesterday, when he'd written a note asking the phantasm's name, the girl had taken one look at the paper and flipped it over, then went back to studying real analysis on the laptop.

The behavior was odd.

But the girl was a ghost. Was her behavior any more bizarre than Fat Nick, Dumbo Jock, or the other spirits haunting Pinedale Central? Zuri couldn't decide. But it wasn't thoughts of the ghost girl alone that kept her awake. It was the trepidation and guilt that she dragged

Luis into a corner where he was in over his head and in peril. He claimed to be an expert on all things phantasmagoric, but Zuri was no fool. He only said such things to impress her. The real experts in her coterie were Edith and John, and they knew enough to want nothing to do with the ghost girl, man in white, and phantasmal hand.

Part of Zuri knew she should stop going to the library. Luis and she could find somewhere else to study and hang out. But she couldn't abandon a sister in need, not even a dead one. The ghosts listed in The Compendium haunted the high school because they had come to a traumatic end on school grounds. What trauma had robbed the ghost of her voice?

Zuri sucked in a breath. She needed only to recall the nightmares featuring the man in white with his bowie knife to have an inkling.

Knocking on the door startled Zuri from her reverie, causing her to utter an undignified yelp. "Zuri? Is everything all right?"

"Yeah, Mom. You startled me."

"Did I wake you up? I'm sorry. I thought you'd want to help with the pie."

"It's okay. I was awake," Zuri said. "I'll be right there."

****

At the stoop of the Torres house, Zuri rang the doorbell while balancing the warm pie plate in her opposite hand. The tinfoil covering the pie couldn't contain its wonderful pumpkin scent that made Zuri salivate in anticipation of the upcoming meal. She hoped the pie tasted half as good as it smelled. Amari hunkered next to her, simultaneously attempting to take in the pristine home and escape the chilly breeze stirring the shrubbery.

"This is a nice neighborhood," Amari said, clearly impressed.

"Try not to embarrass me." Zuri gave Mother the stink eye.

Stomping feet and shouting echoed inside the house. Zuri recognized Luis's voice and assumed the other belonged to his older sister—Maria, three years older and attending community college. His mother was Raquel, a well-known civil rights attorney. Zuri had decided while baking the pie that it was best to refer to her as Mrs. Torres, despite Luis stating his mother was easy-going outside of the courtroom.

"I won't do anything to embarrass you," Amari whispered. "Not on purpose. You need to relax. You look like you're going to punch—"

"Mother," Zuri hissed as the deadbolt clicked and the door swung open, emitting the enticing aroma of turkey and all the fixings.

"Let me through."

Luis's voice was muffled by the door, and there was a sound of a scuffle. A tall, slender, and striking young woman, a person so stunning you'd do a double take while passing by, appeared in the doorway. Zuri felt like a junkyard dog in comparison, wishing she had nicer clothes, designer make-up, and, well, better everything.

"Oh, hello," Maria said. "Come in. You must be—"

"Maria!" Luis bulled past his sister, his fearsome frown transforming into a smile when he saw Zuri.

"Luis!" Maria said in shrill annoyance.

"Children!" A stern female voice came from the kitchen. "Behave!"

"Yes, Mother," the Torres siblings replied in unison, separating themselves.

Not for the first time, Zuri was pleased not to have a sibling. If she did, such squabbles would end in fisticuffs.

"Follow me," Maria said, leading them toward the kitchen, the aromas growing richer with every step.

Luis fell in beside Zuri. "Hello, Mrs. Williams, it is a pleasure to meet you."

Amari beamed at him. "The pleasure is all mine, Luis. Zuri has told me so much about you."

Luis faintly blushed and said to Zuri. "I can't wait to show you my igloo."

"Igloo? Out of ConnectSmithery bricks?"

"Yeah."

Mrs. Torres, dressed to the nines, including a red and white checkered apron, stood at the commercial range in the expansive kitchen. Steaming food sat on a marble countertop alongside bottles of wine and sparkling cider. Amari took in the kitchen with wide, envious eyes. Although Zuri felt the flash of awkwardness, she couldn't blame her mother for being blown away. The space was a dreamscape for anyone who loved cooking.

"Zuri, darling, is that a pie?" the cook asked, who, if anything, was a more elegantly arresting version of her daughter. "Be a dear and set it there with the rest of the food."

After greetings were exchanged and it was determined that thirty minutes remained before the feast, Luis escorted Zuri out of the kitchen and down the hall to his bedroom.

They were pursued by his sister's teasing voice. "Showing off your nerdiness to your girlfriend?"

The remark earned Maria a mild rebuke from her mother, and Zuri was genuinely stunned and impressed when Luis flipped his sister the bird out of Mrs. Torres's sight line, of course. Unlike Zuri's first visit, the hallway before Luis's room wasn't cluttered with pillows and blankets.

Luis noticed her taking in the empty hallway. "The best thing about the igloo is I can sleep inside it."

"You can't be serious."

"Oh, yes, I can." Luis opened the door to his bedroom.

Practically every inch of floor space was taken up by an igloo of blue bricks. The entrance faced the doorway and was large enough to crawl through. There was barely enough room around the sides of the igloo to skirt it with one's back pressed against the wall.

"Go inside." Luis pointed to the arched opening.

"You sure it won't collapse?"

"You're starting to sound like my mother," Luis complained.

"Forgive me for not wanting to be crushed," Zuri said, but nevertheless, flattened herself onto the carpet.

"Go on," Luis encouraged, a smile splitting his face. "It's a tight squeeze. We both won't fit."

Zuri crawled toward the igloo's entrance, which looked remarkably like the mouth of a demon. The channel into the structure was a tight squeeze with the curved walls of plastic bricks pressing into her sides. One wrong move could bring the whole thing down, or so Zuri feared, but as the ripe BO lurking inside the enclosure indicated, Luis had been sleeping here for several days, at least.

The tunnel opened into a domed space, with a small

opening at its peak, allowing in light from the ceiling-mounted fixture. The reek came from a pile of blankets and pillows that took up most of the interior. Crinkling her nose, Zuri prepared to back out the way she came, eager to escape the stench.

"What do you think?" Luis asked.

Zuri almost carped about the smell. "Impressive."

"Yeah," Luis said and started in on a lengthy explanation of the build.

Zuri didn't pay close attention to what he was saying, instead, she enjoyed his voice as she inspected knickknacks pressed against the wall. There was a Rubik's cube, an insanely thick tome that must be a math textbook, and a plastic ring topped with a wide circle and a second smaller circle inlaid on it. The ring captured her attention because all the letters of the alphabet were along the outer edge of the larger circle. Engraved along the edge of the smaller, inner circle were numbers.

"Luis, what is this plastic ring?"

Luis stuttered to a stop in his explanation of the igloo's construction. "What?"

"This ring? What is it?"

"Oh, it's an old decoder ring," Luis said nonchalantly. "Maria bought it for me off the internet as a joke. Stuff like that used to come in cereal boxes."

Clutching the ring in her hand, Zuri backed out of the channel. She was so excited that the BO no longer bothered her. After extricating herself, Zuri sat cross-legged on the floor and held up the ring.

"Are you thinking what I'm thinking?" she asked.

Luis looked dubious. "That we can assign numbers to letters and use them to communicate with the ghost?"

Zuri grinned. "Exactly."

Luis shrugged. "I thought about it, sure, but it seems too easy."

Zuri shook her head. Luis was too clever for his own good. "That's the beauty of it, Luis. The simplicity. It's going to work. How long have you been sitting on this idea?"

"I found the ring about a week ago," Luis admitted. "It just seems like kid stuff. Too easy."

Zuri rolled her eyes.

Chapter 32

Rose's Story

The Thanksgiving feast was an all-around hit. Mrs. Torres was a fantastic cook: the turkey was melt-in-your-mouth delicious, the mashed potatoes were buttery and lighter than air, and even the savory stuffing, typically something Zuri didn't enjoy, was to die for. By the time Luis and Maria served the pie, everyone was full nearly to bursting.

"This looks delectable," Mrs. Torres declared when her son set a plate of pie with an ample dollop of whipped cream before her.

Zuri and Amari exchanged a quick glance, both apprehensive the dessert wouldn't live up to the rest of the evening's fare. The siblings finished serving the pie, and Luis sat on Zuri's left.

She leaned toward him and murmured. "The pie isn't good."

"Looks good to me," he whispered.

"Oh, don't want to share what you have to say with the rest of us, Luis?" Maria said as she took her chair.

Luis's cheeks pinked.

Mrs. Torres batted a hand at her daughter. "Would you stop teasing him?"

"I was telling Luis the pie won't compare to all the amazing food you prepared." Zuri regarded the orange custard topped with whipping cream. "He said it looked good." Shrugging, Zuri smiled wanly at Mrs. Torres and Maria. "Don't get your hopes up."

With a wicked smile, the elder Torres picked up her fork, tines pointed to the ceiling. As she spoke, she stabbed the fork upward in time with her words. "I will be the judge of that."

"Don't be dramatic," Maria said, rolling her eyes.

Luis beat everyone in taking a bite. "This is great!" He exclaimed, words made mushy by the mashed pumpkin and crust filling his mouth. "Seriously, I'm not kidding."

Soon, everyone was eating and laughing at Maria's stories of meeting travelers while working as a night clerk at a local motel. More than once, Amari and Zuri gave each other relieved glances that the pie passed muster despite not being at the same level as the rest of the meal. For a time, Zuri forgot about the ghost girl, encoding messages, and the man in white...almost.

****

The rest of the holiday weekend proceeded with excruciating sluggishness. With the gym closed, Zuri was beside herself with what to do, even after running close to eight miles Friday morning before the gusting wind blew in downpouring clouds for the afternoon. Her go-to distraction of watching Malee Chaiyathorn bash girls into the canvas couldn't keep her occupied for long. Boundless energy and gnawing disquiet hummed through her in nearly equal measure. She wished her mind would go blank, and she wouldn't be plagued by the spectral tween, the man in white, and the phantasmagorical hand. But her mind never settled, instead scampering from one worrisome concern to another. It made her want to punch something or someone.

By Saturday, she was bouncing around her room shadow boxing. Her rambunctiousness ran away from her and soon it sounded like cattle stampeded through her room. The resulting rumpus brought Mother to the bedroom door with her hands on her hips.

Tired-eyed, Amari sighed. "Honestly, girl. I told you yesterday I'm working on my latest column. I'd go to the office if I could, but the Gazette is closed until Monday, like the gym. You kept me up half the night with all your bouncing around and now you're back at it. What's going on?"

The column. The darn advice column that was the talk of the town. Downcast, Zuri said. "Sorry."

Only, she wasn't too repentant, oh, no. Mention of the newspaper column resurfaced dread Zuri didn't have the bandwidth to process. What if someone discovered the true identity of the town's new, super-popular advice columnist? What then? Would Big Jake eventually find out and come with murder on his mind? Amari claimed he wasn't looking for them anymore. Zuri wanted to believe that was true, but she couldn't after the dream where the man in white morphed into her father. That nightmare was an ill omen. Even as her lips trembled, she reckoned she was being silly, but then again, ghosts haunted the halls and classrooms of Pinedale Central. She didn't know what to think—or believe—anymore.

"Zuri, what's wrong?" Her mother reached for her, but when Zuri retreated beyond her grasp, she dropped her hand.

Zuri shook her head. "There's nothing to do with the gym closed and the crappy weather."

To emphasize the point, the rainfall increased to a squall, drumming against the roof.

"Why don't you message your friend Luis? Go see a movie or something. I can drive you," Amari said, expression softening. "If you stay here, you'll be banging around all day. I won't get any work done."

Zuri raised her eyebrows. "You mean go on a date? With Luis?"

Even as the words came out in the most dubious of tones, her tummy fluttered, and her lower abdomen tightened.

Amari shrugged. "It doesn't have to be a date. But…" she grinned, "I saw how you looked at him and how he looked at you."

Zuri smiled, hoping to hide her mortification. "I don't know. I mean…we're friends, sure… but we don't have that much in common, and after…" Zuri slumped, and a shudder ran through her "…after Toby."

"Come here, baby." Amari rushed in and embraced her. "I thought…after seeing you so happy beside him. I know you probably don't think I'm the best person to give relationship advice, but—"

"Mom, you are the town's advice columnist," Zuri chuckled.

Mother hugged her even tighter. "I know you might be scared to bare your heart to someone after that vile Toby boy, but Luis is different. I really believe that after meeting him and his family. You and Luis might have more in common than you know."

"I'll think about it," Zuri said to get Mother off her back.

Amari pecked her on the forehead. "You do that and try to be quiet about it."

Mother left Zuri to her thoughts. Without intending to, she started obsessing about Luis—all the good times, how he was compassionate and generous, and rather good-looking, albeit in a very academic way. In the end, she texted him.

——*do you want to do something? Like see a movie*——

He replied within a minute.

——*Sure*——

——*OK. No talking about ghosts or anything like that.*——

——*To read is to obey.*——

After some back-and-forth, they determined Mrs. Torres would drive them to the theater and pick them up afterwards. When Zuri self-consciously said she'd need to ask her mother for money, Luis texted her not to worry. She set aside her usual stubbornness about accepting charity, instead choosing to appreciate his generosity.

The ride to the theater was more luxurious than Zuri had ever experienced. The cream leather seats were supple and even heated. Inlaid on the dash was a giant touchscreen that seemed to control every aspect of the electric sedan. Most impressive, the road noise was practically nonexistent, giving Zuri the sense she was cocooned inside a lavish unreality. The feeling of displacement was enhanced by the subtle and pleasing scent of citrus and jasmine wafting through the cabin and Luis's top-shelf attire. He looked like he was ready to attend a Hollywood movie opening instead of going to the local cineplex.

Zuri wondered if she should have spent more time picking out clothes, but she only had well-worn athletic gear. At least what she wore had no holes and was freshly laundered. Of course, Zuri shouldn't have bothered worrying, but it did prevent her from fixating on the paranormal.

They watched a superhero movie that was still in the theater after many months. The auditorium possessed the distinct odor of stale popcorn with undercurrents of even more unsavory scents.

The popcorn they ate tasted burnt and was too greasy. Zuri found the movie forgettable, thinking most of the martial arts performed defied logic and the laws of physics. Luis, however, seemed captivated most of the time.

She noticed him glancing at her every now and then, and decided she liked the attention. When the closing credits began, and Luis started to stand, Zuri, heart thundering like she had gone four rounds in the octagon, pushed him back into the chair and planted a kiss right on his lips. After a second of discombobulation, he wrapped his arms around her shoulders and kissed her back.

It was short.

It was awkward.

And it was wonderful.

****

"Her name?" Luis asked, pencil at the ready over a sheet of paper with the alphabet across the top with a corresponding number, one through twenty-six, underneath each letter.

The library was particularly cold, even drafty, that Monday after school. The ghost girl hovered next to them at the study table, her gaze fixed on the closed laptop.

"What else should we ask?" Zuri smiled at the girl from her seat at the table next to Luis.

The ghost glanced between them in consternation and pointed at the laptop. Clearly, she wanted to study advanced mathematics.

"She's impatient," Zuri said.

"Give me a sec." Luis ran his finger along the numbers he had written. "I don't want to give her a garbled message." He flipped the paper around to face the spirit and placed the pencil beneath the code. "What's your name?"

The spirit gave them a stern frown before inspecting the paper. Her features relaxed as she studied the encoded message: 23 8 1 20, 9 19, 25 15 21 18, 14 1 15 5.

After a moment, the girl smiled, picked up the pencil, and wrote in an elegant script: *Eighteen.*

Zuri clapped her hands. "It's working. We're communicating."

Fifteen.

Zuri threw an arm over Luis's shoulder. "I told you it would work."

Luis patted her arm and nodded.

Nineteen.

Five.

"Rose," Luis translated. "Her name is Rose."

Rose glanced up and smiled shyly, then wrote more.

Luis inspected the numbers. "O'Dell. Rose O'Dell."

Rose nodded.

"O'Dell?" Zuri said. "Like Miriam O'Dell?"

Rose gave them a blank look.

"Don't know," Luis murmured. "Maybe."

"Why can't you talk?" Zuri asked and pointed at the

paper.

Rose snatched the paper and pencil, her lips set in a grim line and eyes as intense as thunderheads. This time, her writing was jagged and rushed, all elegance muddied by vehemence.

6 1 20 8 4 18

"Father," Luis said.

Zuri's free hand went to her mouth. "Oh, no. That's…"

Rose pulled down the high collar of her dress, revealing a wide gash along her throat: slashed tendons, mutilated muscle, trachea severed, and a ragged dark red stain below the wound.

Chapter 33

O'Dell House or Bust

Rose's story emerged in a flurry of decimals meticulously decoded by Luis into letters, words, sentences, paragraphs, and finally, a tale of woe.

Of never being good enough.

Of always being too smart and opinionated for her own good.

Of being too bookish and never sufficiently skilled in womanly pastimes: embroidery, cooking, music, and the like.

Being so mathematically inclined, she made fools of teachers, tutors, her brothers, and most damning of all, her father—none other than George O'Dell: founder of O'Dell Enterprises, long-time mayor of Pinedale, and noted philanthropist. His civic deeds of such import, he became known as Good Old George, a benefactor to the community, always with what was best for all in the foremost of his mind.

Luis stopped scribing. "George O'Dell is your father?"

Expression grave, Rose nodded.

"George O'Dell? Is there a statue of him in Pinedale Square Park?" Zuri asked.

"Yes, indeedy." Luis opened his laptop and typed George O'Dell into the search engine, which brought back a plethora of hits regarding the man, Pinedale, and O'Dell Enterprises, one of the largest privately held companies in the United States. Luis clicked on a link to a website that provided a biography of George. "Look. Died in 1947 at age ninety-four."

Zuri stared at Rose. "She might be one hundred years old or more."

Rose shrugged.

"Look at this." Luis highlighted a section of text and read. "In 1899, tragedy struck the family when the youngest daughter, Rose, died after falling into a well at age twelve."

"Did George O'Dell do that to you?" Zuri asked, pointing at the gnarly gash at Rose's throat. It was impossible to look at the wound without feeling her gorge rise.

Eyes wide, Rose pointed to the wound and nodded emphatically.

"Oh my God. I'm sorry," Zuri said.

"Do you think she can…" Luis mimed pulling a shirt collar around his neck.

"Can you cover the wound?" Zuri asked apologetically.

Smiling tightly, Rose pulled up the collar of her dress, covering the grotesque wound, then, taking up the pencil, started writing again and quickly run out of space on the paper. Her face screwed up in consternation, and Zuri suspected the girl was on the verge of tears.

"She needs more paper," Zuri said.

"On it." Luis pulled out several sheets of paper from the main compartment of his backpack, which he placed on the table before Rose.

Visibly struggling to maintain her composure, Rose

finished printing on one page and moved on to another. Zuri wondered if they were asking too much of the ghost—she looked like a child, even though she'd been dead for over one hundred years. Softly drumming her feet against the floor with pent-up anticipation, Zuri hoped what Rose went through was cathartic. Finally, she'd learn precisely what she needed to do to aid the ghost girl. In broad strokes, the pugilist already knew what needed to be done. Stand up to a bully or bullies. One of whom was an abusive, murderous father.

This time, Zuri wouldn't fail to defeat the patriarchy no matter how hard they hit or sharp their blades. But the fingers of her left hand clawed at her thigh, scraping, burrowing, betraying the anxiety she tried to deny. The fear that the man in white, who she believed with almost no doubt was George O'Dell, would be her undoing. That she would fail Rose as she had failed her mother in the kitchen all those years ago. That there would always be someone barring her way, another Big Jake who was too strong, too domineering to overcome.

A sharp snap derailed Zuri's thoughts and made Luis start. Rose wrote with such force that she had broken the pencil's tip, and now she stared at the writing implement with dismay.

Zuri reacted first, retrieving and uncapping a ballpoint pen from her backpack, which she offered to the girl. After a brief hesitation, Rose set down the pencil and took the pen. Zuri felt a chill when Rose's finger almost brushed hers. The ghost finished writing the missive and passed it to Luis, whose clammy hands left wet stains on the paper's edge. His lips moved silently as he interpreted the code.

"Let me decipher this." Luis painstakingly

transcribed the numbers into letters. After five minutes, he put the pen down and reviewed his work, lips trembling. "Okay. I think it's all correct."

He handed Zuri two sheets of paper chockful of neat, cramped script. Zuri read the story twice. Rose was the daughter of George O'Dell, long-time mayor of Pinedale and founder of O'Dell Enterprises. She died at age twelve in 1899, as the website indicated, but her death was not due to falling down a well. Her father had entered her bedroom in the dead of night and attacked her with a bowie knife while chanting, she would later discover, a demonic spell.

Each time Zuri read about the attack her breath caught in her throat, and for a moment, she dreaded she might not breathe again as a mirage of being attacked by the man in white flickered before her eyes.

After slashing and stabbing Rose dozens of times, he carved open her throat to stop her screams. The mortal wound had stolen her voice in death, a voice she had loved to use to sing in church choirs. Only what she experienced she learned wasn't true death. Rose did not ascend to Heaven, burn in Hell, or fade into oblivion. Instead, she was trapped inside a cage—all alone, for minutes, for hours, or decades she hadn't known. Until her father was there with her, his hateful presence was like being cast into a blast furnace. She had thought being alone was intolerable, madness-inducing, but being subjected to his presence was worse, like marinating in a bowl of hate.

But George had erred when he entered the cell. He had left a crack in what had once been impermeable walls. And it was through an infinitesimal gap Rose had seeped to escape the prison or so she had thought. For she hadn't escaped, not really. The tween was still tethered to that cage by a cord she could not sever. Whenever the adolescent apparition dared venture beyond the library, she felt the cable tugging her, drawing her back to the clink. The further she ventured from the bibliotheca, the more powerful the undertow until it was almost irresistible. If she ventured too far, she would undoubtedly be dragged back to the prison. And now, with George prowling the spiritual matrix, Rose feared to leave the book repository because it was here that she felt the safest and the undertow the least.

Rose wanted Zuri's help to escape the prison and find peace, whatever that meant, whether it be Heaven or Hell or the void; the ghost no longer cared which. She only knew for a certainty that whatever waited for her in true death was better than drowning in George's maleficent animosity forevermore or haunting the library, observing life but never participating in it.

Zuri gazed at Rose with tears in her eyes. "How? How can I help?"

Rose wrote a response and pushed the paper to Luis.

Luis inspected the script. "He kept a diary in the library." Luis looked up. "What library?"

"O'Dell House," Zuri said.

Rose pointed at a black-and-white picture on the laptop of the sprawling estate that was her family's home.

****

Deep in the subbasement below Pinedale Central, Good Old George was as busy as his progeny in the library. He had found his trickster, his sorceress, and wormed his way into her mind. He didn't understand her binary world of zeroes and ones, but he knew that with her witchcraft, she could send up a flare that his champion would find irresistible.

He didn't enjoy dredging the female mind, but the trickster was a disaffected youth, full of angst, the desire to change the world for the better, and the bone-deep need to prove herself to her peers. That made manipulating her child's play.

In her parent's dusty attic warmed by the radiant heat of humming computers, CyberWitch hacked into The Pinedale Gazette's network using the default administrator password some IT flunky had neglected to change. How could someone be so dumb? It nearly took all the thrill out of the hack.

Quickly, CyberWitch bypassed the other paltry security measures fueled by a burning desire she didn't fully comprehend. She wanted to dox the struggling legacy media outlet. That would give her all the fulfillment she pined for that her hacktivism didn't provide.

Chapter 34

Starting Pistol

"I told you there's no way we'll be able to get inside," Luis said, loud enough to be heard above the gusting wind and driving rain.

O'Dell House, located on the outskirts of downtown Pinedale, was surrounded by a ten-foot high white wall adorned with ornamental cast iron spears topped with fleur-de-lis. The town had sprung up around the mansion, growing lockstep with O'Dell Enterprises' many business interests. A red and white sign declaring security cameras was displayed on the wall.

Zuri looked along the top of the wall, reckoning she could get up and over once she had a grip on one of the decorative spears. Beyond the obstruction were tall, swaying maple trees devoid of all but the most stubborn leaves. "I don't see any cameras."

"Doesn't mean they're not there," Luis said and cowered when a car sped by. "And look at that sign. Beware of dogs."

"Dogs won't be out in this weather," Zuri said dismissively. "Give me a boost."

"They will be out in this weather. Everyone knows they have trained attack dogs—ones that cost tens of thousands of dollars," Luis complained, but he trotted over to her side. He held his coat's hood in place against the wind. "What do you want me to do?"

"Brace yourself against the wall, and I'll use your knee to give me a boost."

Luis frowned. "This is a bad idea. We should talk to Miriam."

Zuri shook her head unequivocally. "No way. Besides, I'm only taking a loo—"

A speaker crackled to life from somewhere along the wall. "You kids better move along. You're being recorded, and if you trespass, the police will be notified."

Zuri and Luis stared at each other in wide-eyed shock. Her pulse thrummed like an over-revved engine.

"Where?" Zuri mouthed.

Luis shook his head once and grabbed her by the hand, striding purposely down the street through the pattering rain.

****

That same day, over two thousand miles away, in a narrow trash-strewn alley behind a strip club, Big Jake was having a discussion with a man who was down on his knees and blubbering. The light above the backdoor to the club buzzed like a nest of angry hornets and cast a waxy glare and brooding shadows around the backstreet. What the man said next would determine if Jake gave him a beating or beat him to death.

"I didn't short them, Jake, honest," the man pleaded.

Jake squatted beside the man—a boy, really—only a few years older than his daughter. "That's not what the bosses told me, Frankie." Jake rested huge hands with knobby, scarred knuckles on his knees. "Come clean and pay up."

"I didn't short them," Frankie insisted.

Jake shook his head at the gold hoop in the kid's left

nostril. There were many things in life he struggled to tolerate. One was liars, the other was jewelry on men. Lots of people in Jake's line of work wore bling. He wasn't sure why—maybe as a show of wealth, to look tough, or both. The thing was bling only brought trouble in the end, just like lying.

Jake reached a meaty mitt toward the sparkling nose ring, but Frankie flinched. With his right hand, Jake then grabbed the fool by his greasy brownish hair and pulled him close. The boy spluttered and spat, so Jake smacked him a good one with his left hand—hard enough to knock Frankie silly and perhaps loosen some teeth, but without the oomph to dislocate the jaw. He still wanted the boy capable of talking. Then, with a thumb and index finger as thick as fat sausages, he ripped the hoop from Frankie's nose.

The kid bawled and begged while blood ran from his nose over his lips. Jake tossed aside the ring that tinkled softly when it struck the concrete. "Where's the money?"

"I-I-lost it on the game," Frankie said. "But I can earn it back."

Jake shook the idiot by the hair. "Name."

"What?"

"What's the bookie's name?"

"It's…"

Jake's phone buzzed in the back pocket of his jeans. After holding up a finger for silence, the ex-prizefighter retrieved the phone, keeping ahold of the kid's hair to stop him from doing something dumb like run. It was probably the bosses asking for an update. Frankie really did owe them a wad of cash.

Only it wasn't the bosses. It was an alert Jake had put on his estranged wife's name should the handle ever appear on the web. "What the hell?" Jake whispered, following a link.

"What's wrong?" Frankie asked.

With his head throbbing and blood boiling behind his eyes, Jake read the webpage's content. He released Frankie and stood.

"Can I—"

"Go," Jake growled at the hoodlum.

Frankie didn't need to be told twice, lurching to his feet and scurrying onto the main street and out of sight.

Emasculated him.

Abandoned him when he needed her most.

Stole his daughter from him.

The bosses and their money could wait. This was personal.

****

The driving rain continued to fall without abatement from the dark sky, and the wind howled, making the streets seem like dark wind tunnels or the yawning mouths of primordial beasts. Trash from an overturned can cartwheeled through the light and shadows thrown by streetlamps and storefronts, firmly in the gale's grasp. A Styrofoam food container clamped like a clamshell to a light pole. The squeal of tires and a chorus of blaring horns came from several blocks away. Nary a soul tread the sidewalks except for Zuri and Luis, scampering hand-in-hand away from O'Dell House as quickly as possible without looking sus. The few people out in the weather would only notice the teens if they stared out the rain-streaked windows of the quaint shops and eateries lining the streets of downtown Pinedale.

Zuri was thoroughly annoyed with their failed expedition to O'Dell House. To think, she was missing the gym for nothing. Well, maybe not for nothing. In her peripheral vision, she glimpsed her wet hand in Luis's equally moist one, and warmth the weather could not dispel suffused her. She had enjoyed kissing him at the cineplex and could get used to holding his hand regularly.

Luis pointed to a shop sign shaped like a doughnut with pink frosting swinging in the wind. "Let's go inside and wait out the weather."

Zuri wasn't particularly interested in food, certainly not donuts, but escaping the rain was an excellent idea. The scent of baked goods assailed them even before Luis pulled open the door for Zuri. Low conversation filled the small establishment, and most welcome of all, warm forced air circulated around the space. Side by side, the teens approached the display case, showing off what was left from the day's baking: a handful of donuts, a palm-size square of carrot cake, and a smattering of cookies.

"Do you want anything?" Luis asked.

The sweets didn't appeal to Zuri, but she saw hot chocolate advertised on the chalkboard behind the case. A good cup of cocoa would go a long way to warming her up, but the price was outrageous, and she didn't have any money, regardless. "No, I'm good."

"I can pay." Luis removed his phone from his coat pocket. "Someone is texting me like cray cray."

A girl, maybe a year or two older than them, came through a doorway behind the display case leading to the kitchen and asked if they had decided what they wanted. Distracted, Luis asked for a minute while he stared at his phone. "Umm...Zuri." He held his phone out toward her. "You need to look at this."

She took the device and read through Edith's text

message, not fully comprehending its meaning. "Doxed?"

"Like a document dump," Luis said.

"I know what doxed means," Zuri said. "The Pinedale Gazette. Oh, no."

The text message included a link to a social media post decrying that not only had the Gazette's reporters all been doxed earlier in the day, with all their information popping up in anonymous forums and on the dark web, but the paper's website had been hacked. In place of the regular homepage was a page with all the details regarding the true identity of Pinedale's favorite advice columnist, Dolores Clattenburg.

Feeling like a zip tie had cinched her throat, Zuri tapped on the link to the newspaper's website. The page rendered the typical header displaying the outlet's name, but instead of the usual headlines, there was only one: **Amari Williams True Identity of Advice Columnist Dolores Clattenburg.** Beneath that was all the information the paper's human resource department had on her mother.

****

Jake gunned his muscle car across the roadway illuminated by artificial light and the Beaver Moon's waxen luminescence. The engine roared like an enraged dragon, and the analog speedometer jumped and soared. Grimacing, the big man eased off the accelerator and merged onto I-40 East next to an eighteen-wheeler. The last thing he needed was to be pulled over by a traffic cop. He planned to raw dog the thirty-eight hours to Pinedale, stopping for nothing and no one. The flat of energy drinks in the passenger seat beside him would keep him going nonstop night and day.

He was coming for Amari, and this time, he'd make sure his fists were the last thing she felt.

Chapter 35

A Woodland Trail

"I have to go," Zuri said and handed Luis back his phone.

"But the storm—"

She leaned close to him and caught the faint scent of cologne on his neck. Mixed with the sweet smells of the bakery, it made for quite the concoction. "I need to see my mother."

"At least have a hot chocolate first," Luis said, disappointed.

Zuri almost told him what she had witnessed those three years ago in the kitchen. Her mother's whimpering. The rhythmic smacks of fists pounding flesh. Her father's bloody hands and the unbridled rage burning in his eyes. But the contemplation made her tremble and want to cower on her bed beneath the blankets. If she dared speak, she'd break down in public.

"What's wrong?" Luis asked.

Zuri shook her head and gave him a quick kiss on the cheek. "I have to go. I'll see you tomorrow."

As she had hoped, Luis brightened after being pecked on the cheek, even puffing up his chest a bit. It was cute.

"Bye," Luis said, adding. "Be careful in this weather."

But Zuri was already out the door in the beating rain and wind. She ran against the bluster, blasting water droplets into her face and blowing the hood from her head. By the time she got home, she'd be soaked as a drowned rat—she practically was already. It's not like she could afford waterproof outerwear.

The wind howled through the streets, sounding at times as mournful and wrathful as a banshee's wail. At the intersection of Main and O'Dell Ave, the torrential downpour overwhelmed a storm drain clogged with debris of fallen leaves and trash, partially flooding the sidewalk and street. Skirting the floodwater, Zuri loped past Pinedale Square Park, a green space with the trees and shrubbery whipped by the wind and a statue of George O'Dell, right hand raised in a wave and left gripping a cane, prominently displayed for all to see. Lamplight played across George's bearded visage beneath a boater hat.

Zuri slowed and stopped, staring at the cast stone version of her adversary, the man in white—kin killer and sorcerer. A loud crack resounded from somewhere nearby. For a moment, she feared the effigy came to life fueled by eldritch power. But when the man in white did not leap from his perch on the plinth, she realized she heard a tree branch snapping. Nevertheless, Zuri broke into a sprint, battling against the wind, unable to shake the suspicion that Good Old George watched her flee with satisfaction.

Zuri kept a quick pace for the rest of the run home, a solid three miles through unabating rain and wind. Shivering on the front stoop, she fumbled with the house key, which clattered against the concrete.

"Damnit," Zuri murmured, bending to retrieve the

key. How could she take on George's paranormal might or slug it out with Big Jake if she couldn't unlock the front door?

The second time was a charm, and Zuri slipped inside. They kept the heat down to save money, but the duplex was still cozy warm compared to the outside. Zuri stripped off her wet coat and waterlogged sneakers. The aroma of chicken noodle soup filled the space.

"Zuri." Amari came out of the kitchen. "Oh, goodness. You are absolutely drenched. You need to warm up. Come. I made soup."

Zuri retrieved a hanger from the closet by the front door, hung her dripping coat, and hooked it on the door handle to dry. As appealing as the hot food smelled, she wasn't about to be distracted from her mission.

"Did you hear about the doxing?"

"You know about that?" Mother strode back to the kitchen. "Oooh, almost boiled over the soup. Yes, they told us today. I've already frozen my credit to be safe."

Zuri pursued Mother into the kitchen. Amari stood over the stove, ladling soup into a bowl. "What about Dad?"

Amari gave her daughter a sideways glance. "What about him? I told you before you worry too much about him. He has underworld connections. He could've found us at any time. This doesn't change anything. Eat."

The steaming bowl of soup Zuri took from her mother soothed her cold hands with its warmth. What it couldn't relieve was Zuri's nagging suspicion that Amari's nonchalance regarding Big Jake was fatally misplaced.

****

The weather was decent on the walk to school the

following day, cold but dry and relatively windless. Branches littered yards and roadways, evidence of last night's storm. The sun peeked out from between the clouds, its rays pleasantly warm against Zuri's cheeks and even cast sunbeams onto the Blue Ridge Mountains far in the distance.

Breath steamed from Luis's mouth as he spoke. "Our best bet of getting hold of the diary is to talk to Miriam."

"She won't help us," Zuri said. "She thinks we're trash."

"Okay. What about her brother Ryan?"

"What about him?"

"We can ask him for help," Luis said in exasperation.

"No," Zuri replied. Something about the tall, blond young man reminded her of the man in white, which made sense since they were related. "No way. He's less likely to help us than Miriam."

"We can't even peek over the walls without being spotted. There's no way we're getting inside O'Dell House, and you know it," Luis said, voice rising. "We need Miriam's help. I know you have an issue with her. I'll talk to her. You won't have to say a word."

"What makes you think that she'll help us?" Zuri demanded.

"She's stuck up, mean, rich, and entitled," Luis said. "But she's not a bad person."

"She's bad enough," Zuri murmured loud enough for Luis to hear, but he refused to be baited into further argument, and they walked the rest of the way to school in silence.

When they reached Pinedale Central's grounds,

Luis veered off into the parking lot.

"Where are you going?" Zuri called.

"Miriam," Luis said, pointing to the lot where the rich girl emerged from the driver's seat of an SUV gleaming in the morning sun like polished silver.

The scene almost made Zuri gag. With car insurance so expensive, she couldn't even afford to learn to drive; only in her dreams could she operate such a high-end vehicle.

"You don't have to come with me," Luis said. "I can do this myself. I need to talk to her before she meets up with her friends."

After a moment's indecision, Zuri followed Luis across the asphalt to intercept Miriam. She stopped at the curb to avoid being run over by a dually truck spewing stinking diesel exhaust.

"Miriam! Hey, Miriam," Luis called, dodging a sports car crammed with boys.

Miriam locked her lavish ride with a key fob and turned her snobbish gaze on Luis, regarding him like an insect. If there was ever anyone who deserved to be sucker punched, it was Miriam O'Dell. Only respect for Luis kept Zuri from loping up and doing the deed. One good clobber would wipe that supercilious expression from her face.

"Umm...hi...Luis," Miriam said with all the enthusiasm she'd have for a panhandler demanding money.

"We need your help," Luis said, moving right up into the rich girl's personal space.

Zuri came to stand at his shoulder.

"Ahhh. I need to get to class," Miriam said. "Don't you need to get to class, Luis? Has a nerd like you ever been late?"

Luis spluttered, unable to get out a response. Miriam maneuvered around Luis, but Zuri blocked her path.

"What do you want?" Miriam demanded shrilly.

"Rose O'Dell," Zuri said.

Miriam laughed mirthlessly. "What about her?"

"Let me explain," Luis said.

"All right." Miriam took a deep breath. "I'll listen, but can we please walk to class…"

Luis explained the situation as they marched across the parking lot and onto the sidewalk. Miriam appeared to mostly listen, but she kept looking around, afraid her posse would glimpse her associating with social inferiors.

They joined the jostling throng, mounting the stairs leading to the portico. A dizzying array of scents wafted through the air, from woodland-scented deodorant to high-class floral concoctions like what drifted off Miriam. She glanced all around with nervous energy.

Zuri desperately wanted to make a snide remark, but that would only interrupt Luis's narrative.

"Okay, listen," Miriam said, glancing over her shoulder and hunching as if worried she had been spotted. "I can help. But first, you have to help me."

"What?" Zuri scoffed.

Luis gave her a warning look and shook his head.

Miriam smiled condescendingly. "You scratch my back. I'll scratch yours. Meet me behind the school at the trail into the woods." She looked dismissively at Luis. "You know the one, right, nerd? Across the cornfield."

Luis bit his thumb and nodded.

Chapter 36

Watch My Back

Zuri and Luis stood before the expansive woodland behind Pinedale Central. The trees were a mixture of deciduous ones, barren of leaves, and evergreens, all stirring in the breeze. A narrow path almost overgrown by encroaching shrubs and branches wound along the forest floor and was soon lost in the murk. A rich pine scent floated from the trees, declaring the lushness of life, but there was an undercurrent of decay reminiscent of the stench sometimes accompanying Rose. Given the gloomy clouds hiding the sun, daylight would soon subside in the coppice long before darkness fell outside its bounds.

The chill Zuri felt was not due to the wintery breeze or moribund aroma alone. As she had noticed before, the trees beckoned with dozens, no, hundreds, maybe thousands of children's voices to frolic beneath their branches. Zuri shook her head to dispel the interminable singsong but to no avail.

Come play beneath our branches and cavort through our fallen leaves.

"This trail doesn't see much use," Zuri remarked, hoping her voice might drown out the ditty.

Come play beneath us. You want to. You want to.

"I told you people who enter don't always come

out," Luis said, his gaze nervously alternating between the trees and sky. "At least, that's what everyone says."

You want to come play. You want to come play. You'll want to play forever!

"She's not here," Zuri said. "We should go."

Zuri neglected to say that she feared if they didn't leave soon, she would be unable to resist the forest's summons. Even now, the teen fighter found she couldn't turn away from the trees of her own accord, no matter how much she desired to run pell-mell for home.

"We can give her a few more minutes," Luis said, squinting as he stared across the harvested cornfield to the back of the school.

"I don't know." Zuri forced herself to move, sneakers crunching over hacked corn stalks, but she could only pace to and fro without increasing the distance between her and the timberland. "This place creeps me out. Shouldn't we hear birds or something? It's like…it's like…"

She wanted to say it was like the trees ate the woodland critters, but her tongue was tied.

Come play beneath our branches and cavort through our fallen leaves. You will find. You will find. You'll never want to leave.

"I don't know. Maybe," Luis said. "It's cold and breezy. They're probably staying warm somewhere."

Come and play. Come and play. Come and play all day.

Zuri bit her lip hard, wishing the pain would banish the voices. "The…the trees…"

Don't say that. We want to be friends. Come play beneath our branches.

"What?" Luis glanced at her, his brow furrowed.

"What is it, Zuri? What's wrong?"

Her jaw worked. She desperately wanted to tell him about the voices, but the words wouldn't form.

Come play beneath our branches and cavort through our fallen leaves. Once you join us, you'll never want to leave.

Luis took her hand. "What?"

At his touch, the voices fell abruptly silent, and Zuri felt her mental acuity return as if a dense fog that had been clouding her mind lifted.

"The trees were speaking to me," Zuri said.

Luis's eyes went wide. "Cool! What did they say?"

"Not cool." Zuri shook her head and gave him a rundown of her experience.

"If I let go of your hand," Luis said. "You'll hear them again, maybe?"

Zuri tightened her grip on his hand. "I don't want to run an experiment!"

"Okay. Okay," Luis said, smiling reassuringly. "I won't let go."

"Luis! New girl!"

Luis turned toward the sound of Miriam's voice. Zuri discovered she could tear her gaze from the forest and even took a step away from the trees, although doing so demanded all the willpower she could muster. The moneyed blonde approached from the school about halfway across the cornfield.

"She's going to want us to go in there with her, isn't she?" Zuri asked.

"I don't know why else she'd want to meet out here," Luis said, waving to Miss Snooty. "Hey, Miriam. Her name is Zuri, not *new girl*."

"If she wants us to go into the woods, I don't think

I can," Zuri said, a tremor running through her. "The voices…"

"You don't need to." Luis gripped her hand tighter. "I'll go with her and do whatever needs to be done."

"But—"

"I can do this, Zuri, for Rose." Luis gave her a confident smile that didn't reach his eyes. "And I don't hear the voices."

Zuri was about to say that people who enter the forest don't return, but Miriam neared and spoke first.

"Sorry, I'm late. A friend needed a ride home."

"Of course we had to wait," Zuri scoffed.

"I said I'm sorry." Miriam dramatically rolled her eyes. "I see the two of you decided to make it official."

"What?" Luis blinked, nonplussed. He looked at his hand in Zuri's. "Oh, yeah, I guess so."

"Why are we here?" Zuri demanded.

Miriam nodded. "You want to see the patriarch's diary."

"George O'Dell," Zuri clarified.

"Yeah, in the family, we call him the patriarch." Miriam shrugged. "Lame. I know. Don't get me started. Anyway, you want the diary, I need my mother's necklace back."

"The necklace is in the woods?" Zuri asked and exchanged a glance with Luis.

Actually looking shamefaced, Miriam told the tale of surreptitiously borrowing and wearing to school her mother's heirloom necklace to impress a rival overly affluent girl. The show of opulence utterly devastated her adversary, but there was a hiccup. A ghost she only described as a disgusting poltergeist stole the necklace and absconded into the woods.

"The next day, I found this in my backpack after PE," Miriam said, pulling a folded sheet of college-ruled paper from her pocket.

Zuri took the paper. In large, jagged scrawl were the words *to win the necklace, follow the wildwood path.*

"Why not ask your friends for help?" Luis asked.

"Can you imagine any of them going in there?" Miriam folded her arms across her chest. "You know the stories."

"Then, why are you going in there?" Zuri asked.

Miriam shrugged uncomfortably. "Only stories, as far as I know. What about it, Luis? You're besties with John and Edith, the resident ghost experts."

Luis moistened his lips. "Nothing confirmed."

"If I go into the woodland, something bad might happen," Miriam said. "If I don't get the necklace back before my mother finds out, she will kill me. Are you going to help me or not?"

"Sure." Zuri nodded. "We'll help. Right, Luis?"

Luis whispered. "You don't have to go."

"I do," Zuri whispered. "If Miriam is brave enough to go, I am too. Just don't let go of my hand."

If Miriam had overheard the exchange, she didn't comment on it.

"We're here to have your back," Zuri said.

"Yeah," Miriam said with an easy smile. "I trust you. Without me, good luck getting your hands on the diary."

"I guess we should leave our backpacks," Luis said, nodding toward the overgrown path. "They'll get in the way."

He and Zuri started the awkward dance of removing their backpacks while still holding hands. This required them to work in tandem to unsling the strap from one shoulder and then switch their clasped hands.

Miriam giggled. "You two are a little much? Is there a nerd dating rule that you have to hold hands all the time?"

Zuri dropped her bag to the ground. "None of your business."

"A little touchy, new girl?"

Luis set his backpack down. "Hey, can we keep it cordial? We're in this together."

"Cordial?" Miriam snickered. "Aren't you the Southern gentleman?"

Even Zuri cracked a smile despite herself, and some of the tension lessened.

Luis shook his head. "Glad I can be of amusement." He gestured toward the trail. "Lead the way."

"Me first, huh? In case a monster lurks in the trees." Miriam breezed by, heading toward the caliginous path. "You know, it's always those in the rear who get it first."

Zuri almost said the trees were the monsters. "I guess we're all equally screwed then."

Miriam led the way into the woods with Zuri and Luis following hand in hand, close behind. A breeze stirred the limbs, making it seem like the trees were muggers in a dusky alleyway. Twigs, branches, and brambles clawed at clothing, tangled in hair, and scratched bare skin. Miriam was the first to start muttering expletives under her breath, but she wasn't the last. Soon, Luis and Zuri were no longer able to walk side-by-side. The math whiz took the lead, breaking trail for his girlfriend. Zuri clenched his hand all the tighter, dreading the voices would return if she let go.

"Crap!" Miriam exclaimed the second before she

tumbled onto her butt.

"Are you okay?" Luis called.

Miriam groaned. A wind gust agitated the branches, creating a sound eerily reminiscent of children's laughter.

"I tripped on a tree root. I think." Miriam lurched to her feet. "I can't see anything." The bright LED of a cellphone flashlight flared to life. "Do you have phones? Better take them—"

"Miriam, watch out!" Zuri cried, releasing Luis.

Instantly, the voices pounded through her skull.

Play. Play. Play.

Play with us.

"Zuri!"

Luis reached for her, but she darted toward Miriam, who stared at her quizzically. Zuri saw what they didn't: a vinelike branch slithering down from overhead to cinch around the blonde's elegant ivory throat like a garrot. Mariam gasped, her phone flying from her grip, and tore at the woody tendril cutting into her windpipe.

"Help!" Miriam wheezed.

Stay for a while. Play with us. Play with us. Play forevermore.

The phone landed on the trail, shining upward, but the light missed the struggling teen, so Zuri collided bodily with a thrashing shadow. Zuri reached for Miriam's neck but only grasped her arm and wrist.

Don't do that. She's playing. Don't worry. We'll play with you too.

Something started wrapping around Zuri's wrist, and she yanked her arm hard. There was a crack like a splitting twig, and whatever grasped her fell away. Then Luis was there, swatting aside questing branches and brambles and shining his cell phone light at Miriam's beet-red face. The blonde struggled pitifully at the vine asphyxiating her.

Ignoring the voices ululating at her not to, Zuri ripped the vine from Miriam's neck. Gasping for breath, the girl slumped into her arms. The thousands of children's voices shrieked wordlessly at Zuri. The sonic assault would have brought her to her knees and Miriam with her, but Luis clamped onto her wrist. Immediately, the racket ceased.

"Run!" Luis screamed.

"My phone," Miriam said weakly.

"Forget about it!" Zuri yelled, half-guiding, half-dragging the stumbling rich girl along the trail at a run.

Chapter 37

The Eldritch Woods

They ran helter-skelter along the trail, beating back the branches and creepers grasping at ankles and arms. The frenzied movement of the vegetation made susurrations like thousands of children's voices in singalong. Zuri feared the whispering trees penetrated her mind again, even with Luis gripping her wrist. She was ready to shove Miriam, who leaned heavily against her, to the ground, scream like a raving mad woman, and claw at her ears.

"Go! Faster!" Luis gasped. "I see light up ahead!"

His strained voice cut through the arboreal racket, and Zuri realized, to her relief, that whatever she heard— the voices of trees, demonic children, or malevolent spirits—was not rattling around her mind but coming from all around them. Glimpsing the light at the end of the proverbial tunnel galvanized Zuri to dash onward, half-carrying Miriam and half-dragging Luis.

Ahead was a small clearing beckoning like a beacon of hope bathed by the day's dying light. Luis stumbled and fell, yanking hard on Zuri's arm. She nearly went down, too, coming to an abrupt stop to keep from falling on her ass. Branches and tendrils closed in on all sides like the innumerable tentacles of krakens.

"Help!" Luis wheezed.

Pushing Miriam hard in the back, Zuri screamed. "Run!"

The rich girl had recovered enough vitality to lurch forward under her own power, arms whirling to whack aside the encroaching thicket. Vines entwined Luis's ankles, creeping inexorably up his legs. A low branch reached for his neck, and Zuri stomped it in half. She felt branches and twigs tearing her clothes and scratching her skin. Any moment, something would find purchase, drag her down to the forest floor, and pin her like a bug on a specimen board.

Zuri leaned over Luis and started tearing away the vines. "Help me or…"

She broke a twig curling around her throat and threw it aside. Wide-eyed in terror, Luis started ripping away the shrubbery clinging to his legs with both hands. As soon as he released her wrist, the voices returned.

Play, play, playing. What a fun day! You know. You know that you want to stay!

Clamping hands over her ears, Zuri shrieked so loud her throat throbbed, but that did not drown out the children.

Don't go. Don't go. Stay and play for all your days.

A branch slid around her left wrist and cinched tight, slicing into her skin and cutting off the blood flow to her hand. Even worse, a graveyard reek filled her nostrils, and a rotten taste coated her tongue. *I'm going to die here.*

Luis staggered upright, grabbing her left forearm. "Come on!"

The whispering voices died at his touch. Together, they tore away the branch holding her and careened toward the light. Luis somehow managed to keep ahold of his cell phone, its LED illuminating the wild tangle grasping at them on all sides. Ahead, the trail seemed to shrink, the encroaching vegetation gnashing down where the path met the clearing like the talon-filled mouth of an eldritch horror.

"We're not going to make it!" Luis panted.

"Full speed!" Zuri yelled, pulling him along and pushing him ahead of her.

Branches and brambles tore at them. A twig clawed at her face and found its way into her mouth. She bit into it, splintering the wood, and rotten decay coated her tongue. She spat woody particles, desperately clearing her mouth of the taste threatening to make her gag. Creaking and groaning, trees leaned over the trail, the ground cover formed a web impeding the path, and roots uprooted to trip careless feet. Darkness closed around them, the light from the clearing little more than a pinprick and the phone's flashlight a spluttering, dying torch.

"Jump!" Zuri screamed.

They hurled themselves over the jutting tree roots and into the brambly net, crashing through it. Covered in nicks and scratches and clothing slashed and torn, they slammed into the clearing. Luis yelped, and the wind was knocked out of Zuri, but she managed to keep a grip on her boyfriend. Her ears rang with the forest's cacophonous quaking.

Luis yanked her hand, and she wondered why he was pulling on her. Then he screamed, grip tightening in desperation. Miriam trundled up beside them, grabbing Luis's flailing arm and heaving. Her neck was bright red where the vine had choked her.

"We got you, Luis," Miriam rasped and looked to

Zuri. "Pull!"

Calling on her physical reserves honed by hours in the fight gym, Zuri scrambled to her feet and hauled on Luis's arm. A thick limb of shrubbery wrapped around his ankle and dragged him toward the ravenous woodland. Luis kicked and writhed, but the vegetation held him fast, slowly winning the tug-of-war. Focusing on driving all her weight through her left heel, Zuri stomped on the wooden tentacle once, then a second time to the sound of cracking, and it retreated into the forest before she landed a third blow.

Pulling Luis to his feet, the teens retreated to the center of the dell and collapsed from exhaustion. The rustling of the forest died down, but Zuri felt they were being watched and feared if she let go of Luis, the voices would return. Overhead, light slowly faded from the sky. Soon, the glade would be as dark as the forest.

"What time is it?" Luis asked.

"You lost your phone too?" Zuri retrieved her device from the pocket of her sports pants.

Luis pointed to the edge of the glade where they had come from the trees. "I dropped it during the struggle. I'm not going back for it."

"Five ten," Zuri said.

"Sunset is at five thirty," Miriam said, voice still raw. "It will be pitch black out here soon. We can't go back in the woods. Not at night."

"Hey, calm down," Luis said. "Panicking won't help. We still have one phone. We can use the map to avoid the trees and guide us to the road. Your phone has plenty of power, right, Zuri?"

"Yeah, I think so," she said absently, gazing across the clearing opposite where they had emerged. At the edge of the clearing floated a wispy, vaguely humanoid diaphanous form, emitting an unnerving greenish glow. Zuri used the cell phone as a pointer. "What is that?"

"The goddamn poltergeist," Miriam snarled, lurching to her feet. "Where's my necklace?"

"Cooooommmmme," the poltergeist moaned, floating closer to the trees.

"Wait," Luis said. "Maybe we should think about this first? Miriam!"

The rich girl strode unsteadily across the uneven ground. "I did what you said!" she cleared her throat. "We nearly died! Give me the necklace!"

"Cooooommmmmme hiiiiiitherrr." The specter beckoned with a gossamer-like appendage.

Putting her phone away to preserve power, Zuri stood to follow Miriam.

Luis tugged on her. "Zuri, no."

"What if she enters the trees?" Zuri said. "We can't stop her from here."

Frowning, Luis muttered. "Fine, but I don't like this."

With the daylight quickly diminishing, the teens followed Miriam toward the edge of the clearing in near darkness. The blonde girl stopped not five feet from the trees, at the limit of the poltergeist's greenish aura.

Luis squeezed Zuri's hand. "Stop. If we go closer, the trees can reach us."

They stopped about ten feet from the trees, but Zuri saw no cause for immediate alarm. The vegetation displayed none of the supernatural malevolence they encountered earlier.

"Clooooooooosser." The poltergeist frenetically waved a gauzy limb. "Clooooooooosser."

"No," Miriam said stridently, putting her hands on her hips. "Give me the necklace."

The poltergeist made a grating sound like rusty hinges being forced loose. After a few seconds, Zuri stiffened, realizing the specter laughed at them.

"Iiiii doooooon't haaave iiiit."

"Then where is it?" Miriam demanded.

"Iiiinnnnn hhhheeerrre."

With a blast of sickly-sweet air that nearly knocked the teens from their feet, the poltergeist flared bright, its haunting green radiance illuminating the clearing and nearby woodland like a firework. The luminescence was blindingly intense before it dissipated along with the gust of wind. When their vision cleared, the poltergeist was gone, and where it had levitated at the forest's edge stood a cottage. Enough light persisted to make out the brown walls with pink frosted accents, roofing made of colorful circular tiles, and smoke twining from the chimney. The front door was outlined by red and white poles, disturbingly like candy canes minus the hooked toppers. Yellow light spilled out of the square windows on either side of the door. A sweet aroma with an undercurrent of sewage hung in the air like a pea soup fog.

Miriam shrugged and strode toward the door, raising a fist to knock.

Chapter 38

A Witchy Problem

"Miriam! No!" Luis hollered, lurching forward and reaching for the rich girl.

Zuri trudged along beside him, understanding his horrified reaction. The dark energies that suffused the forest path radiated from the cottage alongside the nauseating saccharine smell. It felt as if the looming trees closed in on them there on the clearing, branches scything with malign intent. Even as Zuri prepared to add her desperate appeals to his, she knew it was too late. Miriam would knock on the door and wake whatever monstrosity lived inside.

Miriam's knuckles struck the door but did not make a rapping sound. "What the..." she started laughing like someone on the razor's edge dividing the sane from the insane. "It's gingerbread. What the hell? Gingerbread!"

Luis's free hand clamped onto the blonde girl's shoulder. "Miriam, we should go. Whatever is inside...we don't want anything to do with it."

"No." Miriam shook her head and brushed off Luis's hand. "We came this far. We almost died. I won't leave empty-handed."

Nearly tongue-tied from terror, Zuri nevertheless spluttered. "He's right. We need to leave. It's going to be pitch black out..."

The door silently swung open, and overpoweringly sweet air tinged with odoriferous excrement blasted them in their faces. Miriam doubled over, heaving and clutching her midsection. Zuri's eyes began watering, and Luis moaned in disgust beside her. In the doorway, backlit by the waxy yellow glow of the room beyond, stood a hunched figure in a tattered black robe with a cowl covering their head. As Zuri's vision adjusted, the hooded countenance resolved into a crone's wrinkled visage with a prominent hooked nose with a massive wart on the tip.

Luis hacked, then said. "We've walked into a Brother's Grimm fairytale."

Zuri quavered with the need to do something, namely, run away like her life depended on it, which it likely did. The spectral malevolence radiating from the crone buffeted her like an unseen tide and captured her in a rip current. Luis seemed similarly enthralled, unmoving and his unblinking gaze locked on the scene unfolding in the entryway. Sweat beaded on his face and rolled down his neck.

"Do you have my necklace?" Miriam demanded the only sign she feared the supernatural menace a slight tremor in her tone.

"I do," the crone replied, her voice high, almost alluring, yet sepulchral. "Come inside, my dear, and I will return the necklace."

Zuri knew that going inside meant certain death, but the witch's voice was a Siren's song hooking her spirit. Without realizing it, she stepped toward the cottage's open doorway, her action nearly simultaneous with Miriam's ambulation.

"No! Stop!" Luis cried, pulling hard enough on

Zuri's hand that she teetered and almost fell. "Don't go inside! It's a trap!"

Miriam pulled up short of the doorway and backed off, barely more than an arm's length from the witch.

"Yeah," the rich girl said tremulously, retreating to beside the other teens. "I think you're right."

"Come inside," the crone insisted, beckoning with a gnarled hand. "No harm will come to you, and I will return your necklace. I promise. I know you want it. Desire it. Need it." She cackled. "What will your mother do when she discovers you stole it?"

"I didn't steal anything," Miriam said. "I borrowed it. The poltergeist stole it from me and gave it to you."

"Says the thief," the witch said spitefully.

Zuri found her voice. "Is there anything we can do for the necklace besides go inside your house?"

The witch tapped the wart on the tip of her nose with a finger bent with age, its nail yellowed, and her rictal grin revealed jagged brown teeth. She lowered her hand from her face and spoke. "Yes. A game. A competition. A single question. If you," she waved an arm to encompass the three teens, "answer correctly, I will return the necklace. If you fail… all I require is that you enter my humble abode. Do you agree?"

"Yes," Miriam said. "Yes, we agree."

"You don't speak for us," Zuri said, panic rising. This was as surely a trap as the invitation to enter the house. "She doesn't speak for us."

But even as Zuri spoke, a semitransparent greenish dome rose from the earth, encapsulating the cottage, the witch, and the teens.

"She has already spoken for you, I am afraid," the witch said. "Do not try to flee. Touching my barrier is deadly. If you answer my question correctly, it will lower, and you are free to go with your prize."

Zuri and Luis glared accusingly at Miriam, who shrugged. "How hard can it be?" she pointed at Luis. "We have the super nerd here."

Zuri balled her free hand into a fist and was ready to knock out Miriam's front teeth, but Luis shook his head. Zuri relaxed her hand and clenched her jaw instead. The crone produced a crooked black stick from somewhere in her robe and used it to write in the dirt before the doorway.

Luis whispered. "If we get the question wrong, be ready to run."

Mariam said. "The barrier—"

"Whatever is waiting for us inside the cottage is worse than risking the barrier. Agreed?" Luis said.

The girls nodded.

"I don't trust her. We should be ready to run no matter what," Zuri said.

Coming to an agreement, the teens faced the witch, who pointed with the crooked stick to what she had scrawled in the dirt at her feet. "Solve this. You have twenty minutes."

Zuri and Miriam sighed with relief almost simultaneously. It was a math equation.

"You're up, nerd," Miriam said.

"You got this," Zuri said.

"Can I let go of your hand?" Luis asked.

"We can try." Zuri winced in anticipation of the spectral singsong returning.

Luis released her hand. Zuri drew in a sharp breath, ready to be brought to her knees by the auditory onslaught of the malevolent trees. Relaxing, Zuri breathed easily and smiled. "I'm good."

"Maybe the barrier," Luis said.

"Maybe," Zuri agreed and quickly explained the voices to Miriam in response to a query from the rich girl.

"Jesus." Miriam blanched. "That's terrible."

Rubbing his hands together, Luis knelt in the waxy glare from the cottage's interior and got to work. Five minutes later, Zuri knew because she had checked her phone when Luis first knelt beside the problem written in the crone's shaky script, he had made no visible progress.

Prove that x + y = n

Where x and y are any two prime numbers.

n ≥ 4

"What's wrong?" Zuri asked, curious and nervous. The equation appeared far simpler than the problems she had watched Luis solve daily.

"It's Goldbach's Conjecture," he said.

"What does that mean?" Miriam asked.

"It's never been solved," Luis said despairingly. "There's a million-dollar prize for proving it."

The girls exchanged horrified looks, and the witch crowed uproariously.

"You're cheating!" Zuri shook a fist at the crone.

The witch only laughed harder, even doubling over.

"But you're a genius," Miriam told Luis.

The math boy wonder slumped. "I'm not. It wouldn't help if I was. No one has ever solved this for hundreds of years. How can I possibly hope to solve it in twenty minutes? I don't even know if it can be solved."

"We need Rose," Zuri said.

"I don't know if she can help, but her input certainly

wouldn't hurt," Luis said dubiously.

Zuri closed her eyes and leaned into her connection with the ghost. She didn't know if she could communicate with Rose this way or if the ghost would be able to help if she could.

Rose, can you hear me? We need your help. Please.

"What is this?" The crone demanded, but Zuri hardly heard.

It was as if Zuri was elsewhere, perhaps in that liminal limbo between life and death. Rose did not speak to her, but she felt something vibrating through her very essence like strikes on a titanic gong. Zuri was sure the pulsations rattling her bones were caused by Rose. But what was she trying to tell her? Was it a cipher?

I don't understand.

The throbs lessened to an almost imperceptible pulsing, like a weak, dying heart.

Zuri panicked. *Rose! Don't leave! We need your help!*

A boom resounded inside her like her very skull was a bell being struck by a giant drummer. Her body stiffened then moved on its own accord with Zuri having only the vaguest awareness and no understanding of what she did. When the sound rebounding through her skull abruptly silenced, all sense of Rose was gone, and she swayed on her feet.

Miriam put a steadying hand on her shoulder. "Are you okay?"

"No, no, no," the crone growled.

Blinking, Zuri nodded. "I think so." A numeric sequence was neatly written in the dirt her feet. It looked remarkably like Rose's handwriting.

21 19 15 12 22 1 2 12 5

"Did I write right that?" Zuri asked.

The crone huffed and puffed, clearly desiring to erase the numbers, but that required her to step out of the confectionery cottage's doorway and that, it seemed, was something she could not do.

"Yeah," Miriam said, dropping her hand from Zuri's shoulder. "What is it? The answer?"

"A deception! A lie!" the crone raved. "The wrong answer!"

"Whatever." Luis studied the numbers. "It's the number code for communicating with Rose. Unsolvable. That is the answer." He looked at the witch. "It's unsolvable."

"Noooooooooo!" The crone gasped, and a mighty wind blew from the trees, howling and rattling limbs.

The gust carried the witch, her cottage, and the green dome into oblivion, leaving no trace except a golden necklace encrusted with jewels that fell to the ground where the crone had stood. With the barrier dispelled, the voices of the woodland returned.

Miriam darted forward and snatched the necklace, holding it up so the last glimmer of day sparkled against the gems. "Yes!"

That wasn't nice. She was our playmate. You'll have to replace her.

"The voices," Zuri gasped.

Come play. Come play. Play beneath our branches and in our fallen leaves, and you will find, you will find, that you will never want to leave.

Luis snatched her hand; the voices silenced.

"Thank you," Zuri said, adding silently for Rose. *Thank you.*

"We did it," Luis said, laughing. "We're still alive."

Zuri stood up and took out her phone. "Let's see if we can find our way to that road you mentioned."

****

Deep below Pinedale, George screamed, not only out of righteous anger that his work might be undone, but out of unbridled, unmitigated fear too. He'd be bedridden with the collywobbles if he still possessed a physical form. Unearthly light spilled from the icon that shook upon its plinth in metronomic time with his howls. Even the heavy stone of the walls, arched ceiling, and flagstone floor vibrated. Upon hearing his cry, engorged rodentia convulsed and dropped dead with blood leaking from their orifices. Rats and nightcrawlers bathed in the spectral radiance burst like melons shot by high-powered rifles.

Despite the show of supernatural might, George was impotent. He knew Rose, however briefly, touched a mind beyond the confines of the school grounds. Unlike him, his daughter shouldn't be capable of doing that. If she could do that, she might be able to break the dark magic tenuously binding her to the icon. The sad truth was that George hadn't a clue how to prevent Rose from touching the minds of the living. After all, the loophole in the incantations allowing her to escape was the very same George used to summon his champion. Unless Rose foolishly took on a physical form within the school, allowing him to claw her back, he could only wait for his champion and fret that Big Jake might not make it in time.

Chapter 39

Competing Yarns

Using Zuri's cell phone, the teens navigated to a narrow two-lane road. Thankfully, the route avoided most of the forest, and the strip of trees they did have to traverse to reach the roadway did not harry them. Zuri had never such felt such relief at having the solidity of asphalt beneath her feet. She was even more relieved when Luis released her, and childish voices did not haunt her.

"No voices?" he asked.

"No," Zuri said, laughing and they hugged.

After a minute they broke the embrace. Luis stared into the night sky, which was now well and truly dark. Miriam held up the necklace, the jewels glittering in the weak luminescence from a distant streetlight at an intersection up the road.

"Was it worth it?" Zuri asked.

"Hmmm?" Miriam appeared mesmerized by the necklace. An angry red welt encircled her neck like a choker where the vine had abraded her dovelike skin.

"Almost dying," Zuri said. "Was it worth it?"

"Oh," Miriam said, lowering the necklace. "Making sure none of the jewels are missing. Was it worth it?" she shrugged. "We're still alive. My mother won't kill me. So, yeah, it was worth it."

Zuri wanted to lay into Miriam verbally and follow up the upbraiding with a roundhouse kick, but Luis intervened. "She's right, Zuri. We survived, and she will uphold her end of the agreement. Right, Miriam?"

They both looked at the rich girl, who carefully placed the necklace in the front pocket of her tattered jeans. It was a tight fit. "Of course, I'll get the diary tonight. I promise," Miriam said and gently bit her lower lip. "First, I'm hungry. Do you want cinnamon rolls? I want a cinnamon roll. And don't worry, I'll pay. Obviously."

The cashier at Irene's Cafe eyed them suspiciously while ringing up the three cinnamon rolls and drinks. She, however, took Miriam's black card readily enough.

"Are you kids, okay?" She asked, tone half concerned citizen and half mother hen.

"Oh, this?" Miriam pointed to her throat and vaguely gestured to the numerous scratches on her companions' bodies and tears in their clothing. "We were playing in the woods. Hide and seek."

Expression curdling, the cashier handed Miriam her card. "Someone will bring out your food."

Miriam led them to a table in the back, well away from the few patrons seated at the front near the window looking out onto the street. Zuri and Luis sat beside each other, and Miriam sat across from them. The rich girl crossed her arms on the table and leaned forward.

"Tell me why you want the patriarch's diary," Miriam said.

"To help Rose," Zuri snapped.

"Whoa, settle down," Miriam said, rolling her eyes. "I know that. I want to know the deets. Luis was vague when he asked for my help. I mean, Rose O'Dell died a long time ago. It was a family tragedy at the time, but that was over one hundred years ago. It's like…part of the family lore now. Part of the patriarch's lore. If she wasn't his daughter, I wouldn't know anything about her. Not even her name."

A teenage waitress brought their cinnamon rolls and drinks. The sweet, confectionery scent Zuri detected upon entering the eatery was overwhelming, with the three enormous frosting and butter slathered buns on the table. The gingerbread house with the crone in the doorway flashed in her mind, and she suspected eating would be out of the question.

"Hi, Miriam," the waitress said, placing a steaming cup of tea before the blonde girl. Zuri and Luis both had glasses of water.

Miriam's cheeks reddened. "Hi, Suzie."

Probably embarrassed to be seen with us, Zuri thought uncharitably and took a sip of water to rinse the foul flavor of rot from her mouth. The waitress went about her business.

Miriam picked up the giant cinnamon roll in both hands and chomped down on it. "Oh, my God! This is good. Try it."

Daintily compared to the socialite, Luis sampled the baked good. "Wow." He tore into it with gusto. "This is great."

They looked at Zuri expectantly. Grimacing, anticipating the confection to taste rotten, she picked up the roll in both hands. It was gooey to the touch. Shutting her eyes, the teen pugilist took a nibble. Cinnamon and sugar coated her tongue without a trace of anything remotely disgusting. Still, Zuri found the roll a little too sweet for her liking, but her stomach cramped with hunger, so she ate along with the others.

Miriam had consumed half her cinnamon roll when she wiped her sticky fingers on a napkin and sipped the still-steaming cup of tea. "I feel much better. I was starving. Spill the tea. I want to know everything."

Luis swallowed the last bite of his food and glanced at Zuri. After a moment of consideration, she nodded. Clearing his throat and sipping water, Luis launched into the appalling tale of Rose's demise. Miriam listened with rapt attention, eyes wide and mouth forming an O. Zuri thought it made the affluent teen look as dull as a goldfish. At the appropriate points in the yarn, Zuri added her input, namely descriptions of her early encounters with Rose and, with greater difficulty, her nightmare featuring the man in white.

"Wow," Miriam said and chuckled mirthlessly at the story's conclusion. "That's not the story I've been told."

Zuri dropped the remaining cinnamon roll onto the plate. It hit with a thunk. "You don't believe us?"

"Whoa. Whoa." Miriam raised her hands, palms outward. "I didn't say that. My family's lore is different. That's all."

Beneath the table, Luis took Zuri's hand and gently squeezed. "Do tell."

Miriam quickly detailed the false circumstances surrounding Rose's death that they had read on the internet, adding at the end. "Of course, the patriarch is only spoken about in the most glowing terms." Miriam rolled her eyes. "Like he was Jesus Christ instead of a titan of industry. Anyone who made that much money can't be a saint, right? He gave away millions, but that's nothing compared to the billions he made."

"Not a saint?" Zuri scoffed. "I'd say so. He

murdered his daughter."

Miriam leaned forward. "Exactly. That's evil. I want in. I want to meet Rose."

"The book first," Zuri said.

"No worries. I'll get the book tonight, like I said. I'm a woman of my word. But tomorrow...I want to meet Rose. It will be a family reunion. She must be my great, great aunt or something."

****

The windshield wipers thrummed back and forth at maximum speed barely able to keep up with the torrential downpour pinging against the car. Visibility was terrible. Being night out on an unlit back road didn't help. It was Jake's ill fortune to encounter, according to the weatherman on the radio, a once-in-one-hundred-year rainstorm that flooded I-40 for the next fifty miles through Texas. He already made horrible time due to his enlarged prostate—gulping energy drinks kept his eyelids sewn open and meant he had to piss at every rest stop and then some.

But he drove on with a white-knuckle grip, enraged but undeterred. Fantasies of Amari, winning journalistic awards and achieving all her dreams, and his resentment for her abandoning him when he needed her most, fueling his volcanic fury.

This time, when he started punching, he wouldn't stop until he obliterated her from existence.

****

Miriam crept down the grand staircase five minutes after midnight. At twelve o'clock sharp, she had slunk into her mother's sitting room and replaced the necklace in the jewelry case atop a restored eighteenth-century dresser. It was easy as pie, honestly, and she was ninety-nine percent certain—okay, maybe ninety-five percent—Mother hadn't noticed the necklace missing. The woman owned more jewelry than any ten people needed.

The staircase creaked and Miriam paused her descent, listening for other movement. All she heard, was the interminable tick-tock of the grandfather clock at the base of the stairs. Behind her the light of the Cold Moon spilled in from a tall arched window. Her elongated shadow cascaded over the stairsteps like a multitiered waterfall. The light pooled on the parquet floor. Taking a deep breath, Miriam continued down the stairs. She'd show the new girl that Miriam O'Dell kept her word.

With only two steps to go, Miriam halted again. This time, she heard sharp clicking against the floor, and a muscled Doberman pincher walked into the pool of light. The dog stopped, gazing at her attentively with glinting eyes and stub tail wagging.

Miriam squatted. "Bruno, you startled me, you big monster."

Bruno ambled up to his young mistress and licked her on the face. Miriam giggled and scratched him behind his pointy ears, just as he liked. She loved Bruno and all the other guard dogs she had shared her life with. It was one of the many things Miriam and Mother butted heads on. The O'Dell matriarch saw the dogs only as a layer of protection, keeping the undesirables at bay. But to Miriam, they were playmates, companions, and family. Mother couldn't stand that.

"Come on, boy." Miriam stood and strode across the parquet floor to the French doors to the library, framed by waist-high planters replete with flowering orchids.

To her surprise, the glow of lamplight suffused the gap between the doors and the floor. Who would be in there at this hour? Not Mother, she was in bed. Father maybe? Sometimes, he stayed up this late reading or conducting business, but when he did, he preferred his study upstairs. It couldn't be Ryan. Last she heard, he was staying in Raleigh to concentrate on completing a research paper for school. She didn't have a clue what the paper was about and didn't care. She didn't know what her brother majored in and suspected he didn't know either.

Miriam patted Bruno on the head for reassurance. "Someone probably left the light on."

She took the cool metal handle and pushed open the door, revealing a small ballroom converted into a library with books from floor to ceiling. In the back, a ladder leaned against the shelving built into the walls to allow access to the highest books. A massive fireplace was on the left-hand wall near the center of the space. Across from the fireplace stood a large square table polished to a brilliant gleam. Miriam had spent innumerable hours at that table studying with friends, tutors, Mother, or alone. A most unwelcome individual sat at the table, looking up from his laptop.

"You're up late," Ryan said.

"I thought you were in Raleigh," Miriam said coolly.

Ryan gave her a rakish smile. "Too many keggers in Raleigh. If I don't raise my GPA to at least a 3.0, Dad is going to kill me."

You mean cut your allowance. "Poor boy."

Miriam strode purposely to the fireplace, the place of honor in the library where all the family histories were displayed. Bruno cruised alongside her.

"You suddenly have an interest in the family history?" Ryan chuckled.

"Something like that," Miriam said, quickly finding the patriarch's diary, a slender notebook that had been restored several times. The leather cover was soft and supple in her hands.

"I thought you despised the patriarch," Ryan said.

"I do," Miriam said without thinking, turning for the doors.

"It gets pretty wild at the end. I think he must have gone craaaazzy," Ryan said. "Had a real active imagination."

"You've read this?" Miriam asked, heading toward the door with Bruno, a bulwark at her side.

"Dad made me. You know, you'll run the business one day, so you have to read this kind of crap." Ryan stood. "Hey, you're not supposed to take the patriarch's diary out of the library."

Miriam turned on her older brother. He was tall, athletic, and uncharacteristically stern.

"I'm taking this, and you won't tell a soul," Miriam said.

Ryan arched an eyebrow. "I won't—"

"That's right. You won't, or I'll tell Bruno to bite off your balls."

Detecting the distress in her voice, Bruno sidled closer to her and tensed. Despite all their training as protectors of the O'Dell family's lives and property, the Dobermans—Bruno, Roxy, Bolt, and Zeke—loved Miriam. She was pack, and they would do anything for her. She knew it, and Ryan did too. More than once, when they were younger, Ryan had ended up treed after

Miriam set a dog after him. The episodes had always been their little secret and were to this day.

Ryan's eyes widened, and he deflated, flopping into the chair.

"You better not lose or damage it," her big bro called at her back.

Chapter 40

The Hidden Path

The following morning, a dour one with the mercury barely above freezing and dark clouds portending a day of pelting rain, Zuri and Luis practically ran to retrieve their backpacks before school. The remains of shredded corn stalks crunched beneath their feet as they scampered across the field to find their backpacks where they left them. Then they jogged to the school parking lot, damp from the overnight precipitation, to confront Miriam as she emerged from her luxury SUV. The socialite wasn't alone; the vehicle was crammed with members of her posse, which Zuri was certain would make the encounter more awkward than it should be. But she and Luis were undeterred. They had faced down a demonic forest and an evil witch spirit to gain access to Good Old George's diary. They weren't about to allow a gauche high school clique to deter them.

Miriam spotted them through the windshield. Her eyes went wide, and she quickly shook her head once in the negative before rejoining the boisterous conversation of her crew. Zuri was about to shake her head in response, but the growl of a revving engine startled her. Luis literally leaped a good quarter foot off the ground. From their right came the blare of a horn. Zuri stopped and turned to glare at the smirking jock behind the wheel of a souped-up sports car. Not one to risk being run over, Luis scampered out of the way over to Miriam's vehicle. After flipping the driver the bird, Zuri joined her friend. The car accelerated past, engine roaring and spewing redolent exhaust.

"Hi, nerd," a freckled redhead chirped as she approached from the side of Miriam's car. The quick up and down look she offered Zuri reeked of disdain. "Hi, new girl. You have the most interesting style."

The comment cut deeper than it normally would but after having last night's outfit shredded by the maleficent woodland, Zuri was down to wearing thrift store yoga pants with holes in the knees and a threadbare hoody over a plain T-shirt.

"What happened to your face?" the girl asked Luis as three more preppy girls gathered around. "That's a nasty scratch? You two like it rough?"

Miriam slid out of the vehicle and shut the door. "Hey, I need to talk to Luis and Zuri for a sec. Don't wait for me. I'll catch up."

Her friends did as Miriam bid, meandering in an animated throng toward the school's entrance. Zuri enviously noted that Miriam wore a black turtleneck covering the abrasions on her neck. It looked as luxuriously soft as cashmere or an equally fine material. "Do you have it?" she demanded.

"I want to meet Rose," Miriam said.

"We know," Luis said.

"I want to meet her first. Then I'll show you the diary," Miriam said. "I told you. Whatever is going down, I want in."

Zuri's first instinct was to give the rich girl the experience of being punched in the gut by a future MMA champion, but once again, Luis kept his cool and defused the encounter. He took Zuri by the hand. "Come to the library after school."

Miriam nodded, and Luis led Zuri toward the school.

Zuri offered the affluent blonde one long glare over her shoulder. "Don't be late."

****

At lunch, Edith noticed the scratches on Luis's cheeks, sparking an inquest. John, masticating a roast beef sandwich like a cow chewing cud, even examined the math whiz after hearing the remark. "Yeah. I see that," John said, words slurred due to the food in his mouth. "What happened?"

Zuri played with the iceberg lettuce salad drenched in ranch dressing with a plastic spork, fearing anything she might say would reveal they were helping Rose after promising not to.

"Does it have anything to do with the ghost girl, Luis?" Edith demanded, setting aside her container of Greek yogurt and giving him a critical stare.

"What? No way." Luis flashed an incredulous smile. "On the way home yesterday, I tried to help a stray cat. I thought it was hurt. Stupid me. It scratched me and took off like a rocket."

Zuri moved her left hand, which had a prominent red scratch along the back from the pinky's knuckle to the wrist, onto her lap.

Edith arched one eyebrow. "Really?"

John swallowed, his throat bulging as the food slid down. "You don't like cats."

"I thought it was hurt," Luis said defensively.

"We called animal services," Zuri said.

Luis nodded enthusiastically. Edith eyed them suspiciously, but John appeared satisfied with the explanation. "Why didn't you reply to my texts?" he asked Luis.

"When did you text? I forgot my phone at home," Luis lied. His phone was lost on the dell next to the satanic trees.

"I did some research about the en passant move's origin last night," John said, and he launched into a detailed history of the chess move. His enthusiasm reached such lofty heights that he uncharacteristically set aside his lunch and neglected to finish it before the bell sounded, summoning the students to class.

Chess didn't particularly interest Zuri, but the same wasn't true for Edith, who listened intently. Soon the inquiry into the origins of Luis's wounds was completely forgotten.

****

To Zuri's considerable surprise, Miriam was waiting for her and Luis beside the library's entrance after school. The socialite appeared distinctly uncomfortable, shifting her weight from foot to foot and playing with her blonde locks with the pointer finger of her left hand while texting with her right hand.

Luis led their winding advance through the crowded hallway of dispersing students full of buzzing conversations and aromatic with perfumes and body odor occasionally mixed with stale cigarette stank. As they closed in on the entrance, Luis called a greeting. Miriam looked up from her phone to glance around nervously and stopped playing with her hair. Locating them in the crowd, she grinned briefly and turned for the doors.

Once again, Zuri was surprised by Miriam. She actually held the door to the library open for them. They quickly traversed the open area before the front desk, where Mrs. Binder spoke quietly with a pair of upperclassmen. Zuri took the lead, guiding the group to the usual study desk in the back of the collection.

Zuri unslung her backpack, set it on the floor, and sat down in the first available chair. Luis followed suit, sitting next to her, pulling his laptop out of his backpack, and setting it on the table.

Miriam regarded their surroundings curiously. "Now what?"

Luis removed a college ruled notebook and a ballpoint pen from his backpack and placed them beside the computer.

"We wait." Zuri pointed to the chair across from her. "You should probably sit. Rose will come on her own time."

Luis flipped open his laptop. "This should help attract her. She's more fascinated by real analysis than I am, and that's saying something."

Miriam raised her eyebrows. "Okay."

The blonde girl shrugged off her backpack and sat across from Zuri.

"Do you have the diary?" Zuri asked.

Miriam sighed in evident annoyance. "I do. I told you. I'm a woman of my word."

"Take it out," Zuri said.

Miriam opened her mouth to speak, but Luis said quickly. "Rose is the one who told us about the diary. She's…she's shy. You might make her nervous, but if she sees the diary—"

"She'll come." Miriam nodded and leaned over to

root around in her backpack. She sat up holding a thin leather-bound volume. "Here it is." She slid it across the table to Zuri. "Be careful with it, please. I'm not supposed to take it out of the family library, let alone the house."

"Like the necklace," Zuri said pointedly, picking up the diary. The cover was soft and supple.

Miriam self-consciously rubbed the neck of her lavish turtleneck. "Something like that."

Zuri detected the necrotic stench in the air and the temperature drop the instant before Luis said, "She's here."

The girls turned toward the stacks to observe grey mist seeping out of the shelving and from between the books. The spectral fog gathered into a dense cloud between the shelving and the study desk.

"Is that…is that Rose?" Miriam hugged her arms to her chest to ward off the chill. "Ewww, that smell."

"It used to be worse," Zuri said. "It won't be so bad once she's fully formed."

Slowly, the fog swirled into a nebulously hominid shape. As this occurred, the odor and cold slightly decreased. By the time the mist coalesced into a deathly pale girl in a high-collared dress with a hoop skirt of whirling fog, the noisome odor and chill were practically undetectable.

"Oh my God," Miriam said. "She looks exactly like in the family photos. Except for the fog skirt."

"We have the diary." Zuri proffered Rose the slender book.

The ghost snatched the book from Zuri, leaving behind a tingling cold where her ethereal digits brushed the pugilist's hand. The phantasmal tween paced back and forth before the teens, flipping through the diary. Occasionally, she studied a page intently before shaking her head in disappointment and continuing her search.

"What is she searching for?" Miriam asked.

"The location of where she is bound to a statue or something by black magic," Zuri said.

"Wait a sec." Miriam clapped her hands. "I perused the diary last night—super disturbing. Page..." She snapped her fingers. "Page 145. The patriarch refers to an idol in a subbasement below Pinedale High."

"I've never heard about a subbasement," Luis said.

Rose was so intent in her study of the diary she took no notice of their conversation.

Zuri waved a hand before the spirit's face. The ghost paused her pacing and looked up from the diary in annoyance.

"Page 145," Zuri said. "Check that page."

Frowning, Rose flipped to page 145. As she studied the page, her eyes went wide and she visibly stiffened. Looking up, she pointed at the page and nodded emphatically. After some back and forth that included number codes written by Rose, they determined the ghost didn't know how to access the subbasement.

"Does the diary give a hint how to access the subbasement?" Luis asked.

"Not that I could tell," Miriam said.

"What about the fire evacuation map?" Zuri said. "There's one by the library's entrance. Maybe that will give us a clue.

"Okay. Worth a try," Miriam said, and Luis nodded in agreement.

After they explained to Rose their intention and she surrendered the diary to Miriam, the teens speed walked to the front of the bibliotheca, leaving the ghost behind. Mrs. Binder softly hummed from somewhere out of sight behind the front desk. Zuri led the way to the evacuation map posted next to the entrance inside a hard plastic holder affixed to the wall. The teens considered the map.

Zuri pointed to a stairwell near the shop classroom. "What's down these stairs?"

"Huh," Luis said. "There's a door there marked faculty only. I didn't know it led to stairs. I've never seen it open."

"Let's go see where it leads," Miriam said.

Chapter 41

A Ghostly Hand

The teens burst from the library into the empty hallway, running full tilt for the shop classroom and the nearby staircase at the opposite end of the school. Their footfall echoed in the otherwise eerily quiet corridor. Zuri led the way at first, but soon Miriam, with the diary clutched in her left hand, passed her, moving with the practiced efficiency of a top runner. Unable to accept being outrun by the rich girl, Zuri redoubled her effort, breath coming in bellowing gasps and a stitch forming in her side.

With every step Zuri fell behind. She could accept Miriam being more gorgeous, wealthier, and smarter than her, but physical prowess was her bailiwick, and being in a losing position was a blow, especially when the socialite glanced over her shoulder and smirked. That haughty grin was sharp glass lodged in Zuri's throat.

From behind Zuri came breathing that sounded like a freight train lumbering down tracks. Slowing, she allowed Luis to come up alongside her. Sweat glistened on his face.

"We can walk," Zuri said.

Luis shook his head, expression determined. Zuri was impressed by his grit. From down the hallway came the thud of a door closing. Soon, the crotchety shop teacher, Mr. Cashburn, appeared at the junction up ahead. He looked up from his phone at the sound of the teens sprinting through the passage. "No running in the hallway!" he barked in a voice graveled from years of smoking.

The teens stopped running.

"Sorry, Mr. Cashburn," Miriam said sweetly, accelerating to a speed walk as soon as she passed the teacher.

The shop teacher gave Zuri and Luis the stink eye when they crossed paths in the hallway.

"Come on," Zuri whispered to Luis, and they power-walked to the intersection. There, they turned left to find Miriam before the door labeled faculty only in black capitalized lettering next to the shop classroom.

"It's locked," Miriam said.

****

Welcome to Pinedale.

Big Jake blinked, unable to believe his eyes.

Rubbing his gummy orbs, Jake slowed the muscle car and stared at the green sign planted in the ground at the city limits.

Pinedale.

It was real. Not a mirage.

Finally.

His destination.

His destiny.

Riding shotgun, the flat of energy drinks was empty. The spent cans clinked on the passenger-side floorboard.

Now to the high school to track down his wayward daughter.

No.

Jake shook his head.

That wasn't right.

First, he needed to visit his wife. But when he came to the first stop sign in the small burg, he nearly disregarded the GPS instructions squawking from his phone and almost turned left instead of heading straight.

Little did he know that turn would've taken him to Pinedale Central. Jake suspected his near mistake was his exhausted mind playing tricks on him, but of course, it was Good Old George summoning him to do the vile spirit's evil will. Unbeknownst to him, he was George's champion, a willing dupe, but the ex-boxer had unfinished business with his wife to take care of before answering the dead man's call.

Jake removed a .38 special from the glove box and placed it on the passenger seat, then drove straight through the intersection en route to The Pinedale Gazette.

****

The three teens stared at the locked door. Zuri punched the heavy steel door in frustration. Pain lanced through her hand and up her forearm. Grunting, she shook out her hand, and gradually, the good hurt dissipated. It reminded her that she could fight as long as she was alive.

"Like that's going help," Luis said.

Zuri glared at the math whiz like he was a moron. "Thank you for that information."

"Now is not the time for a lovers'…" Miriam trailed off when Zuri rounded on her. "Time to argue, mansplain, whatever. Do we have any idea where to find the key?"

"I got it," Luis said. "I bet Hank, the janitor, has it. On that huge key ring, he keeps on his belt."

Miriam grinned crookedly. "How exactly are we going to get that away from him? Have Zuri knock him out?"

"No!" Luis said and eyed Zuri. "Don't do that. What's the rush? Right? We can strategize. Come up with a plan to get the key and get past the door another day."

"No." Zuri shook her head.

The teens looked at her questioningly.

"We have to do this now," Zuri said. "Don't ask me why. Don't ask how I know. I just do. We need to get through this door. We need to reach the subbasement. And we need to do it *now*."

Luis gestured toward the door. "But how?"

"Ah." Miriam moistened her lips. "I'm probably going to regret saying this. But maybe…ummm, we can use the tools in the shop to break down the door."

"Like that won't cause a bunch of noise and bring Hank or someone else running to investigate," Luis said.

"No," Zuri said. "We don't need to break down the door. Be quiet. Please."

Miriam arched an eyebrow, remaining silent. The math whiz started to speak but stopped under Zuri's glare. After a beat of quiet, Zuri concentrated on her connection with Rose, like she did in the clearing before the diabolic gingerbread house.

Rose, we need your help getting to the subbasement. There's a door…but it's locked…

A tremor pulsed through Zuri followed by chill air flowing downward from the ceiling.

"God, why is it…" Miriam said, glancing up.

Gray mist descended from overhead toward the teens. They retreated to avoid contact with the cold, nebulous cloud that emitted a faint moribund odor.

"Is that…Rose?" Luis gulped.

"I hope so," Zuri replied.

The fog rolled into the door, seeping around the edges until it was entirely gone from sight, leaving behind only a feeble smell reminiscent of roadkill baking in the sun. The teens looked at each other in puzzlement.

"What now?" Miriam asked.

Zuri replied. "I—"

A mechanical click announced the deadbolt's withdrawal. Luis moved first, grabbing the handle, turning it, and pushing the door open.

****

From somewhere near the entrance to the Gazette's office space came raised voices. The racket was enough to break Amari's concentration on her work, and she checked the time in the upper right-hand corner of the computer monitor, almost four—about one hour before quitting. Part of her wanted to hop up like a prairie dog and gaze out over the cubicle farm to get an eyeful of the commotion, but she had enough time to put the finishing touches on the article before five as long as she kept powering through.

Blinking, she focused on the text document, scrolling to the top. It was time to edit. My boyfriend is abusive, but I love him. Should I leave him? *Yes, don't make my mistake, girl.*

The question was still posed to and answered by Dolores Clattenburg, but that was all mummery. The word was out. Pinedale's favorite advice columnist was none other than Amari Williams. She was happy people knew she was the woman behind the penname, dispensing indispensable wisdom.

When she was most honest with herself, which was usually while lying awake in bed at two a.m., she was a little nervous Jake might discover she had found success and seek her out with clenched fists. But she also believed that he wouldn't come looking for her now.

That's when she heard a bellowing shout that made her gasp and hold her breath. She spun in the chair to face the cubicle entrance, the article forgotten.

Chapter 42

Supervised Exploration

The door marked faculty only opened onto an
unfinished stairwell with stairs leading down. The teens
scurried inside, and Luis allowed the door to shut with a
loud clank that echoed through the space.

"You're going to give us away," Zuri said.

"Sorry," Luis mumbled.

The only hint that Rose had been there moments
before was the weak aroma of decay lingering in the air.
Recessed lighting, buzzing like flies on a day-old
carcass, provided illumination. Zuri glanced over the
railing. The stairs went down and down and down, like a
mineshaft leading to hell.

"Looks promising," she remarked.

Luis joined her at the railing. "Gives me the creeps."

Zuri understood what he meant. Something was off
about the stairway like they were about to slide down the
feeding tube of an unearthly monstrosity instead of doing
something as mundane as traversing dozens of steps.

"Only one way to go," Miriam said, starting down
the stairs.

Hand in hand, Zuri and Luis followed. After only
two flights, the temperature dropped precipitously, and
by the third flight, Miriam's teeth chattered. The aroma
of decay did not worsen—nor did it dissipate as they

expected.

A stern voice came from above as they neared the fourth landing. "What are you kids doing here?"

They froze, recognizing the voice of Hank, the janitor. Only it was his voice as they had never heard it before, with all the friendliness withered and gone, replaced by disapproval.

"Where did he come from?" Zuri whispered. "I didn't hear the door or anything."

Not even the clink of the innumerable keys dangling from the giant keyring hanging from Hank's belt.

Luis shrugged and held her hand tighter.

"Crap," Miriam said. "I hope he doesn't report us. My parents will kill me if I get in trouble."

****

Amari was glad she hadn't drunk that last cup of coffee, or she'd be peeing her pants right about now as she stared at her estranged husband eclipsing the cubicle's entrance. The intervening years had done nothing to diminish his massive frame; his enormous fists looked as bone-pulverizing as ever. When they first met while she was a college student in L.A., his impressive physique had turned her on, making her heart race and body tingle with electricity, and that aura of dangerous tough guy he always exuded had made her feel safe. Now, all she could think was how she was about to be beaten to death. She saw it in his eyes, the cruelty and the pain and the finality. She hoped no one tried to be a hero, to intervene. That would only end with Jake killing more people.

"Get up," Jake said. "You're coming with me."

Swallowing a lump in her throat, Amari shook her head. "No. I know what you're here to do. Just get it over with."

Jake's grimace showed crooked teeth. "I want…" He shook his head. "No…ahhh…" He smacked his palms against his temples. "You're coming with me. We're going to see our daughter."

Despite being cold with terror, head pounding and abdomen knotting, Amari found the courage to spit. "Never! I won't have you killing me in front of her!"

Jake reached around to the small of his back and pulled out a shiny revolver, cocking the hammer. "You're coming with me, or I will kill every person in this building."

****

The teens responded to the janitor all at once.

"The door was unlocked," Luis blurted only half a lie.

"Don't report us, please," Miriam wheedled.

"What are you doing down here?" Zuri demanded.

Hank frowned, the expression turning his usually good-natured countenance rather maniacal. "You kids need to leave now."

The teens exchanged a look and, despite their reservations, came to an unspoken agreement.

Zuri faced the janitor. "No."

Hank crossed his arms over his chest. "Listen. You kids don't want to get in trouble. Right? You leave now, I won't report you. Refuse…well, that's a one-way ticket to the principal's office."

"But…"

Zuri fell silent as gray mist seeped from imperfections in the wall, precipitated by the stairway becoming even colder and the odor of rot intensifying.

"Rose?" Miriam whispered.

Zuri shook her head, and Luis shrugged.

Hank retreated a step up the stairway, staring wide-eyed at the cloud. His eyes didn't blink, and after that initial ambulation, he didn't move as if he were in extreme concentration or a trance.

"What's going on?" Miriam queried.

"Are they communicating?" Luis whispered.

Hank relaxed, dropping his hand to his sides and smiling as the fog percolated into the wall. "Okay. I'll tell you what. I'll let you explore, but I'm coming with you—to supervise."

****

Jake sped through Pinedale. The muscle car's V8 roared, providing harmony to the melody of Amari's muffled protestations from where he had stowed her, wrists and ankles zip tied, in the trunk. He braked hard to take a corner past a minimart at high speed, tires squealing and the vehicle's rear end fishtailing.

The school. The school. The school.

He needed to reach the school, or the throbbing behind his eyeballs would cause them to explode like twin geysers. He slammed the accelerator into the floorboard, and the speedometer reading climbed. He darted through an intersection at a red light, narrowly avoiding being T-boned. A chorus of honking horns resounded in his wake. Weaving through traffic, he knew how to reach his destination, even without the aid of the GPS.

George reeled him in like a fishhook was lodged in his lower lip.

****

After going down innumerable steps, the teens and adult finally reached the end of the stairs at a closed and locked door. Hank unlocked the door after selecting a key without even a glance from the enormous keyring at his belt. A musty odor escaped the room when the janitor pushed open the door and stepped inside.

A second later, overhead lights flickered on. The teens entered the space, not knowing what to expect. What they found was nothing even remotely paranormal, at least at first blush. The room was neither large nor small and unfinished. Along the walls was metal shelving, the kind that could be found at big box stores nationwide. The shelves were crammed with cardboard boxes, some labeled while most weren't. Piled haphazardly on the floor were more boxes.

Luis meandered around the room, poking at the boxes and shelving. "What is kept down here?"

Hank shrugged. "School supplies. Old textbooks. Stuff like that."

"Is this the subbasement?" Zuri asked.

A tremor ran through Hank, and he looked at her sharply. "Is this a what?"

"Subbasement. Is this the subbasement?" Miriam pronounced each word carefully as if she was speaking to someone for whom English was a second language.

Hank glanced at the rich girl in irritation. "No, this is the basement. You kids have seen it. We should go."

"We just got here," Miriam said, flipping through her ancestor's diary.

"I have another question." Zuri eyed Hank. "Is there a subbasement?"

Hank nervously looked around the room. "I don't like it down here. We should go. I agreed to let you kids explore. You did. Time is up."

"You didn't answer my question, Hank," Zuri said.

"Is there a subbasement?"

Hank clasped his hands against the side of his head. "I don't know. I want to leave. You need to leave. Please."

"Listen to this," Miriam said excitedly and read from a page in the diary. "My symbol marks the path! At my symbol, recite this chant! I think it's in Latin…some of it, anyway."

"What is the symbol?" Luis asked.

"It's probably a cornucopia—that's a symbol of wealth and abundance," Miriam said, smiling broadly. "A cornucopia has been included in the branding for O'Dell Enterprises since its founding."

"Cornucopia? Is that one of those things sort of shaped like a ramshorn?" Zuri asked.

"Yeah, sort of," Miriam nodded and faced Hank. "Have you ever seen a cornucopia down here?"

Shaking his head, Hank backed into the doorway. "We need to leave. You kids stop what you're doing."

"Luis, look for the cornucopia along the walls," Zuri said. "Miriam, figure out how to say the chant. I'll search the floor for the symbol."

Zuri started pushing aside boxes.

Chapter 43

A Bit of Witchcraft

Zuri tried to push aside an enormous cardboard box, discovering it wouldn't budge. It was heavier than any of the boxes she had moved thus far.

"Huh." A corner of the box's top was ripped, allowing her to peek inside. Stacked neatly and still shrink-wrapped were thick, hardbound Algebra Two textbooks—there must have been at least fifty crammed inside.

"You kids need to stop," Hank said stridently from the doorway. "We need to leave."

The teens ignored his protestations, continuing the search for the cornucopia and deciphering the text in the diary. Zuri crouched low and jammed her shoulder into the box, heaving. Inch by inch, the container slid across the floor. God, she was happy she didn't have to haul around tons of huge textbooks in her backpack. The laptop was much lighter.

By the time she had the box shifted to reveal the floor beneath it, sweat rolled down her cheeks. But the effort was worth it because carved into the floor that had been hidden by the box was a shape like a horn or a cornucopia.

"I think I found it! Oh my God, I found it," Zuri said, wiping sweat from her brow.

Miriam looked up from the diary. "Seriously?"

Zuri pointed to the symbol that appeared untouched by the hand of time. "Check it out."

Miriam weaved through the boxes to the pugilist's side. "That's definitely a cornucopia."

Luis scrambled toward them, tripping over boxes along the way. When he reached the girls, he squatted beside the symbol and said, "Wow!" He traced the horn of plenty, including the bounty spilling out, with his fingers. "It's like…it's like there are no imperfections. It's not worn or anything." He looked at the girls. "That's strange, isn't it? The symbol has been here for over one hundred years."

Miriam shrugged. "If this has always been used for storage—"

"Don't touch that!" Hank snapped.

Without hearing or sensing him moving, the janitor had walked up behind them and stood at Miriam's shoulder, staring at the cornucopia. "That is an evil sign!" There was a ranting quality to Hank's tone.

"It symbolizes abundance," Luis said dismissively.

Zuri leaned over and grabbed Luis by the wrist, pulling his hand away from the symbol. "He's right. This cornucopia is associated with George. He is evil."

Shrugging, Luis stood, giving the janitor a suspicious glance. Hank had stopped ranting now that nobody touched the horn of plenty, although he swayed, and his unblinking eyes seemed as wide as silver dollars.

"Any luck with the chant?" Luis asked.

"I think so," Miriam said, moving closer to the other teens. Her right pointer finger tapped a page below words in a language Zuri did not recognize. "*Diablo* is devil. I know how to say that. *Del*, maybe that's the? I'm not sure about *Aperta*?

"Let me see," Luis said, and Miriam turned the diary, giving him a view of the page. His eyes narrowed in concentration, then went wide, and he took a sharp breath. "*La puerta del diablo*. Ummm… in Spanish, that means the devil's door. This isn't Spanish. You're probably right about it being Latin, but it's close enough. That definitely means devil's door."

Zuri started chewing on her lower lip and crossed her appendages before her chest, rubbing her upper arms. Suddenly, the coldness pervading the basement made the temperature seem like only a handful of degrees above zero.

"*Aperta*?" Luis frowned. "*Aperta*? Hmmm…open, maybe? Like…like, *abre la puerta del diablo*. I think this means open devil's door or open door of the devil. *Aperta Puerta del Diablo*."

"Don't say that!" Hank's wail startling the three teens, so Miriam fumbled and nearly dropped the book. "It's evil! It's evil!"

Luis was nonplussed. "*Aperta Puerta del Diablo*? Those are just words."

Hank pointed a trembling finger at Luis. "Evil! You will unleash evil upon the world!"

No sooner had the words left his lips than the janitor spun and ran pell-mell from the basement, taking the stairs two at a time. He fulminated about evil being unleashed and running rampant through the school, through the town, and eventually over the entire world. The teens listened with aghast expressions until the sound of his footfall and raving faded from hearing. They exchanged looks of both puzzlement and foreboding.

"Okay." Miriam took a deep breath. "I don't know

if I want to do this. I mean we were lucky to survive the woods, right?"

"You don't have to come," Zuri said, even as memories of the clawing creepers and branches made her shiver. "I'm going to help Rose."

Luis's voice cracked as he spoke. "I'm with Zuri."

Miriam shook her head. "I'm here to save Rose too. All the way. Whatever it takes. She got screwed over by the patriarch. By my family. It's the least I can do. It's just…" she pointed to the doorway. "Whatever that was with Hank. That was creepy as hell, and so is this diary." She shoved the book into Luis's chest. "You read the incantation. I can't pronounce the Latin properly."

Luis took the book and glanced at Zuri. She nodded, determination firm.

"Okay, here it goes," Luis said and started to read. "Lucifer, rent the path. Beelzebub, gape your maw. Asmodeus, unlock your flesh. Leviathan, claw open your eye. Belphegor, forget your indolence. Satan, smote thy door. *Aperta Puerta del Diablo*."

Nothing happened. The teens looked at each other.

"I think I pronounced it all correctly," Luis said and faced Zuri, offering her the book. "I think you need to say it. You're the one with the connection to Rose."

"I don't know," Zuri said uncertainly and took the book. She studied the page. "How do I say this last bit? The Latin words."

"*Aperta Puerta del Diablo*," Luis said.

Zuri repeated the phrase five times before Luis approved, and Miriam said. "Close enough…probably."

"Thanks for the vote of confidence," Zuri said and started reciting. "Lucifer, rent the path."

As soon as she spoke the words, heat flared from the

diary, and the floor beneath them shook. Zuri tap danced to maintain her balance. The cornucopia emitted an eerie green luminescence.

"It's working," Luis said. "Keep reading."

"Beelzebub, gape your maw."

The diary grew so hot Zuri flinched. Miriam let out a piercing scream as the floor around the cornucopia cracked. The teens retreated, Luis guiding Zuri with a hand on her forearm. The fractures around the symbol formed a circle like a gaping mouth. The horn of plenty was untouched by the spiderweb of cracks and continued emitting the green glow.

"Asmodeus, unlock your flesh."

A resounding thud like a mammoth deadbolt sliding out of place echoed through the basement. The heat from the book made Zuri's hands throb, and black smoke rose from the pages, smelling like burning flesh.

"Leviathan, claw open your eye."

Where the bounty spilled from the cornucopia, came a thunderous snap, and an evil eye opened, subsuming the abundance. The uncanny light altered, forming a sickly green column shooting up from the center of the glaring aperture. Zuri discovered she could no longer deliver the words. Each time she tried the syllables died stillborn in her throat.

It was that eye.

That vile orb.

Watching. Peeling her epidermis like an onion to blister her very soul.

"Don't look at the eye!" Luis said.

Miriam maneuvered, blocking Zuri's view of the orb, although she still saw the green column rising overhead to pierce the ceiling. "Belphegor, forget your indolence."

The floor rumbled beneath them like monstrous gears turned, clinking and clanking into place. Her hands burned like she held them centimeters above a lit candle. Smoke gushed from the book, and a flame leaped, blackening pages and racing toward the remainder of the incantation.

"Satan, smote thy door. *Aperta Puerta del Diablo*!" Zuri screamed. She dropped the diary which immediately burst into an inferno at her feet and was quickly consumed.

Simultaneously, the green light from the devilish aperture went out, and the overhead lights flickered but remained on, only dimmer. The cracked floor around the cornucopia started to transmogrify to a clamorous symphony of rending and cracking stone, forming a spiral staircase down into the dark and endless deep.

Zuri glanced over her shoulder toward the entrance to the basement. Despite the deafening racket, she could have sworn she heard voices—an argument. But her companions showed no sign of hearing the voices, so she decided she must be hearing things and shook her head. She turned back to the supernatural staircase, now fully formed with the cornucopia, Leviathan's eye still blazing from within, adorning the top of the support column.

Miriam coughed, waving a hand to clear the smoke from the burned diary. "Do you have a light? It's like pitch black down there."

"I have my phone." Zuri fished the device from her pants pocket, looking over her shoulder again toward the doorway. Did she hear voices?

"What is it?" Luis asked, loudly.

Zuri shook her head. "I thought I heard something."

"My ears are still ringing," the math whiz said.

Zuri faced the spiral stairs and flicked on the phone light. The darkness consumed the light like a black hole.

"Let's go," Zuri said, and the teens started descending the stairs.

"Zuri!"

They had only gone three steps when a voice Zuri knew too well bellowed her name.

Chapter 44

Rats

Deep in his sanctum, George knew his defenses had been breached. He didn't hear the sound of the ancient machinery fueled by magic turning. Oh, no, he felt it in every atom of his spiritual essence. Big Jake, his champion, his dupe, was late to the showdown. That wouldn't do. That wouldn't do at all.

Time. That was what Jake needed, a bit more time.

"Come to me, my children." George's voice spilled from the idol almost as resonant as it had been in life.

Hissing shrieks, like the sounds of angry rats, only much louder, answered his call. George prepared to unleash his horde upon the intruders, but then he felt a kindred soul nearing his sanctum.

"Ahhhh," he breathed in both relief and satisfaction. Instead of releasing his minions, George held them in check and tapped his reserves of necrotic power.

Green light burst from the icon, bathing the rodent horde in its unholy radiation.

"Grow fat and powerful, my children, fat and powerful," Good Old George crooned.

****

The room and stairs spun like a roulette wheel. In one reality, her mother sprawled on the floor with blood pooling around her head when the roulette ball clattered to stop. In a second, Big Jake pulled the revolver's trigger, blasting a hole in her mother's skull. And in the third, he drove the revolver's barrel into her mother's temple while tears streamed down the woman's face. But what reality was Zuri destined to tread?

"No, no, no!" Zuri screamed, falling to her knees on the spiraling steps, once again, as helpless as she had been in the kitchen three years ago, listening to the wet smacks of her father's fists hammering her mother's face.

Jake shouted, but the words were lost in the clickety-clack of the roulette ball and the moist thuds of his fists crunching into mother's cheeks. Zuri was vaguely aware of Luis and Miriam coming alongside her. Luis kneeling and wrapping an arm over her shoulders, and Miriam, raising her hands out in front of her and pleading. Zuri was aware of all this as if it happened far away in another place, even another dimension.

Big Jake's yowl brought Zuri tumbling from the titan's grip of past trauma back to reality. Amari had her mouth clamped around the meat of his muscled forearm. Blood formed red streams on his skin. Instead of shooting Amari, Jake raised the pistol overhead and brought it down toward his estranged wife's crown.

Zuri rose to her feet, brushing aside Luis's grasping hands, dropping her phone, and charging. Jake brought the gun down onto Amari's skull with a crack, and she went limp. When he removed his bloody arm from around her neck, Amari slid boneless to the floor.

Big Jake turned on Zuri. Surprise flashed in his eyes.

He still expected her to be the thirteen-year-old cowering while he beat her mother, and the hesitation that caused was all Zuri needed. When Jake swung the revolver around to take aim, Zuri delivered the most perfect high kick of her life, as good, she would decide in retrospect, as any landed by The Jade Tiger. Her foot connected with his wrist, and the gun flew from his hand, landing several feet away and spinning across the floor.

Snarling his fury, Jake launched himself at her. Zuri tried to dodge, but his arms were as fast as striking adders. An open palm smashed into the side of her head, dazing her, and she wobbled backward. Jake lurched toward her but stumbled over Amari's limp form, and Zuri scurried out of reach. Blinking, Zuri shook her head to regain focus. In her peripheral vision, she glimpsed her friends rushing to her aid.

"Stay back!" Zuri said. "Stay back! He can punch hard enough to kill."

"Watch out!" Luis yelled.

Jake charged, looming as large as a professional linebacker. Zuri moved, but she was still dazed and too slow. She braced herself for impact, maybe a fist, a flying knee, or his freight train of a body slamming into her. But then Rose was there, rising out of the floor fully in humanoid form, a spectral girl forever twelve years old. Jake passed into her phantasmal body and fell crashing to the floor, as if he had run into a brick wall.

Rose floated over to Zuri, staring at Jake with stern disapproval.

"Thank you," Zuri said, swaying.

Luis scrambled to her side and wrapped a steadying arm around her waist. "It's okay. It's okay. He's down...for now, but we should go."

Jake pushed himself to a seated position and stared at Rose with glazed eyes. "So cold."

All his bare skin was red as if exposed to subzero

temperatures.

"Mom," Zuri said, rushing to Amari's side, with Luis supporting her.

Zuri dropped to her knees beside Amari, who, thankfully, stirred. A welt the size of a golf ball with blood trickling from it marred her right temple.

"Mom, please be okay." Zuri placed a hand on her shoulder. "Please be okay."

Amari's eyes fluttered open, and she groaned. "Is that you, girl? Help me up?"

"Are you sure?" Zuri asked, but Amari began sitting up, so she, along with Luis, provided assistance.

"Guys! Watch out!" Miriam shrieked.

Zuri turned to watch Big Jake, his face screwed up into a fearsome sneer, stalking toward them. His movements were herky-jerky, almost like a marionette, and a faint greenish mist rose off him. Zuri squinted, sure her eyes played tricks on her, but the mist remained—almost too indistinct to see. Rose moved to intercept Jake but was repulsed as if she ran into an invisible barrier. The spectral tween stared at Jake in consternation and attempted to grab him, but her hand could not pass through the green haze.

Girding herself, Zuri stood and was pleased to find her legs steady and her mind clear. She always knew it would come to this in the end. That one day, she would have to face down her father in a grudge match.

Luis said. "Zuri, no—"

"The gun, Luis," Amari said urgently. "Get me the gun."

Zuri clenched her hands into fists and assumed a fighting stance.

"Zuri Williams, you should not have come," Big

Jake said, but she instantly knew that although her father spoke, the words belonged to the man in white. "All you needed to do was stay away—to keep your nose out of my family's business. Now you're all gonna die!"

Jake rushed forward, and a single deafening gunshot rang out. Jake stumbled and fell to the ground with blood blossoming on his right shoulder. "Goddamn! You shot me!"

Zuri relaxed her fists. The green mist surrounding her father was gone, and whatever supernatural power that had played him like a puppet snapped. Ears still ringing, she glanced over her shoulder. Amari stood with the smoking revolver held in both hands, her expression fiercely determined.

"I don't know what's going on here," Amari said. "But go. Do whatever you kids are here to do. I'll keep him here."

Zuri ran to her mother, and the women embraced.

****

The teens descended the spiral staircase in a tight group. Rose floated above the steps ahead of them. Miriam held Zuri's phone, shining the light back and forth, but as Zuri observed earlier, the stairway absorbed the luminescence. Their primary light source was the pale glow cast by Rose.

At first, the stairway was smooth and uniform, as if carved with robotic precision. But after a few turns, the stairs became roughhewn and dank, even slippery slick. The teens slowed their descent to avoid falling, but Rose continued at the same pace, forcing them to speed up or risk being left behind in the darkness. The further they descended, the air became ripe with the reek of decomposition. The stench was so powerful that Zuri breathed through her mouth, which only coated her tongue with a rotten flavor. She started spitting in a doomed attempt to clear her palate.

"Do you hear that?" Luis asked.

"I can barely hear anything," Zuri said. Truth be told, her ears were still ringing from the gunshot.

"Don't shout," Miriam chided.

Zuri hadn't realized she had spoken loudly and remained quiet.

"What is that?" Luis asked.

"I don't know…it…it doesn't sound good," Miriam said.

Zuri concentrated on detecting what the others heard. There was a faint noise, barely detectable above the wet plops of their feet against the steps. Zuri gasped. The distant sound reminded her of the susurrating branches of the devilish woods.

Rose continued around the bend, threatening to leave them in darkness.

"Come on," Luis said, scampering after the ghost and quickly out of sight.

The girls followed more cautiously.

"What the hell!" Luis screamed.

"Luis!" Zuri called and loped down the steps with Miriam at her side.

Only the dimmest edge of the radiance cast by Rose lit their way. Zuri clearly heard the ominous racket Luis and Miriam had been on about. It was the hissing shrieks of dozens of voices mixed together to form a roar echoing up the spiraling passage.

They came around the curve to a horrific phantasmagoria. Dozens of gargantuan rats the size of back-alley tomcats bounded up the stairs, claws scraping against stone and teeth gnashing. From their throats came the hissing caterwauling. Rose's ghostly light reflected in their maniacal eyes. Those in the lead clawed and bit at Luis, who crab-walked backward up the steps and kicked at the diabolical rodents.

Zuri rushed forward and grabbed Luis under the armpits, pulling him to his feet. She kicked the nearest rodent in its bulbous snout, sending the squealing creature cartwheeling over the writhing bodies of its grotesque brethren. More rodents dashed forward, snapping teeth and slashing claws. Zuri and Luis kicked the vermin while retreating up the steps.

"Rats! Rats!" Miriam wailed behind them. "Oh, my god!"

Light flared, illuminating the stairs like the noonday sun. Squinting, Zuri threw an arm before her eyes and turned her head away from the light. Beside her, Luis groaned, and from behind, Miriam whimpered. But most disconcerting of all was the terrorized squealing of the rats.

When the light faded, the vermin horde littered the steps in deathly repose. Rose's dim radiance reflected in scores of dark, glassy orbs. It was immediately apparent something was wrong with the ghostly girl. Her light was duller than Zuri ever recalled, and her shoulders sagged. Her almost always somber expression was now also exhausted as if the paranormal spark fueling her spiritual essence burned low.

"Rose killed the rats," Miriam said and giggled like someone on the cusp of madness. "With the light."

"Are you sure they're dead?" Luis said. "Look what they did to my jeans."

The denim was shredded from his ankles to his

knees, but it looked like he had avoided taking any wounds.

"They look dead to me," Zuri said and glanced at Rose, meeting the girl's tired eyes. "We'll finish this. Whatever it takes."

Rose nodded.

"Let's roll," Zuri said.

"I'll stay behind," Miriam said, hysteria entering her voice. "With…with Rose."

Zuri nodded to the rich girl. The rats had been too much for Miriam.

Chapter 45

The Evil Sanctum

Hand in hand, Zuri and Luis slowly shuffled downward. Each step they descended took them a little further from Rose's dim glow. Ahead, only a yawning abyss awaited. Soon, they were literally stepping out into the black, unable to glimpse the ground directly beneath their feet. Rose's light was lost to them behind the bend. Zuri pressed her right hand to the damp wall of uneven, cold stone.

"What is it?" Luis asked.

"The wall almost feels icy," Zuri said. "We need to be careful not to slip."

"We could step out onto anything or nothing," Luis whispered.

"I know," she said but continued onward, driven by duty and the bone-deep desire to put an end to George's evil once and for all.

The unwholesome reek hanging in the air was even worse than the impenetrable murk, sickly sweet with decay and ripe with defecation. It was a smell to make noses twitch, eyes water, and foul enough on the tongue to induce gagging. But they soldiered on, groaning in revulsion, hacking, and heaving.

"What's that sound?" Luis asked.

This time, Zuri had noticed the noise, a distant thrum

like that from a power substation. She had been about to remark on it herself. "I don't know," she said. "Maybe we're near the subbasement."

"I'm not sure if that's a good or bad thing," Luis said.

Zuri squeezed his hand. "It means that this is almost over. No matter what, it's almost over."

The thrumming intensified as they continued until it seemed to vibrate their bones. Zuri thought this must be what it's like to have a beehive inside your skull. The din was maddening, even making her teeth tingle. Its unrelenting nature sapped her will and nearly made her turn back. But when she slowed, Luis tugged her onward.

"I see green light up ahead," Luis shouted to be heard over the racket.

Zuri squinted. "I see it!"

A faint shimmer reflected off the damp stone of the wall and stairs. Galvanized, Zuri sprang forward, pulling Luis along. They spiraled down while the sickly green light grew ever stronger.

"Watch out!" Luis gasped, yanking on her arm.

Zuri slowed and ducked beneath the web of a hairy spider the size of a bowling ball. She clenched her teeth so hard that her jaw ached as they passed beneath the arachnid, dreading that the monstrosity would drop down upon them with fangs glistening with venom. But the beast did not stir. Was the spider stupefied by the thrumming noise, spellbound by the green light, or dead in its web? They did not know, nor did they care.

They broke into a jog, eager to put distance between themselves and the spider and feeling confident now that they could see their surroundings painted with ill light. The green aura became brighter as they corkscrewed deeper into the bowels beneath Pinedale High. The thrumming grew until it was deafening, threatening to drown out even thought. Ahead, the radiance was as bright as a sunlit day—if the light emitted from the burning star Earth orbited was an unholy green.

Zuri squeezed Luis's hand, and they slowed their advance until they stalked like hunters.

"Come out, Zuri Williams." Somehow, the resonant voice was easily heard through the din. "There is no need to play games. I know you are here. I can feel you."

Zuri straightened and strode forward, but Luis pulled her back, shaking his head.

"No!" He mouthed.

Eyes wide, Zuri gestured toward the light and mouthed. "I have to. Rose."

Luis shook his head unequivocally.

Rolling her eyes, Zuri yanked her hand free from his and continued into the light, not caring if Luis followed. She wasn't sure what awaited her at the spiral staircase's terminus, but she knew George O'Dell was a bully and that she had already stood up to him once while he possessed Big Jake. She could stand up to him again and best him with or without Luis's help.

Zuri rounded the corner alone and entered a circular chamber with a domed ceiling. In the center of the chamber stood a roughly five-foot-high stone pedestal. Upon it sat a devilish bust with grotesquely distorted male features and curving ram horns protruding from the skull. The green aura emanated from the statuette's eyes, nose, and ears, and the thrumming came from its mouth, which gaped in a perpetual scream.

"I know what you want, Zuri Williams." The voice came from the screaming icon. "You want to be a champion. I can grant you the strength needed to achieve your dreams. All you must do is walk away and leave Rose with me. It is right that Rose should be with me. She is my daughter."

Zuri shook her head and marched toward the icon, intending to pick it up and smash it against the floor. But she got no further than several steps before her progress was impeded by an unseen force. She moved forward two more steps before she could go no further, like she pressed against an invisible wall. Zuri drew back and punched the barrier. Her arm was about half extended when her fist was arrested. She didn't feel like she struck anything. Instead, resistance slowly built, as if her fist moved through ever deeper water, with the pressure slowly building until it was too great to overcome.

"Luis Torres, I am glad you have come to join us," George said from the icon.

Zuri glimpsed the math whiz standing in the arched entrance, wide-eyed and gawking.

"I know what you want, Luis Torres," George crooned. "You want the notoriety of being a renowned mathematician."

Luis cringed and shook his head. Even frightened as he was, Zuri was buoyed by his presence. They could win. They could stand up to the bully together.

"Oh, but you do, Luis Torres." George's mean-spirited laughter was gleeful. "You want to prove Goldbach's Conjecture and many other formulas. I can help you with that, Luis Torres. My power can unlock your greatest potential, granting you the capacity to solve any mathematical problem you set your…"

Zuri saw why George trailed off. A pale white light intruded on the stairway behind Luis, battling the sickly green for domination. Miriam descended the stairs, Rose levitating at her shoulder.

"Rose!" The icon raged, all pretense of good humor dispatched. "You treacherous harlot! Turning your back on your family! Betraying me!"

The words echoed through the chamber, so painfully loud Zuri grimaced. But she also noticed something that was either new or she had overlooked. Twining through the unnatural green luminescence was a tendril of intertwined green and pale white light.

"Miriam O'Dell, are you a harlot too?" George demanded. "Will you make paupers of your family? It is my magic that ensures the success of O'Dell Enterprises for perpetuity. Will you endanger that for the sake…for the sake…of an ungrateful child too smart for her own good? You're an O'Dell. A daughter of privilege. Without me—"

"A fortune built upon murder is not a fortune worth having." Miriam's words cut through the din, strong and clear. The infernal thrumming faded in intensity. "If O'Dell Enterprises is so decrepit that it will fail without your black magic, so be it!"

The icon roared in response, but it was no longer deafening. It seemed Miriam possessed the power to speak truth to her vile ancestor. The exchange continued, but Zuri focused on the intertwined light. It was a tether flowing from the mouth of the icon to wrap around Rose's waist. Zuri reached for the tether but hesitated and glanced at Rose. The sad, somber girl nodded once, and Zuri knew what she must do.

Zuri took hold of the ghostly tether with both hands and gasped in pain. The light was biting cold, but she did not release the fetter. Instead, she moved along it hand over hand. She still felt resistance as before, but it was no longer impenetrable.

"What is this?" George shouted as Zuri closed in. "Turn back, Zuri Williams! Turn back now, and I will spare Luis Torres! Continue, and you will die! He will die!"

Intense green light gushed from the icon's mouth, blinding and blizzard cold. Zuri stumbled backward but retained her hold on the ghostly rope burning her hands. Soon the light faded and the icy blast with it. Vision returning, Zuri smiled and trekked onward despite her throbbing hands.

"No," George said in a wavery voice.

"Yes," Zuri replied grimly, finally coming into range to deliver what she hoped would be the fatal blow.

Wincing, Zuri removed her left hand from the tether. Her palm was burned red and blistered, but nevertheless, she wrapped her right wrist with the paranormal shackle, clenching her teeth as her skin burned.

"Please, don't do this. All I have done is for my family," George begged.

"Rose was your family, and you murdered her." Zuri placed her weight on her left heel and spun to the left, delivering a spinning roundhouse kick with her right leg. Pain exploded through her foot when she struck the icon. The statuette wobbled precariously and teetered backward. When her foot touched the ground, sharp pain lanced through the limb, and she crumpled to the stone floor.

"Noooo!" George wailed as the icon fell over and tumbled from the plinth.

When the devilish face impacted the floor, it shattered like porcelain. Instantly, the green aura winked out and the thrumming abruptly stopped with a loud whoosh of putrid air. The only light left was from Rose floating between Miriam and Luis in the archway. A smile of pure ecstasy graced the girl's face making her seem more beautiful than Zuri had ever known. Rose turned that radiant, joyous expression on Zuri and waved while fading into oblivion.

Experiencing a lightness of being like no other, Zuri returned the smile with a pained grimace and waved a blistered hand before Rose ceased, plunging them into blackness.

"We did it!" Luis shouted. "We did it!"

"Yeah, we did," Zuri said weakly. "Do we have any light? My foot is hurt. I think…I need help."

"Hold on," Miriam said. A dim glow from a phone screen illuminated the faces of the rich girl and Luis. "Got it."

The phone's light flared, spotlighting Zuri. She held up a hand and squinted as Luis ran to her aid.

Chapter 46

Champions

Zuri missed a week of school after the events in the subbasement, recovering from the harrowing experience. Primarily the time was spent in bed sleeping or watching clips of Malee Chaiyathorn.

She daydreamed about following in the footsteps of her hero to become a mixed martial arts champion, but she couldn't glimpse her bandaged hands and cast-encased right foot without fearing that when she recovered from the injuries, she wouldn't be able to kick as hard or punch as powerfully as before. The doctor told her she would make a full recovery, but such assurances could not fully dispel her worry that she had freed Rose at the expense of her dreams. That was a terrible price to pay if that were true, but one she would learn to accept if need be.

Amari stayed home with her over those days, recovering from the blow to the head that left her concussed and dealing with headaches. Fans of Dolores Clattenburg would have to wait a few days for her next advice column. There were also matters with the police to sort out. Big Jake was in the hospital under police guard on charges of attempted murder, but there would be more questions to answer for Amari, Zuri, Luis, and Miriam.

Mrs. Torres drove Zuri to school on her first day back. Zuri sat in the front next to the civil rights attorney while Luis lounged in the back with her crutches. Upon arriving at school, she half expected to be hauled off to the principal's office, but Luis insisted she needn't worry. Hank heralded them all as heroes despite his bizarre behavior in the basement. Luis also had a warning for Zuri.

"People might look at you a little differently," Luis said. "Miriam's been spreading the word that we're heroes just like Hank is."

Zuri discovered people did look at her differently, and not only because of her bandaged hands and crutches. The disparaging whispers of new girl and less flattering words had ceased. Students who had never given her a second glance offered to share their notes since she couldn't write or type with her hands bandaged.

During lunch, Luis stood in line for her food while she sat at the usual table with Edith and John.

"I wish you had told us what you were doing," Edith said accusingly. "What if something happened to you or Luis?"

"Something worse in your case," John said between bites of ham sandwich.

Miriam sauntered over to join them, saving Zuri from needing to justify herself. Edith and John were so awed by the popular girl's presence, they fell silent and merely nodded along as Miriam recounted the tale of Zuri facing down Good Old George. For her part, Zuri was a little embarrassed—Miriam made her seem far more heroic than she recalled.

Once the school day ended, Zuri and Luis returned to their study table in the library. He pulled out the chair for her and took her crutches and backpack after she sat, setting them on the floor. After taking out his laptop and opening a web browser to a page full of real analysis, he tutored her on algebra.

After a spell, Zuri glanced over to the stacks to where Rose used to appear and sighed.

"I miss her too," Luis said.

Zuri faced Luis and gazed into his kind, brown eyes. "She's free. It's for the best."

Smiling, Zuri leaned over and cocked her head. Luis mirrored her movement, and they kissed long and sweet.

A word about the author...

Dan Rice pens the young adult urban fantasy series The Allison Lee Chronicles in the wee hours of the morning. The series kicks off with his award-winning debut, Dragons Walk Among Us, which Kirkus Review calls, "An inspirational and socially relevant fantasy."

While not pulling down the 9 to 5 or chauffeuring his soccer fanatic sons to practices and games, Dan enjoys photography and hiking through the wilderness.

To discover more about Dan's writing and keep tabs on his upcoming releases, visit his website: https://www.danscifi.com and join his newsletter.

https://www.danscifi.com